THE OTHERS

ALSO BY CHERYL ISAACS

The Unfinished

CHERYL ISAACS

THE OTHERS

Heartdrum
An Imprint of HarperCollinsPublishers

HarperCollins Children's Books, a division of HarperCollins Publishers,
195 Broadway, New York, NY 10007

HarperCollins Publishers, Macken House, 39/40 Mayor Street Upper,
Dublin 1, D01 C9W8, Ireland

Heartdrum is an imprint of HarperCollins Publishers.
The Others
Copyright © 2025 by Cheryl Isaacs
Letter from Cynthia Leitich Smith © 2025 by Author Consultant CLS, LLC
All rights reserved. Manufactured in Harrisonburg, VA, United States of America.
No part of this book may be used or reproduced in any manner whatsoever
without written permission except in the case of brief quotations embodied in
critical articles and reviews. Without limiting the exclusive rights of any author,
contributor, or the publisher of this publication, any unauthorized use of this
publication to train generative artificial intelligence (AI) technologies is expressly
prohibited. HarperCollins also exercises their rights under Article 4(3) of the
Digital Single Market Directive 2019/790 and expressly reserves this publication
from the text and data mining exception.
harpercollins.com
Library of Congress Control Number: 2024950183
ISBN 978-0-06-328744-0
Typography by David Curtis
25 26 27 28 29 LBC 5 4 3 2 1
First Edition

FOR MY FAMILY,
KONORÓNKHWA

ONE

THE OTHER SHOE—THAT WAS THE PROBLEM.

I left the sidewalk and turned into the entrance to the park, giving a quick wave to the lanky summer staff at the gatehouse, trying to focus on the *crunch, crunch* of my footsteps on the gravel path and keep my mind clear. But a lot of objectively bad things had happened to me recently, and for a natural-born pessimist, the recent past was not past enough, making the mantra of *what if, what if, what if* loop through my brain like a particularly unsettling train on a track. The sun was high in an impossibly blue sky, warming the back of my neck, and on the breeze came the heavy sweetness that was the signature scent of a sweltering summer just getting started. It was a beautiful day, perfect conditions to spend with friends and revel in the moment. But I appreciated none of it.

I was waiting for the other shoe.

The one that would drop, that would fall from the sky and squash whatever I was enjoying, snatching my happiness away like it was something I'd stolen. And I *was* happy, for the first time since my dad had left, since I'd been consumed with running, and then when I'd stumbled into a waking nightmare and almost lost everything for good.

Two weeks ago, I'd been on a seemingly perfect run through

the vast forest that encircled our town when I'd stumbled onto an eerie pond, and immediately after, strange things had started to happen.

Long a legend, the black water was supposedly a small pond that only revealed itself to the unlucky few and, once disturbed, unleashed the faceless Ragged Man to wreak a cycle of danger and darkness until whoever had woken it managed to put it back to sleep. It was a story I'd heard all my life and dismissed as small-town fiction until it all turned out to be horrifyingly real.

People in town started to go missing only to return as the Unfinished—faded, mindless drones—but the black water's mental grip kept people from suspecting anything more sinister than the town having a lot of runaways. Bad turned to worse; worse became unthinkable when my best friend Key disappeared. Only a few of us—my other bestie, Stella; my boss, Frank; and my new friend, Foster—were free of the black water's influence and could see what was going on. We stopped it by fighting the Unfinished and following ancient instructions to destroy the Ragged Man.

But even that hadn't brought Key back, so I'd gone into the black water to get him.

And then the pond had broken its banks and grown.

Now things were back to normal—as normal as they apparently ever got in this town.

I stomped up through the parking lot, seething that this was something I was compelled to do on a day like this, to see with my own eyes where the nightmare had started and ended.

People in town were calling it the Big Pond—previously undiscovered, they thought, but I knew it was just the latest iteration of something else, something smaller and darker and much more dangerous. Now I'd heard it was just a pretty pond.

We'd see about that.

At the west side of the parking lot, I stopped at the edge of the new path cut through the brush by the park crew, the gravel they'd dumped carelessly not really necessary. Anybody could have easily followed the shredded and torn branches left behind from the machines, naked white pulp exposed like broken bone visible through flesh. The whole thing was barely a ten-minute walk from the parking lot. Much shorter than the route I'd taken the day I found it, the one that I couldn't remember and had never found again.

You only find it if it wants you.

I shivered at the memory but forced myself to walk the new path, the goose bumps on my skin and sick twisting in my stomach at odds with the brightness and beauty of the day.

Crunch, crunch, crunch.

Cut right into the brush, the new path was like a corridor, outraged green and damaged branches rising like a wall on either side of me. Whatever was in there, I'd never see it coming. The closer I got, the more the little voice inside told me to turn around and run, certain that I'd find something dark and dripping at the end of the path, a ruined face torn open in a gaping smile.

Welcome back.

I shook out my hands and sped up, trotting the last little bit until the bushes on either side of me opened out onto a broad clearing, a sudden release from the claustrophobic path, and there it was.

In front of me, the pond lay clear and sparkling, pretty and inviting—not evil at all. When I'd pulled Key out of the water, the pond had grown, like I'd pulled a plug, but instead of water draining out, more had flooded in. Much more. The pond was now easily twice its original size, almost the size of the soccer fields where I sometimes ran sprints. From the end of the path, I could just glimpse the newly submerged long strands of grass that swayed gently under the surface; the last time I'd been here, those grasses had been a treacherous meadow. On the far side of the water, the pines still stood guard over the end of the original path, the one I'd been unlucky enough to stumble on, but no one would be taking that route. Whoever visited would take this new shortcut.

"Like an express lane to hell," I muttered to myself, rising up on my toes to see more without actually getting closer. I could just make out a couple of orange safety cones on the opposite shore and what looked like some pipes sticking out of the water's edge. I squinted briefly, but cones and pipes weren't what I was looking for. They weren't what I dreaded seeing.

To my right, a man and a preschool-age boy with matching baseball caps and fishing rods stood with the water lapping at their feet. I looked down at the toes of my running shoes, sinking into the crabgrass, gravel still under my heels, and decided against another step forward. This was far enough.

I'd been in that pond when it was smaller, but my memory of it was as murky as the water had been. I had only the vague sense of pressure, of cold wrapping itself around me tighter and tighter, squeezing until everything went dark. I'd gone in deliberately for a very good reason, but I'd never go back again. The man and boy might think there were fish in the pond, but I still had bad dreams about what was in there before.

At a flutter in the corner of my eye, I froze and held my breath. I didn't dare turn to track it, fearing I'd see something dark and brooding just behind my shoulder, staring at the back of my skull with eyes like pits that had no bottom. I stood still as a stone, because I knew this forest held things that would give chase if you ran. At a little glimmer of movement on the ground, I flicked my eyes down and felt icy cold flood my veins.

The pond was breaking its banks. Tiny trickles, slivers of glistening silver were slithering out and onto the scrubby grass of the shore, threading their way blade by blade, questing closer and closer to my feet at the end of the gravel path.

On the other side of the pond, the man showed the boy how to cast his line. Two practice throws and then the bobber hit the water with a *plop!* The boy squealed with delight.

At the end of the path, my body thrummed with panic rising fast, threatening to surge up from my stomach and take my brain completely offline. But I was stubborn, and so I fought back. I swallowed hard against the constriction in my throat. What I saw wasn't real. The pond was not branching out; it was not making its way toward me.

"It's not real." I muttered, but I still couldn't look away. It was just lingering trauma, that's all. Residual anxiety from everything I'd been through. The pond was not sending out tendrils to wrap around my ankles and drag me under the surface, to keep me in the cold and dark forever.

"It's not." I swallowed hard and closed my eyes for a moment to slow my pulse, taking a long breath in and reminding myself that I had woken up. The nightmare had ended, and I hadn't lost anything—not even the trails I'd half feared would be ruined for me forever. I had run them and enjoyed them as much as ever.

I opened my eyes and looked down. No tendrils. A glance over my shoulder showed only the path.

"It's fine." I nodded, one part of me reassuring another. I drew in a breath that was long and only a little shaky.

Things were more than fine: It was summer, school was over, FallsFest was about to start, and Key was home and healthy. I had learned a lot about myself and about just *being* myself, not keeping every little thing a secret locked up tight. Key and I were officially "something"—TBD but on the way to OMG. My life was pretty much perfect. Which was why I had to keep reminding myself to unclench my jaw.

Because nothing was perfect.

Life was good again, except for that other shoe. I didn't want waste another second thinking about what had happened. I wanted to move on.

One last look at the pond, and I turned on my heel. As fast as I could without running, I went back down the path laid with fresh gravel, out of the parking lot, and onto the sidewalk, where my chest immediately loosened and my mind turned toward brighter things. The black water was in the past; all that remained of it was the Big Pond, and I'd come here to satisfy myself that it was truly harmless. It checked out, as far as I could tell, but I was used to things not being quite what they appeared.

It's fine.

It's fine.

I shook my hands out and willed my heart to slow, putting all the bad memories into a room in my mind and shutting the door. I wasn't running from anything anymore; I was going forward. I hopped over a crack in the sidewalk, even though my mom wasn't there. She'd always made a game of watching my footsteps when I was little. One crack stepped on and I'd be startled by a loud "Ow!" sending us both into fits of giggles. I missed those times, that feeling of lightness and unexpected joy; I was determined to get at least some of it back.

The neighborhood felt quiet and lazy, everyone on a summer schedule or in a summer state of mind. The trees and grass were every shade of green; a hundred kinds of flowers bursting with color and heady fragrance swayed in gardens. My body drank it all in. This summer was going to be perfect.

I crossed to the next block, and then my day got better because a man and a dog were coming toward me. No day could be perfect without meeting a dog—no offense to the cat currently out like a light on my bed. As the pair got closer, though, my enthusiasm dimmed.

There it was.

The other shoe.

The pert little Westie trotting toward me used to be walked by a woman. But she'd been one of the first the black water had stolen, and now the other end of the leash was held by a bear of a man who looked like he hadn't slept well in a year: unshaven, with rumpled clothes and vacant eyes. I'd woken from my nightmare, but he hadn't; he never would, and so as much as I wanted to cross the street to avoid them, as penance I forced myself to stay on course and pass right by. As much as I'd been through, I'd been lucky to come out of it in one piece.

The dog raised his little nose to me for an instant before returning to more interesting aromas; the man's zombie stare didn't seem to clock me at all. I only started breathing again when they'd passed by. I was in a hurry now to get where I was going, to recapture the summer euphoria I'd been feeling earlier that morning, fragile enough to sag under the weight of one man and his dog. I had to buoy the happiness levels of Summer Me, and I knew of one sure way to do that.

TWO

THE FRONT YARD OF KEY'S HOUSE WAS A RIOT of color, his mom's garden strategically crammed with plants that would take turns blooming all summer. The porch sported massive clay pots overflowing with blooms in purple, pink, white, and yellow that enveloped me in a cloud of fruit-scented sweetness as I waited at the door.

"Avery!" Key's dad drew me into a bear hug on the porch and released me on the mat inside the foyer. "My dear." His giant hands warmly clasped my shoulders, and he bent to look into my eyes. "You don't have to knock, wait to be let in like some stranger!"

I nodded sheepishly, but we both knew I was incapable of just walking into their house.

"Key! Avery's here!" He went down the hall, surprisingly light on his feet for a man that size.

I sat on the arm of the plush yellow sofa and breathed in the signature scent of the house—mango and cinnamon. The living room blinds were shut to keep out the worst of the heat, and from the TV came the low chatter of a cricket match—an inscrutable sport Key's dad had tried to explain to me many times.

"My son"—he returned, shaking his head—"is a little out of sorts. I don't think he's sleeping well. Maybe you can ask him."

The last part was less of a suggestion than a request. Since Key and I had finally been open with how we felt, his parents had accepted our new relationship as something they'd known about all along, and I'd officially been welcomed into their circle of People Who Care for Key. In his brief hospital stay after I'd pulled him from the pond, this had included texts from his mom to ask the nurse for warmed blankets, reminders that her son preferred orange juice over apple, and to please rinse out the containers his homecooked food had been transported in. Apparently, I was now the Decipherer of Moods as well.

"That's okay," I assured his dad. "I'm used to his grumpiness." Not super true, because Key was only occasionally grumpy and usually with good reason. His off moods were never the kind of mysteries that needed to be investigated, either because they were so short-lived or because he'd straight up talk about them. Secretive grumpy was more my thing. But we were so glad to have him back at home—"Clean as a bean," according to his doctor—that we would all happily endure any crankiness Key had to offer.

When Key emerged from the darkened hallway, I silently acknowledged his dad was right. Key did look out of sorts. There was an unfamiliar hardness to his expression, and he walked into the room without looking directly at me or his father.

"Oh, Avery!" Key's dad raised a finger from where he'd resettled on the sofa. "My niece's birthday party is the end of this month. You should come."

Key slipped on his shoes and did the impatient "let's go!" thing with his eyebrows.

"I'd love that. Bye, Mr. Rogers." I waved as Key took my wrist and half pulled me out the door.

"Have fun!" his dad called after us. "Not too much and not too late!"

On the porch, with his dad safely on the other side of the door, Key rolled his eyes but opened his arms to me. "Hey, Ave."

I would never get tired of this—wrapping my arms around him, solid and warm, breathing and with me. "How are you?" I asked into his shoulder, a shadow of tension in the words. I felt protective of him in a way I hadn't before, but he had just gotten out of the hospital after being abducted by a swamp demon from another dimension. So.

"Fine." Key kissed my temple, but that's all I got. Even as I stood there, close enough to feel his heartbeat, I was very aware that I was holding another body containing another brain, other thoughts and feelings—a boundary I couldn't breach. All I could know was what he told me, and I had to believe it or not. Was he really fine, or did he just not want to worry me?

"You ready for FallsFest?" I stepped back and smiled into his eyes.

"FallsFest is not ready for me!" He pumped one fist and whooped, but I looked at his face and again thought his dad was right: Key hadn't slept well. I wished he'd tell me why. But those were other thoughts and other feelings in a body that didn't belong to me. Remembering all the times I'd done the exact same thing, I couldn't blame him. It's true—payback is a bitch.

I took his hand, and we jumped off the porch together, heading downtown. If Key wanted to pretend he was fine when he wasn't, I'd let him. Key had never been a mystery to me. All I had to do was wait, and sooner or later, he'd tell me the truth.

By small-town standards, FallsFest was a pretty big deal. The annual festival in Crook's Falls had been the focus of my summers since I was a little kid. Setup started two weeks before the opening, anticipation building every day as the rides, carnival games, booths, and vendor area got closer to completion. Mom always complained about the parking spots lost to trucks, generators, and coils and coils of cables, but I knew she looked forward to it almost as much as I did. It was like a vacation that came to town.

When the crew had first started stringing up lights around the town square two weeks ago, my life had been different. I'd been different. Getting through the end of the school year and training for a scholarship had been my priorities, but now everything had changed.

Key squeezed my hand as we waited for the light to change. "I am not going on that." He raised the hand holding mine to point out a ride I thought of as "Spinny," even though every year he tried to convince me that it was actually called a Gravitron. Key's brain housed weird facts like this. People paid actual money to stand against the walls of the circle, spinning faster and faster, trusting gravity or magic or their own perceived invincibility to stop them from dropping out onto the pavement when the ride rose up on its side. Every year, I stopped and watched, shaking my head in disbelief. It was still called Spinny to me, and there was still no way I was riding it. But I was pretty ride-averse in general, given my trust issues. Not everyone was like that.

"You went on the Spinny when you were a kid." I knew this because Key's dad had offered up the fact during one of the many "let's embarrass Key" moments I'd shared with him in the hospital. The story ended with Key draped over a trash can, a scene his dad had mimed, wiping tears of laughter from his eyes at the same time.

Key pursed his lips and tilted his head, acknowledging the fact. "When I was a kid, I didn't look at how the Spinny is anchored. Which is . . . not very well. Besides, I don't think the Spinny and cotton candy go together for me anymore."

I clucked my tongue sympathetically. "You're very old."

"Speaking of junk food, I don't know how much work I can put in tonight." Key patted his belly gently. His voice was light, but he was looking across the street, not at me. A faint note of alarm sounded far in the back of my mind. "Haven't been piling it in lately."

In the hospital.

His parents had made all his favorites and brought them to him, worried that he wasn't eating enough. But really, he hadn't been in the hospital long enough to be in danger of wasting away. I hadn't said anything to anyone but personally suspected the slight hollows around his eyes and gauntness in his cheeks noticeable to only me and his family were due to something else; eating enough was not the issue.

"Are you . . . okay?" Not the word I was looking for, but I wasn't sure the word I was looking for existed.

"I'm fine." A little sharpness in his voice this time.

Fine. That word again.

He smiled quickly and pressed his other hand over mine in reassurance, but his eyes slid left and down. This had been happening a lot—me asking the same question and him unwilling to give a real answer. It was new and strange behavior for him.

"Okay." I nodded, letting it go for now.

We passed by the food truck lot, usually parking for the library but now filled with a dozen colorful food trucks selling everything from crepes to grilled cheese. I had no idea how they'd managed to get all the trucks to fit in so precisely, but the whole block smelled amazing, a blend of sweet, spicy, and savory. We started to wander up and down the aisles that were quickly becoming clogged with people.

"Where's Stella meeting us?" Key asked.

"Huh? Yeah, yeah." Stella could wait. My nose had caught the scent it had been waiting for all year. I led Key on, faster through the maze of trucks, chasing down the big prize of FallsFest. For me, anyway. We wound through two rows of trucks before I spotted the red-and-white-dotted sign. "Here!"

"She's meeting us here?"

"Who?" Still pulling him through strolling snackers.

"Stella."

"Who cares about Stella? Key—" I waved at the sign. "Mini donuts!"

"Oh God." Key face-palmed, preparing, I knew, to bring up all the other FallsFests when I'd overestimated my ability to consume the tiny, perfectly fried and sugared donuts that were made right in front of us, traveling on a tiny conveyor belt until they fell in a sugary puff into a paper bag. Since I'd started training seriously, I wasn't usually one for junk food, but these donuts . . . I could not walk by them. They were my weakness.

"Can you wait?" He asked it like he didn't know the answer.

I stared at him. "Do you not understand? They're mini donuts." I mimed the shape. "They make them right in front of you and they're warm and sugary—"

"Stella might want some, too," he reasoned.

"Since when are you worried about Stella?" I dropped his hand like he'd burned me, faux outrage. A little drama never hurt.

"True." He took my hand again and stepped up to the window. "Cinnamon or white sugar?"

I rolled my eyes. It was like he'd never met me.

Once I had the little sack of donuts in my possession, we strolled down the block of trucks, evaluating this year's offerings for later.

We crossed over to the town square, where a crowd was waiting for the opening ceremony and gawking at the fountain that was flowing for the first time in my life. The fountain occupied the center of the tree-lined square and had been a bone-dry eyesore for decades. It had always seemed an unexplainable extravagance to me, such a large and ornate fountain for such a small community, like the town was pretending to be something it wasn't, or maybe something remembered but long gone.

My whole life, the fountain had done nothing but provide good lunchtime seating around the edge of the concrete basin. It was ten feet across with two tulip-shaped bowls that rose out of the center, supported by a column like tiers on a wedding cake. At the very top, a steady stream of water gurgled and fell, creating an ever-shifting array of beads and sheets of water that ended up in the basin to start all over again.

Now it was full of water, clear and glittering, trickling down gently, a constant musical cascade into the basin, where a few coins already gleamed on the bottom. It had started running recently enough to be a FallsFest novelty. Key stretched out his arm and let his hand cut through the curtain of water, gazing down thoughtfully and watching the droplets distort the surface so much that there were no reflections. I knew he was probably interested in the patterns of light and shadow, artsy stuff that would make beautiful photographs. Looking around at all the people, colors, and lights, I wished he'd brought a camera. It would be good for him to get back into the photography saddle. Key without a camera was just a bit weird, like a flightless bird.

"Avery!" Hearing my name at such volume startled me. I turned and saw my mom and her ihstá Lily, but it was my ihstá Ru who'd bellowed my name across the square. Mom looked a bit embarrassed but just gave her sister a hip bump and waited for Key and me to thread our way over to them.

The last time I'd seen my auntie Ru was when I was nine and we visited her place, which at the time I'd thought was a farm—it was so wide-open and green compared to our little house and patch of grass in town. I'd had fun playing with my younger cousins until Ru had casually called my mom an apple—red on the outside and white on the inside. I remembered the moment, the sudden wave of tension that swept through everyone, even though I hadn't really understood what the term meant at the time. Ru had been laughing and didn't seem to mean anything by it, but Mom had gone very still and quiet. We'd left soon after, and I hadn't seen Ru since. Maybe Mom had gotten so mad because deep down she was afraid there was some truth in it. After all, she'd raised a kid who didn't know fancy from jingle, or if it was okay to use the word *Indian* in reference to tacos, and had to constantly remind my great-aunt Lily to speak English because I couldn't follow her Kanyen'kéha.

Mom could hold a grudge like her life depended on it, but it seemed Ihstá Lily had finally gotten her wish of Mom and Ru getting back to being sisters. Since the day I'd pulled Key out of the pond in the forest, something in my mom had changed; she'd been mending fences, and I was glad. It was nice to see Mom with her sister again, even if Ru was a lot sometimes.

"Shé:kon." I bent to kiss Lily, who was riding in style in a wheelchair for the evening, in case she got tired, wearing a lilac linen dress and sitting straight like a queen on a throne. She wasn't able to see much over the crowd, but her eyes were bright and excited.

"Oh, Avery!" Lily's bony fingers grasped my wrist tightly. "Aren't you beautiful." Lily was always a confidence booster.

"Did someone say 'beautiful'?" a voice boomed behind me.

"Hi, Ihstá." I turned to Ihstá Ru.

"Niece!" Ru grabbed my shoulders and pulled me in for a hug like she was trying to juice me, Mom smiling her quiet smile over her sister's shoulder.

Ru was the older sister by two years, and she and my mom could have passed for twins except that one twin was shorter and significantly louder than the other. To my eyes, Ru hadn't changed in the years we'd missed each other. She still had boundless energy for learning other people's business, stacks of rings on her fingers, and silver hoops in her ears, and today's selection of T-shirt was a red *Land Back* with the sleeves cut off.

"And you must be Key," Ru said with a smile, like she knew a secret. But if Key and I had ever been a secret, we weren't hiding it any longer.

"Hi." The only word Key got out before suffering the same juicing fate, but Key came from a large and loud family of huggers, so he was well prepared.

"Hey, Key." My jaw dropped as my mom raised her arms to Key for her own gentler, quieter hug. Over her shoulder, his eyes went wide. This, he was not prepared for. If this was the influence Ru had on my mom, I was all for it. Mom had always loved Key, but Mom was definitely *not* a hugger. Like I said, after the pond, something in my mom had changed.

"You staying for the opening?" Mom didn't hug me, but she did elbow my ribs affectionately just to show that she hadn't changed *that* much.

"Uh . . ." Speeches? Not really part of the plan, but I checked in with Key, who shrugged and glanced back at the fountain.

"Trust me." Mom nudged me again. "You'll like it." She seemed so happy and light, with her sister and aunt, I couldn't refuse. If a few minutes of listening to the mayor blather on about town history made Mom happy, I could do it.

We weaved single file through the growing crowd, Mom clearing the way and Ru following with Lily's chair. The stage was set up in the space adjacent to the fountain, a spot normally empty except for a few people reading or just sitting on the benches lining the area. I often ate my lunch here on break from the bookstore.

"Enjoy responsibly, folks," a cop drawled as we neared him.

My stomach tightened at the sight of the cop in the baggy uniform. He had been in the room when I tried to get help for Key and no one listened—or was able to. That part probably wasn't his fault, but everything else I disliked about him was. *Folks.* I hated that word. And what did he mean, "responsibly"? And why did he look at *us* when he said it?

My nose wrinkled in disgust, but I kept a lid on it. This was a good day. We were here to have fun. I kept my back to him as I passed by, though; I had no time for this idiot probably getting time and a half to slouch in a golf cart nursing a giant blue slushie. Ru caught my eye and shook her head at the sight before a tap on her shoulder made her turn to a smaller, shinier version of herself.

Pearl greeted me with a quick lift of her chin, her eyes flicking over me and Key before saying something to her mom in a voice too low for me to hear. It wasn't much of a reunion, but the last time I saw my little cousin, we were young enough to be climbing trees and pretending to explore an alien planet. We were pretty much strangers now, our moms' fallout affecting us, too. If it had taken this long for Mom and her sister to sort things out, it was going to take my cousin and me even longer.

Pearl was now a mini Ru, short in stature but with a big presence. With jet-black hair that fell in a glossy cascade almost to her waist, she had Ru's big eyes and, apparently, her audacity.

Ru shook her head. "Oié:ri."

Ten. Ten what?

"Tewáhsen," Pearl insisted with a pout and batting of her lashes.

Ah. Now I knew exactly what they were negotiating.

"Wísk." Ru made it sound like a threat.

Pearl held up her palms in surrender. "Okay, okay." Smirking at her win, Ru pulled a ten-dollar bill from her pocket and held it out. Pearl tried to pluck it with the tips of her fingers but found that her mother held it fast. Pearl rolled her eyes, but they were both smiling.

"Nyá:wen, Mom." Pearl blew a kiss that Ru caught in her fist and pressed to her heart, gave me a wave, and was gone, disappearing into the crowd that had gathered.

"Such a little mercenary." Ru shook her head but there was nothing on her face but love.

I wasn't in the habit of asking my mom for spending money anymore; that's what my bookstore job was for. It did hurt me a little, though, to know that if I did ask, it would have to be in English. Maybe *hurt* wasn't the right word. *Shame? Envy?* When it came to my culture, it was hard to sort out my true feelings.

"You're not going to hit me up, are you?" Key nudged my shoulder with his.

"Excuse me?" I bumped him back. "I don't need your money." I sniffed.

"Just like you don't need me to walk you all the way home." He nodded. "So old-fashioned."

Our agreement was to part at Maple and South, which was almost all the way, with me texting as soon as I got in, but it was a compromise Key still didn't love.

"I'm not offended." He pretended to wipe a tear away. "You don't need me."

"Of course I do." But I couldn't say those words quite yet. *I need you.* Baby steps.

"But really, how would you defend me?" I pressed. "With your superpower of . . . ?"

"Uh . . ." He rubbed the bridge of his nose with one finger, as he always did when thinking, like he could coax an idea out of his brain and down to his mouth. It was a question I knew he couldn't answer—too many choices.

"You're fast!" he crowed.

"Yeah. That's *my* superpower," I pointed out.

"Exactly. So whatever was chasing us would get me first."

"Your superpower is being slow and easy prey?" Just checking, for the next time this topic came up, because with Key, it would.

"You'd be home with your feet up while the beast was still crunching on my bones." He mimed gnawing.

The idea hit a little too close to home, setting off a shiver that radiated out from a place I'd kept locked up the last two weeks. I wrapped my arm around his to put an end to the conversation and surveyed the crowd. Scary things lurk even in small towns. I knew that better than anybody, but that didn't mean I wanted to rely on someone else to see me to my front door every single night. To me, that didn't feel like safety; it felt like living in fear. And I was done with that.

THREE

"IS THIS ON? CAN YOU HEAR ME?" THE MAYOR tapped the mic and then clapped and rubbed his hands together in excitement, like he didn't do this every summer. The stage was set up on one side of the town square with the fountain to the right and the vendors' booths ringing the space. Mayor Lewis was a smooth-skinned, still-young man, with a bright smile and always impeccably groomed, and even tonight he looked cool despite the heat. He was the kind of person too put-together to sweat, like he good-naturedly willed himself not to. Although he had a regrettable habit of doing the finger-gun thing as a greeting, the mayor was popular. Even Ru liked working for him. He seemed genuinely interested in making everyone happy and, according to my mom, was therefore doomed to fail. But he tried. Mom liked him, and she didn't like anyone even remotely connected to politics. "What a great turnout and a beautiful evening," he said, adjusting the mic like a pro. "I'd like to welcome everyone to the official opening of FallsFest Fifty! Let's get the festivities started with a few words from Foster Miller." He backed away, leading the applause with his hands raised over his head.

Foster? Mom shot a quiet smile my way. Foster had never struck me as the type for public speaking, but that was definitely him slowly mounting the podium steps, leaning on his cane with one hand and the mayor's arm with the other before shooing him away at the top step.

Chatter died down, and everyone hushed as Foster surveyed the crowd and nodded at us with a smile. He tugged at the hem of his favorite pale blue shirt, and I noticed that he was wearing a pair of soft olive pants that I didn't recognize. He'd shopped for the occasion. After years of no one wanting to listen to him, Foster finally had the spotlight. He'd never struck me as the attention-seeking type, but even from where I stood in the crowd, I could see the glimmer in his eye; he was definitely loving this, and I couldn't help but smile.

Although I hadn't known him long, I'd grown to love him, prickly though he could sometimes be. Foster had been through so much in his life. He'd helped me put the black water to sleep, but he was also reconnecting me with my family and my culture in a way I never expected. I'd gotten into the habit of going out to his little house on the edge of town, curling up on the love seat in his living room and listening to stories—some I'd heard before but never really paid attention to, others that were new to me. It was nice, like I was making up for lost time. It felt like that was true for him, too.

"I'm going to start with the words we say before all else." His voice was soft, even amplified. "I'll try to make it the shortest ever." He smiled and then closed his eyes.

He started speaking in Kanyen'kéha, but the only part I understood was the repeated phrase *now our minds are one*. Ru leaned closer and began to translate—allegedly for Key's benefit, but just loud enough for me to hear as well. Ru had taught her daughter to speak the language, but Mom hadn't taught me. One more difference between them.

"He's giving thanks for Mother Earth," she whispered. "The waters, animals, trees." Key listened intently, and so did I, trying to catch some of the words I knew as Foster spoke, because I was thankful—more than I'd ever been in my life. "And the Creator," Ru finished, but Foster paused and then kept speaking, a smile playing around the edges of his mouth, ending with a sentence that brought a few scattered chuckles from those in the audience who understood, including Ru, who choked a little on her blueberry lemonade.

"What was that?" I hadn't gotten any of it.

Ru shook her head and cleared her throat. "Just a little joke—if your banana bread is too dry, don't use so much white flour."

I didn't get it.

Ru shrugged. "It's just funny to say stuff in public that the white people don't understand."

I bristled.

"Oh, not you, honey." Ru patted my hand, clearly embarrassed and maybe apprehensive. That was all we needed—another incident for someone to take offense and rupture my family again. I wasn't insulted and Ru knew it. Both of us shot looks at my mom where she stood beside Lily, because Mom was the unknown variable. She was standing very still, her long dark hair stirring in the breeze, but she wasn't looking at us. Her attention was focused on something off to the side, past the edge of the crowd; she stared expressionless before her eyes dropped down to the ground.

I saw what—who—she was looking at and for an instant considered pretending I hadn't. It would make things easier. But in the end, I couldn't do that. It seemed too petty and not who I wanted to be.

"I'm just going to—" I murmured to Key. He followed my eyes.

"Oh. Yeah, sure." Key pressed his palm to the back of my neck. "Take your time." Key was one of the few who knew that while I didn't make a big deal of my fractured relationship with my dad, the distance he'd allowed to grow really hurt me. After he'd moved out of the house, calls had gotten fewer, pickups had been missed, weekends had been canceled, and I'd started to think it was for the best to just let our relationship wither and die. But deep in my heart, I knew that wasn't what I wanted. Key had encouraged me many times to try harder to reconnect, and maybe I was finally ready.

My dad stood between a bench and one of the maple trees lining the square—on the periphery, which was how I viewed him now. He seemed smaller than the last time I'd seen him. Both of his hands were bunched up in the pockets of cargo shorts that were a little too big for him, and they stayed there when I walked up. He radiated the desire to disappear.

"Hey, Dad."

"Hi, Ave." He looked like he was straining not to do something or not to say something. There was music and laughter and noise all around us, but as usual, my dad and I were in our own little pocket of silence.

He'd been trying recently. I knew Mom had told him about Key and . . . everything. We'd talked on the phone a few times, but with Key in the hospital, I was now the one who was too busy to meet. All the missed pickups and canceled weekends—now the shoe was on the other foot, and the saddest part was I wasn't sure Dad minded. Everything seemed so hard for him, and I was so exhausted; I kind of wanted to tell him not to bother, but even after everything, after how deeply my dad had hurt me, a small part of me couldn't help hoping.

"Key looks good." Dad's voice sounded like his throat was very dry.

"Yup." I turned back to see Key chatting with Mom and Ru. "Same old Key. Good as new."

"That's good." Dad seemed to be studying something on the ground, but all I saw were interlocking bricks, an intricate pattern that had no obvious beginning or end. "I've not been good."

His voice was very quiet, soft in a way that hurt my heart.

"I've not been good to you, Ave." His head was still hanging low, and that one little sentence was enough for tears to prick my eyes. "I've been struggling since your mom and I split up. I can't seem to . . ." He jiggled the keys in his pocket, a note of confusion in his voice. "I can't seem to get moving again, and I didn't want you to see me like that. But it's my problem, not yours. I didn't handle it well; I didn't realize that you might think you're not the most important thing in my life. So . . . I want you to understand what's going on, and know that you are. The most important thing. Still. Always."

He looked up, searching my face, waiting for a response, but all I could do was blink.

Because he was right. That's exactly what I'd thought—that he didn't care, that he had better things to do. And here he was, telling me that our relationship had fallen apart because he was falling apart. It made me sad for us both. And relieved. And pissed off.

"I know I can't make it up to you." His hands finally came out of his pockets to rub the back of his head. "I know that's not possible. But I'm getting some help now, and I was wondering if maybe we could . . . start over. I'll do better this time, I promise." He held my eyes, looking terrified by what he might find there.

I wanted to tell him how much he'd hurt me. I wanted to remind him of all the times I'd waited and he hadn't shown up. The texted, last-minute excuses and promises about the next time that never came. If he'd only told me what was going on instead of trying to shield me from it in the worst possible way.

But I believed what he was saying; he was sharing now, and if anyone knew how difficult that could be, it was me, the queen of withholding. I was angry with him, but I missed him more, and so of all the things I wanted to say to him, only one whispered word made it out of my mouth.

"Dad."

One step forward and I was in my dad's arms again, immediately a child once more. It felt like the ghost of who we once were—careful and tentative—a different species from the hug I'd gotten from Key's dad. But if this was something that could be revived—me and my dad—I would take it. I thought I'd lost us forever.

I would let him try again. To be honest, I would probably let him try a million times.

I stepped back and found Key at my side.

"Hey, Mr. Ray. Good to see you." He shook my dad's hand and smiled. Key always knew how to defuse any tension, how to tactfully change a subject, how to rescue me when I was about to dissolve into a puddle of tears in the middle of FallsFest, alarming my mother and never ever living it down. His hand slipped into mine. I was lucky to have this.

"Really good to see you, Key." Dad peered around Key. "No Stella?"

"She'll be here," I assured him. Even Dad, as out of the loop on my life as he was, expected Stella to be around me somewhere.

"Well, I'll leave you to it, then." Dad shuffled nervously, hands back in his pockets, and I realized he'd come here specifically to see me and that maybe he didn't want to run into my Mom. Definitely not Ru.

"Okay." I nodded but waited to see what he would do. It was weird, but I didn't want to scare off my own father.

"Okay." Dad stepped forward and wrapped his arms around me again, a little surer this time. "I'll text you. I promise."

What was the saying? If I had a dollar for every time I'd heard that, I'd be rich.

But I didn't want to be rich. I just wanted my dad back. I watched him go, my heart swelling, so many people milling around now that two steps and he was swallowed up by the crowd, the space he vacated quickly filled by others.

FOUR

I WAS STILL SNIFFLING A BIT WHEN I SPOTTED a cloud of blond curls bobbing along in the crowd. "Key. Stella's here. Key?" He'd been right behind me, and I'd be lying if I said my stomach didn't drop into my shoes when I turned and he wasn't there, bringing back bad memories of when he'd disappeared, but in a few seconds I traced my way through the crowd and found him back at the fountain.

"It's so weird," he said softly, staring at the water trickling from one level down into the basin. "To see it with water."

"Hey, friends!" Stella had several of our classmates trailing her, including my lanky cross-country teammates Sian and Derek, the latter a sweet overachiever who'd been very obviously smitten with Stella all year.

"How are your splits?" Sian sidled up to me, always talking shop. She was long, lean, and always in motion. In her cropped T-shirt and shorts that used to be sweatpants, even her clothes seemed like they were halfway to somewhere else.

I shrugged. "Not really keeping track. Just some nice long runs."

"Right, right." Sian nodded and raked her hand through short auburn hair. "Summer runs. Junk miles. Hey." She stepped in, giving me a close-up of the dusting of freckles across her face, and lowered her voice. "Any chance you could take Mopey here off my hands?" She tilted her head toward Derek. Running was Sian's first love, but matchmaking was pretty high on the list, too.

"I am not getting in the middle of this." I raised my hands to ward off any involvement. "That would be up to Stell, and I don't think she's interested in anybody."

"What does that mean?" Sian may have gone a week without crushing on someone, but I couldn't say for sure.

"It means she isn't interested in anybody." I raised my shoulders and let them drop. I didn't know how else to say it.

"Hmm." Sian considered the idea. "Fair. Okay. I'll try to temper expectations." She turned to collect her crowd, everyone assuming that Key, Stella, and I would break off on our own. "Hey. If you want a team run anytime . . ." She mimed *Text me*, rounded up her group, and headed off toward the rides.

It had been this way for so long—me, Key, and Stella, our own little party—it almost felt kind of rude sending everyone else on their way. Almost. These days, I found myself even more possessive of the time the three of us had together. It wouldn't last forever, and I'd had a glimpse of life without my two friends. I hadn't liked it much. In fact, it had sucked pretty hard. That's why now I was determined to hold on to them for as long as I could.

"Okay." Stella clapped her hands like a cheerleader and turned to Key because he was the King of Sugar. "Where should we start?"

"Well." Key rubbed the back of his neck. "What do you want to do?"

Stella shot me a look, because we always kicked off the night with junk—before any rides or games, always junk first to toast a new summer. We'd followed the same pattern cruising FallsFest our whole lives.

"She means food, Key," I prompted, shushing the little flutter in my stomach.

"Oh." He seemed to think about it. "I'm actually not that hungry."

Stella laughed, then stopped short, realizing he wasn't kidding. Key not hungry on the first night of FallsFest? The very idea was ridiculous. The fluttering in my stomach increased.

"We just finished a bag of donuts," I said, a ridiculous explanation that Stella raised her eyebrows at, but I had to try to cover for him. Key would feel bad if he realized how weird he was being. A bag of mini donuts split between us was nothing. FallsFest was one of the few times I abandoned my training and was open to eating junk, and Key was a certified bottomless pit. Maybe he really wasn't ready to be out and about like nothing had happened. In the awkward pause, I swallowed against the tightness in my throat.

"How about the swings?" I suggested. They were Stella's favorite and a mellow ride that wouldn't require a lot from Key.

"Is he okay?" Stella whispered to me as we navigated our way to the swings.

If Stella had suspected in the space of ten seconds that he was not okay, then Key was definitely not okay, an idea I didn't want to think or talk about.

"Just tired." I nodded and then quickly changed the subject. "Derek's sweet."

Stella gave only the tiniest eye roll, knowing both exactly where I was going with this and that I should know better. I'd never really understood Stella's independence. I was independent, too, but my independence was ultimately based on fear; Stella's was confidence and self-knowledge all the way to the core. Drawing a blank, I tried again.

"So is Sian." Just throwing it out there. Maybe I didn't know Stella as well as I thought I did.

"She is adorable!" Stella responded immediately, clasping her hands together. "But I'm good, Ave." Giving me a grown-up smile. "I don't know . . . I'm good on my own." And I knew she was.

But I wasn't. I knew that about myself. I'd tried to be, for a long time, but I had learned that I needed people—Key, specifically. If Stella was a comet flying free through space, I needed an orbit.

Key turned back to us, spreading his arms wide. "Swings!" Being goofy by announcing what was right in front of us. Chains clinked as people strapped their kids and themselves into probably the only ride that was universally enjoyed, something so tame that even I was on board.

We claimed three swings in a row, with me in the middle, and I breathed in the first of the evening air, scented now with burnt sugar and a hint of sunscreen. The music started, our feet lifted off the ground, and the swings took us up and out, drifting in a gentle arc.

"Summer!" Stella whooped to my left, making me smile.

It was just a small-town carnival ride, but on this night, it felt like more. I'd struggled so much and for so long, and now I was flying, wind in my hair and a friend on either side. This was my life now, and I liked it. I wanted to hold on to it. The swoop of the swings sent the silver turtle around my neck to the back, but when we got off, tilting and wheeling together as we got our land legs back, I righted it, let it hang against my chest like it was supposed to, where it had for years.

Once we got off the swings, Key was the chatty, mildly bratty, sugar-obsessed FallsFest version of himself that I'd expected all along. He wrapped his arm around my waist, pulled me in, and loud-whispered into my ear, "*Sugar.*"

Stella followed suit on the other side, rising up on her toes to giggle. "*Sugar.* We must consume *sugar.*"

I shoved them both away, shaking my head in faux disgust, not a tense fiber in my body, and loving every second.

We wandered with no particular plan, because that was the core beauty of summer—doing as we liked. The first night of FallsFest was my favorite. It was always the most crowded but also when the vibe was purest. Even if you'd been to FallsFest every summer of your life, as we had, the first night was when everything was new again; the air smelled sweeter, the lights twinkled more brightly, and this year I really felt that. It was a new summer but also a new me—what I'd been through had set me on a different course, more willing to learn, more open and less afraid. And there was the added bonus of a new me and Key.

With every stop we made, Key seemed more himself, interested in everything edible and seeming happy and relaxed. He and Stella went on a ride with cars that rotated and flipped upside down while I held their drinks and watched like an indulgent parent. I stood in front of the ride with a silly smile on my face, listening to Stella's big laugh and Key's frantic but comically low-pitched *OooohNooooo!*

Next up was recovery ice cream—soft serve swirls all around—

and then we witnessed Stella spend two tickets testing her strength with an oversize hammer and actually ringing the bell. Key and I looked at each other, impressed.

"Small but mighty." I shrugged.

"Now I'm a little scared of her," Key acknowledged.

Stella coolly collected her prize and sauntered by us.

"How did you do that?" Key asked, still amazed by her feat.

Stella flashed one delicate bicep in reply. "Roller coaster?" she suggested.

After the roller coaster, which was actually for little kids but a solid tradition for us, our sugar levels started to dip, and the vote was for cotton candy.

I passed this time—literal mouthfuls of nothing but sugar was a step too far for me. We made our way to the carousel, the dead center of FallsFest. The carousel looked out of place in the midway filled with loud, flashy rides and games—it was a Victorian-style throwback, complete with a sweet tinkling melody, pale-pink-and-gold scrollwork painted around the canopy that reminded me of the underbellies of clouds at early sunset, and ornate horses that rose and fell gently as they circled the mirrored center. *Quaint* was the word. When I was little, I'd ridden those horses with my dad standing beside me. I'd lifted my face to the colorful glow of the lights and pictured myself riding a mighty steed, flying across the open plains. Then I'd discovered running and learned how to fly on my own.

We stood in the glow of the carousel, sugar dissolving on our tongues, watching even the adult riders temporarily transformed into wide-eyed children. I grabbed a few chunks of Key's cone of blue fluff and a small piece of Stella's pink, to balance things out, but I didn't have their tolerance; running was a harsh mistress, so I hadn't eaten this stuff since we'd been here last summer. I was content to stroll, enjoying the cooling air on my skin and the warm bloom of happiness in my chest. Stella and Key trailed me back through the vendors' area in the square with their cones like two sticky toddlers.

"I'm going to check in on Frank," I said over my shoulder as we made our way through the sugar-addled crowd. "You can wait here if you want." Frank would be swamped on his own, and I wanted to see if the display tables I'd set up inside the store and out on the sidewalk needed adjusting or restocking.

"We'll come with." Stella's lips were stained pink, making her look like a kid who had gotten into her mother's makeup.

We continued through the vendors' section, tables surrounded by fabric booths of all colors arrayed around the fountain. Key got hung up at a table selling handmade kaleidoscopes, always transfixed by anything with a lens, which made me wonder again about the absence of his camera. Maybe he hadn't wanted to risk it on the rides? Stella lingered to chat with a white-haired woman selling colorful dragonflies delicately worked in metal, and I stopped at a booth selling jewelry.

The table was covered with cream fabric, setting off the jewelry—some silver, but mostly beaded earrings, pendants, and barrettes in every color, lined up on the table and sitting patiently, waiting to go to their new homes. The vendor was a woman older than my mom but younger than Lily, sat on a folding camp chair behind the table, tapping at a tablet with one calloused fingertip. She was wearing a ribbon skirt and a white T-shirt, made vibrant by her brown skin, that read *Beaders do it better* in big, looping multicolored script. I picked up a pair of pale blue-and-green-beaded earrings—small ovals with a delicate fringe of beads.

"You related to Ru?" the vendor said without looking up from her tablet. "You look like her."

"She's my auntie."

"My sympathies." The woman chortled, put down her tablet, and sat up. "Twenty dollars for you. Nice piece." She pointed at the silver turtle around my neck. The twenty was in my hand without a thought, a warm, fuzzy feeling spreading through my chest and up into my face at having a family connection recognized.

"Nyá:wen," I said softly.

I still couldn't see Key or Stella's hair anywhere, but just as I put my earrings in, the two of them burst through the crowd.

"There she is!" Stella yelled, like Key wasn't right beside her.

Stella skipped—actually *skipped*—over, immediately noticing the new addition to my outfit.

"Ooh! So pretty!" She reached out one sticky finger to touch the earrings, but I slapped her hand away.

Key smile and nodded. "She sure is."

I decided to take the compliment, even though I knew he'd misunderstood, thinking Stella was referring to me. Which was unlike him. He should have noticed the earrings. He noticed everything. I tried not to let that slip bother me, but the series of small but noticeable moments of weirdness were adding up.

As we approached the curb, Key glanced back, hand raised halfway to his face with one finger sporting a blue fluff of cotton candy. Even though his view was obstructed by people milling around, I had the creeping sense that he was looking at the fountain. I couldn't explain to myself why that should disturb me—it was just a fountain, after all—so I pushed the thought away whole, shoving it into the locked room in my mind while wondering how much more I could cram in there before the door gave way. One sharp *crack!* and all my fears would come spilling out. Surely it could hold one more worry. Just one.

In front of the bookstore, the sidewalk sale display I'd made was a good distraction from unwelcome thoughts. It looked pretty intact, but the graphic novels seemed to be selling well. Frank probably hadn't had time to come out to check and replace them. Even though it was my night off, it would take two seconds to do myself. I headed to the door, marveling at the sense of ownership I'd come to feel for the store.

"You can't come inside with that." I stopped at the entrance, turning back to point at Stella, who froze with a fluff of pink candy peeking out of the corner of her mouth. Stella was not someone who wolfed down treats—she savored, which could sometimes be inconvenient for the wolfers among us.

"Fine. I'll browse out here." She lifted her nose like I'd offended her and ambled toward the sidewalk sale table.

"But don't touch!" I'd spent hours selecting books for that table, carefully putting together an array of topics and types to interest the largest number of people and entice them to come into the store. I was taking bookselling seriously these days. Who was I?

"And you—" I turned to Key.

Key shoved the remainder of his cotton candy in his mouth,

dropped the cone in the trash, and held up his empty hands like a challenge. I shook my head at him but couldn't help smiling as I hauled the big door open. Even when he was annoying, Key was undeniably cute.

"Hey, Frank." I tapped the front counter and Frank turned to me with the same smile I got every day, like he was thrilled to see me—the most consistently genuine smile I knew.

"Well, hello, young lovers!" Frank was checking out a customer and looking particularly snazzy, silver hair combed back and dressed up in white sneakers, pressed khakis, and a pale green guayabera shirt for the opening night of FallsFest. Frank took care of himself, was always impeccably groomed and fit, but tonight he looked extra good. He was securely in his Hip Grandpa era.

"Frank . . ." I groaned. He'd been teasing Key and me for years, and he was really never going to let it go now that there was actually something to tease about.

"Frank." Key jerked his chin in some weird kind of bro-speak greeting that Frank, even at his age, automatically returned.

"Key." Frank slipped the books into a paper bag and waved the customer out. "Come again!"

Three sharp bangs on the window made me and a few browsers jump. Frank startled and turned, pressing one hand to his chest. On the other side of the window, Stella bounced on her toes and waved to Frank with both hands, her hair wild from the rides and mouth stained bright pink, looking absolutely unhinged. Frank waved back and turned to me.

"Sorry," I said. "She's had a lot of sugar."

"And what about this one?" Frank pointed at Key, who instead of coming over to the counter as he usually did, had stationed himself at a small table of local photography books and was slowly flipping the pages of a collection of waterfall photos.

"Sugar." I shrugged. "Just on the crashy side." But I wasn't sure about that and felt the door in my mind starting to creak and bulge under the pressure.

"Hmm." Frank tugged at the hem of his shirt.

"Foster still around?" Changing the subject for the second time tonight to take the focus off Key, I poked my head down an aisle. It was getting late for him, but if Foster were still out and about, he'd probably be in the bookstore. After years of not talking, the events with the black water had brought Foster and Frank back together; they were thick as thieves these days.

"No." Frank straightened a pile of flyers on the counter that didn't need straightening. "He went home. He's pretty worn out." He smiled again, but this smile was tired; there were more lines around his eyes than there had been a couple of weeks ago. Fighting the black water and getting Key back had been hard on Stella and me, but Frank and Foster hadn't had much gas in the tank to begin with. I hoped Foster was okay. I wished Frank would tell me so.

It felt like we all had a lot of questions for one another, but no one was brave enough to ask. We were all intent on putting the black water in the past. Fine with me.

Stella popped her head in the door, making sure her sticky fingers remained safely outside. "Round two?"

There were still more rides, more food and things to do, but I glanced at Key, who'd been flipping through the same book for the last few minutes. "I think it's last stop."

"Hmm." Stella followed my eyes and nodded in agreement. "Okay."

"You're sure you'll be okay alone?" I had to check in with Frank, although if he said he wanted me to stay, I didn't know what I'd do.

"Pfft!" He waved me off. "Go. Enjoy!"

"If you insist, boss."

"I insist." He reached out to take some books from a customer ready to check out.

"The graphic novels out front could use some restocking," I said tactfully.

"Listen to you." Frank clucked his tongue and chuckled. "Bossing me around."

"I wouldn't dare." I pressed my hand to my heart. "Key, let's go. One more ride."

He didn't move.

"Key?" I frowned and went over to where he stood at a display table, frozen in the act of turning a page in a photography book but staring at the laminated plastic *FallsFest Special!* sign. "Key!" I touched his shoulder gently and he startled, a grin stretching across his face so instantly that it looked uncomfortable.

"Are we off?" He slipped an arm around me and guided me to the door and out without waiting for an answer.

Something was off about him tonight, something so minor that not everyone would notice, something small that came and went, like the sun peeking out from behind clouds, reassuring me he was fine one moment and worrying me the next. I couldn't put my finger on it, but something was not right.

FIVE

ON THE SIDEWALK, STELLA WAS WAITING AS patiently as the sugar rushing through her bloodstream would allow. "Where to?" She bounced on the balls of her feet.

"Let's try something different this year." Key tilted his head and gave me the heart eyes. "Because this year is different."

Stella pretended to gag at the mention of romance, but I laughed, relieved that he was himself again, just like that. Maybe he'd gotten his second wind. Maybe I should stop second-guessing every little thing.

"Well," Stella said. "There aren't many choices because there isn't much left, and we all know Key's not going to go on the Spinny, no matter how *different* this year is." She raised her eyebrows at Key.

"True," I confirmed. FallsFest didn't really have any surprises left for us. We did it every year, thoroughly and completely. It was only fun because we made it fun.

"Ooh! The fun house!" Stella grabbed both of our hands, struck by inspiration.

"Stell." I wasn't sold on the idea. "It's so creepy and not in a good way."

Key wrinkled his nose. "I don't know . . ."

"Come on. It's new, so it'll be a true fresh start," Stella reasoned. "After everything."

41

Key shrugged and swung my hand back and forth in an exaggerated arc, people-watching as we walked, suddenly gone quiet. I couldn't keep track of his mood tonight. It could be the sugar in his blood rising and plummeting. It could be.

The fun house didn't appeal to me, but Stella was right—it was pretty much the only attraction that we'd never tried. The fun house was a traditional part of any carnival, but somehow new this year. I didn't like it for that reason. Things at FallsFest weren't supposed to change. It was supposed to be one glorious part of summer that repeated year after year. Change made me suspicious, and this particular fun house looked out of place: a little sketchy, run-down, and tired, unlike everything else at FallsFest.

As we made our way toward it, I could feel Key drifting off again. All night he'd been here one moment and gone the next, hyped and into FallsFest and then suddenly acting like it was his first time. I tapped the back of his hand with my finger to get his attention. He smiled at me like he'd just woken up.

He kind of had.

We'd had two very different experiences of the black water. I was still haunted by what had happened, how close my little world had come to collapsing in on itself. But as far as Key was concerned, not much *had* happened. He remembered walking home from my house and then waking up in the hospital. That was a lot of time to be missing, but to be fair, my memory wasn't all that clear because *too much* had happened. It bothered me, though, made me frown and hold his hand a little tighter; his lack of memory made him vulnerable somehow.

The fun house was tucked away in a corner of the midway. It

looked like a cargo container, and I wasn't immediately impressed. How much fun could something that size contain? The cut-out reclining body of a clown attached to the container made it seem much larger than it actually was. The clown was lying on its side, one red-and-yellow-polka-dotted arm sweeping toward us, black double metal doors incorporated into its face, an open mouth and a grin full of too many tiny teeth, ready to consume. I shivered.

In front, a plywood ramp jackknifed up to the entrance. We walked up to the top of the ramp and onto metal grating that shook under our feet, where I handed my ticket to a bored-looking guy with a pencil-thin ponytail in knee-length cutoffs and a Rush T-shirt. I followed Key into the clown's mouth that cackled a recorded laugh and released a gust of stale air when the doors opened.

"I don't think I'm going to like this," Stella said mildly behind me.

"It was your idea," I pointed out.

"I'm just saying."

Inside the clown was pitch-black and dank; I could feel the syrup of a thousand spilled sodas sticking to my shoes but couldn't see a thing. I let go of Key's hand to stretch both arms in front of me, disoriented and searching for a direction to go, but as the doors clunked shut behind Stella, a spotlight turned on over a plain wooden doorway in front of us with an anticlimactic *click*.

"I vote we go this way." Key pointed at it, turned the knob, and opened the door, like being inside a hungry clown didn't bother him at all.

"Onward!" Stella raised one fist, braving her fear of the dark, but if anything, I was the one who wanted to turn around and leave. There was something wrong with the air inside—it was oddly dense and pressed against my chest. It reminded me of something I couldn't quite remember, but neither Key nor Stella seemed bothered, so I kept my mouth shut and followed Key through the door.

It took me less than two minutes to discover that a fun house was definitely not a house so much as a series of hallways and corridors painted in head-swimmingly intense colors with walls that slanted at impossibly steep angles and unstable floors that shifted unexpectedly under my feet.

"Is this it?" Behind me, Stella lurched from one side of the violently green-and-purple hall to the other. "Are we having the fun yet?"

"Key?" I called to him ahead of me, fingers of each hand touching the walls on either side, head down, determined to navigate the treacherous floor. "Stell wants to know if she's having fun."

"Um." Key tried to brace himself against the walls, but no matter how carefully he stepped, the floor shifted under his weight. "I'm actually starting to think this is kind of dangerous. Don't twist an ankle here, Ave."

I followed Key down a red-and-yellow-striped corridor that appeared to be shrinking but found a normal-size door at the end. My heart sped up with every step, and not in a fun way. Shouldn't we have been done yet? How much more of this place could there have been? I stepped through and came out on the other side in a hall of mirrors.

Alone.

Except for the endless versions of me stretched out in every direction.

"Key?" My voice bounced back to me like another reflection. I waited, but he didn't answer, and when Stella didn't come through the door behind me, I turned back only to find not a door, but another mirror, this one elongating me into a strip so thin, I was almost nothing.

"Okay," I whispered, trying not to panic.

The mirrors had to be an even eight feet tall, which wasn't possible. The fun house wasn't that big. Yet above my head I could see nothing, felt no presence of a ceiling, just the same cavernous darkness I'd sensed at the entrance. The different versions of me—some normal but some thin and wavy, squat and wide; one had no eyes and another had too many—stood in every direction and uncomfortably close. I extended my right arm like a sleepwalker and took a few hesitant steps, unsure of what was mirror and what wasn't. If I misjudged and walked face-first into a mirror, it seemed unlikely that it would break, but in watching the other versions of me reach out their arms, I didn't want to touch the mirrors, consumed by the premonition that they would reach out and grab me. There was something disturbing about my misshapen reflections, and then I realized what it was—I wasn't able to make eye contact with any of them. They seemed to be watching me rather than looking back *at* me. But watching from where?

"Key? Stella?" I didn't like it, the way my voice didn't travel, like it was being sucked into the reflections and shunted off to some other place. I stumbled into a dead end, turned around, and tried to go back the way I'd come only to hit another mirror. How did they even fit so many mirrors in here? I must have seriously misjudged the size of the fun house.

"What the..." Nothing about this was right. Swallowing against the knot of panic rising in my throat, I made a quarter turn, nervously touched the silver turtle around my neck, and tried again. I had been through scarier things than this. "Key? Stella?" I watched the reflections swallow my voice down their distorted mouths. There was no reply and a vision of me wandering in here forever flashed through my mind—absurd but intense.

Two steps forward—*bump!*

One step right—*bump!*

Two steps back—*bump!*

My damp fingertips should have left smudges on the mirror but didn't. The air was stale and still. I was trapped in a closet-size space surrounded by nightmare versions of me, watching, waiting to see what I'd do next.

And I couldn't find a way out.

One sliding step to the left, then another, almost in time with my thumping heart. I cautiously went sideways down a passage I'd found, half-convinced that if I turned to face forward, the maze of mirrors would shift and rearrange to block me. Two more shuffles brought me into an open area with dozens of me's. And Key.

"Thank God."

He didn't respond to my voice; his eyes didn't move when my reflection joined his in the mirror.

"Key."

He stood motionless in front of one mirror, nose-to-nose with a slightly wavy version of himself. His eyes were vacant; his mouth hung slightly open. Something in me pinged, a distant reverberation, a ripple in a puddle warning of a storm arriving soon.

"Key." I slid my damp hand into his cool one, relief flooding my body when he slowly turned his face to me. But his gaze was unfocused, disoriented. When Key did register my presence, he squeezed my hand.

"Are you here?" he whispered fearfully.

"I'm here," I whispered back, dread coiling in my stomach. "We should have taken you home." He had almost drowned in the pond before I pulled him out two weeks ago. He'd been in the hospital. "You're just tired."

"I'm tired," he repeated mechanically.

"You're fine." But he wasn't; he hadn't been all night, and now neither was I. My heart pounded as he looked into my eyes like I was a fragment of a dream he was struggling to remember.

"I'm fine," he said, his voice strengthening, the soft smile I knew so well blooming across his face.

Of course he was. He was fine. Why did I even need to tell myself that? He squeezed my hand and gestured at the mirror, shaking his head. The warp in this mirror bisected my reflection so her head was slightly off-center from her shoulders. With Key's hand as an anchor, I tried to hold her eyes but couldn't. A little whirl of agitation spun in my chest; this felt disturbingly familiar, like a word on the tip of my tongue that I couldn't quite grasp. There was something wrong here, and I was looking right at it, but no matter how many times I scanned my distorted reflection, I just couldn't spot it.

Key had raised his free hand toward his reflection, but I tugged it away before he could make contact with the glass.

"Let's get out of here." I turned around and saw the most beautiful thing in the world right then—*Exit* in neon red.

Stella was somehow waiting for us outside. "I did not like that."

She scowled. "There was very little 'fun' in that fun house. What took you so long? Wait"—she raised her hand to ward off potential intimate details—"I don't want to know."

"How did you get out so fast?" Stella must be a better maze runner than Key and me.

"It was a waste of a ticket." She pulled out her phone to find out where Sian and the non-party-poopers were. At an immediate *ding!* in response, she clasped her hands in front like a guide at the end of a museum tour. "Everyone's heading to Laila's. Her dad's just firing up the grill. Sure you don't want to come?"

Laila's dad was an amazing midnight griller, but Key was visibly flagging, and after the fun house, I didn't feel capable of keeping the Party Avery version going much longer.

"You go, Stell."

Stella nodded, always understanding my limits to socialization. "You go have private time, kids." Two air-kisses and she was off. I wished I had that much energy to be social, but for me, being around people was draining, not energizing like it was for Stella.

After seeing Stella off, Key and I walked toward home together, our roles reversed for the first time that night, with him suddenly chattering on about summer plans—movies we'd watch, food we'd eat, laying out the weeks ahead like a smorgasbord of fun. He was being peak Key, totally himself, but I was now a quieter version of myself. As we'd agreed, at the corner of Maple and South, he gave me a hug and a loud smack of a kiss before a softer, real one.

"Text me when you get home," he sang softly, his masterpiece that never changed.

"Yeah, yeah." I sang back the only acceptable chorus, but it wasn't me I was worried about.

There were no lights on in my house, and when I stepped through the front door, it was silent; even my mom was still out somewhere with Auntie Ru, making up for lost time. In my room, Buttons stood up on my bed and stretched each leg in turn, giving a quacky meow, cranky that I was delaying his bedtime.

"Okay, okay."

I texted Key the thumbs-up emoji to let him know I'd made it home alive and got ready for a shower, letting my clothes fall to their rightful place on the floor. I let the scalding hot water loosen my muscles and imagined the tension leaving my body, circling and then going down the drain. I stepped out of the shower and into a steamed-up room. I'd once again forgotten to turn the fan on, resulting in a tropical bathroom climate. Mom was always on me about it, but really, someone should make a shower that automatically turned on the fan—why did that not exist?

I flapped the towel to dispel the steam and then bent over to towel-dry my hair, the most attention it was going to get. When I flipped right side up, I stopped short at the sight of a smiley face drawing that had emerged on the fogged-up mirror. I smiled back at it, because Mom generally refused to set foot in my bathroom, but who else could have made it? I added angry eyebrows to the face, turning it from happy to devilish, flicked off the light, and went into my bedroom.

In bed, I lay back, squishy pillow cradling my head. My cat was curled and purring contentedly in the crook of my arm while I watched the gauzy white curtains billow and dance in the cool night breeze and thought about tonight. FallsFest with Key and Stella had been fun: I had a slight stomachache, always the hallmark of a good time. Stella was Stella, certain in her choices, comfortable in her skin. And Key—he'd just been tired. He'd said it himself. My fingers found the turtle pendant around my neck and held it, warming the silver against my skin, aware this was a nervous habit I'd picked up sitting with him in the hospital.

I let go of the turtle and snuggled deeper, letting the blanket wrap me in a comforting hug. I'd see Key tomorrow and he'd be fine; this nagging worry would go away, vanish from my mind like a bad dream. This summer was going to be great; I was sure of it. It would be a perfect, happy summer, and it would start the second I forgot about the girl in the hall of mirrors when I'd stood next to Key, the one reflection that wasn't bizarrely altered, that looked almost true. The girl who looked just like me, with one small difference that was keeping me awake.

The girl in the mirror—her neck had been bare.

SIX

THE NEXT DAY, I'D GONE FOR A QUICK RUN close to home, walked to work, swept out front, tidied the front counter, and had the sidewalk sale table display set up to perfection by the time Frank arrived. His parking space was in the alley right beside the back door, but his car was electric, so the only thing heralding his arrival was the opera that he blasted on the drive in. A month ago, I would have lazed around at the counter, reading something I'd plucked from the shelves, and only sprung into action when I heard the aria of the day at high volume, followed by the clank of the heavy metal door at the back.

But things were different now. I was different. I found myself a lot more invested in the store, so I'd redone the table displays inside and outside the store, giving second-day FallsFesters something different to browse, a new reason to come in and spend some of the money that summer weather seemed to loosen up as vitamin D worked its magic. I'd gone through last night's sales, noting with satisfaction the titles that had flown off not only the shelves but also the table displays I'd set up. It was almost like I was good at selling books.

At the counter, I turned on my stool to look out the window, soaking in this moment of quiet before it got busy. It was another sunny, impossibly blue-skied day, like the mayor had ordered up the perfect weather, special for FallsFest. Soon, downtown would be bustling, but for now it looked pretty normal. It was easy to tell by the wistful looks on their faces which people were headed to work and who was starting a day of summer fun.

But the soft smile on my face felt more content than anything else. I hadn't always taken work as seriously as I was currently, but the bookstore had never felt like work because I enjoyed it so much. I spun back around to face the store, thinking that must be a good sign, enjoying what you do. This new perspective on life that I had—I was beginning to really get into it. I'd been so tense, so angsty for so long, but all that had changed.

New Me was seated on my stool behind the counter, stamping the *Frank's Books* logo onto brown paper bags when Frank walked in from the back door, wearing his customary khakis, bowling shirt, and a gray alpaca cardigan under his arm, in case of extreme air conditioning.

"You're late." I didn't even look up.

"That should be my line." Frank stashed his cardigan under the counter and looked around, seeing nothing that needed to be done. "Did you—"

"Sweep? Change the displays? Sort new orders? Yup."

We stared each other down.

"You're so responsible these days," Frank observed.

"Are you saying I was irresponsible before?" I stopped stamping and narrowed my eyes at him.

"No, no. Of course not." He patted my shoulder. "You just seem more . . . grown-up now. After . . ." He waved his hand to reference all the stuff neither of us wanted to talk about. "All that."

So I'd grown up? Fighting off a soul-stealing swamp demon from hell will do that to you. I slipped the stack of new bags into their little nook under the counter and looked around for something else to do.

"Maybe someday you could have more responsibility around here," Frank said so casually that my head snapped up, immediately curious as to exactly what he meant. "I'm no spring chicken. It might be good to have a partner." He shrugged and walked over to switch out one of the books I'd added to the front table display, like what he'd just said hadn't thoroughly blown my mind.

A partner. I hadn't even finished school.

"Someday," he amended, angling the books just so, still not even glancing my way.

Of all the possible futures I'd entertained in my head, running this bookstore had never been in the playlist. I ran my hand over the shiny counter, suddenly appreciating the grain of the old wood in a new way. Frank joined me behind the counter.

"Key was quiet."

Three little words that derailed my thoughts of the future and brought them back to the present with a thud. My hand stilled, my lips pressed into a thin line. Frank was voicing the thought that I'd fought all morning to keep out of my head, the reason I'd been such a whirlwind of activity. "He's been through a lot," I said tightly. In the silence that followed, Frank didn't have to say it: we all had.

The bell over the door jangled, and my auntie Ru stalked in, chin up like she was expecting a fight. She tugged at the neck of her *Decolonize* T-shirt, came up to the counter, looked Frank dead in the eye, and slapped down a five-dollar bill.

"I've avoided this place for years." She pointed her finger in Frank's face, the words coming out in a rush. "But now I'd like to be able to visit with my niece, so here it is—when I was thirteen, I stole a pack of gum and two Hershey's bars. I'm paying for them now. Better late than never. So are we square?"

Frank looked to me for help, but I had none. "How—how many years ago was this?" he stammered, as much in fear as confusion. Ru could be pretty intense.

"Are you asking me how old I am?" Ru leaned forward, one eyebrow up in her hairline and going from intense to intimidating in nothing flat.

"No!" Frank waved his hands, unsure how he'd come to be the focus of an increasingly tense encounter. "But this used to be a hardware store, and a general store before that. I didn't—I only bought it recently, after my wife died."

"I know," Ru said patiently. "But you're here now, so you'll have to accept on the previous owner's behalf. Are. We. Square?"

"Um, yes?" Clearly unsure what he was agreeing to but desperate to end the exchange, Frank nodded. Ru stuck out her hand and he shook it.

"Cool." Ru looked pleased, then took a hard right into sympathy. "Sorry about your wife."

"Thank you." Frank turned away, holding on to the counter like he was about to faint with relief.

Ru turned to me, her business with Frank evidently concluded. "How's it going, niece?"

"Good." I smiled. "If you're here to give me money, too, really good."

"Can I get either of you an espresso?" Frank wiped his forehead, looking queasy.

"No thanks." Ru shook her head.

I raised my hand. "I'll take one."

Frank excused himself and shuffled down the photography aisle toward his office, mumbling under his breath. Ru and I watched him go.

"Did I break him?" Ru asked.

"He'll survive." I said, swinging my legs on my stool and waiting, because I knew Ru hadn't come in here solely to settle an old debt with Frank. I was very good at waiting for people to crack, and being newly un-estranged wasn't going to stop me from subjecting Ru to my talents. I stared at her with a small smile dancing on my lips until she sighed and rolled her eyes.

"You are your mother's child. Okay." She threw up her hands in surrender. "You probably don't remember this, but years ago I said something I regret."

"I remember," I said evenly. When Ru had called my mom an apple that day, she'd knocked my mom's life off course. It had changed her relationship with her family, how she saw herself, and, in turn, how I saw myself.

Ru looked up. "Well." She spread her hands flat on the counter, her many silver rings scraping softly against the wood. "I wish you didn't, but here we are. It was a stupid thing to say. I've apologized to your mom and now I'm apologizing to you."

"Why now?"

Ru traced a whorl in the wood grain with the tip of her finger. "After everything that happened, all those people disappearing, it reminded me that—time runs out, you know?" She looked up at me. "And I thought, maybe if you thought you could talk to me, about your friend going missing, I would've listened differently than your mom."

Differently? If she was saying what I thought she was, interesting. But also too late. I'd taken care of the black water and gotten Key back without her.

She was quiet for a moment, but it didn't last. "Saw you talking to your dad last night."

I had to laugh. A seamless transition from apology to getting up in my business.

Ru raised her hands defensively. "I know, I know. But you've only got one dad. Don't let that relationship go without a fight. You'll regret it later, trust me."

Was Ru talking about my mom, or did broken relationships trail her like water in the wake of a boat? For once, I decided to just let it go. Leave it alone.

"Are we good?" She looked into my eyes.

I nodded. She was right—time runs out. I needed to gather as much family around me as possible; I'd learned that much.

Ru gave the counter a friendly slap and hitched up her artfully torn jeans. "Okay. I'm off. I got other people's lives to stick my nose into before work, you know. You're just my first stop."

I turned on my stool to wave to Ru through the window as she strode down the sidewalk, off to be nosy somewhere else and then to her job at the town hall. My ihstá Ru was a lot, but I liked that she was so direct—she had something to say and she said it. Pretty much the opposite of me, although I was working on that these days. The fact that she seemed to be trying to make up for lost time helped me a lot to forgive her. I was glad Mom had her sister back, even if that meant Ru was going to be forever in our business and spouting opinions like a tree dropping fruit. I let my hands settle into my lap. What had I been so tense about this morning? Everything was fine.

In front of the big window, a toddler sporting a jet-black bowl cut and butterfly face paint swung her mother's hand while the mother browsed the selection of kids' books I'd set out on the display table. The kid waved big at me, showing off a butterfly sundress to match the face paint. I waved back and gave the outfit a thumbs-up. Had I ever been that carefree? It felt like I'd been worried about something or other for years, taking up space in my mind and draining my energy.

Speaking of energy . . .

"Frank?"

The bell jingled as two young white men walked in, looking for a sci-fi series I'd never heard of. I sent them in the right direction and went to the back to see what had happened to my promised coffee. "Frank?"

The little office at the back of the store was made smaller by the too-big furniture Frank insisted on. The massive desk with two chairs in front and one on brass wheels behind, I politely referred to it all as "vintage," but Frank countered was "quality." Craftsmanship and solid materials, he claimed, were victims of modern society's insistence on bigger, faster, more. I actually didn't disagree, and if it made him happy to sit at his ornate wooden desk doing the accounts on a sleek laptop worth thousands, well, it was his store.

He could do what he liked. I had enough contradictory aspects to my personality to keep my mouth shut.

I poked my head around his office door, to find Frank standing in front of the shiny and very expensive espresso machine, another nod to "quality." Not an unusual sight. What was unusual was the way the cup dangled from his left hand and the length of time he stood there, simply staring at the gleaming metal beast.

"Frank?"

He took a deep breath like he was surfacing and turned, his eyes a little vacant.

"Are you okay?" I stepped through the door, frowning. I had always tended to worry about his health, but since the black water, that worry had intensified and popped up at the slightest provocation.

"Yes. I just—it looked odd, but . . ." He shook his head to clear it and pressed a button that made the machine gurgle. "Sorry, dear. I must be tired."

Everybody was tired; everybody was weird.

So I made it weirder.

"I went out to see it," I said quietly. He didn't need to ask what. "There's a path from the parking lot. It's not temporary like they said—they put gravel down and everything."

Next would be a sign that said *Big Pond* and a freaking arrow pointing the way.

"Oh, for God's sake." Frank slammed the lid of the machine.

If anything, the pond should be filled in, buried and forgotten, not made into a park attraction.

"Yeah." I dropped into one of the chairs in front of his massive desk. "I think they're promoting it for fishing."

Frank shook his head and made the angriest cup of espresso I'd ever seen. "The almighty dollar, no doubt."

"No doubt," I said wearily. Permits, parking, and profits.

The machine hissed and Frank opened a box of delicate cookies that looked like crispy lace. The bell over the front door sang out so I got up but lingered in the doorway, the room dim due to the new cream curtain Frank had put on the window beside his desk.

"Do you think . . ." I leaned against the doorjamb and twisted a strand of my ponytail so tight that it doubled over onto itself, another new habit I'd picked up recently. "Do you think Key could have like, some kind of . . . damage?"

Frank spun around to face me, tiny spoon in one hand and a frown on his face. "What do you mean? The doctors said he was healthy, didn't they? That's what I heard."

"Yeah, clean as a bean." I nodded. "He's just different." I didn't know how to say any more and I didn't really want to. Speak of the devil and all that.

"Avery." Frank placed a tiny cup and saucer on the desk in front of me. "He—"

"If you tell me he's tired, I'm going to lose it," I snapped, yanking my finger free of my hair. "I know him. Yes, he's tired, but it's more than that."

"And you're afraid it's . . . that." Unruffled by my outburst, Frank sat down with his own cup.

"No, no." I shook my head. There was no way it was what Frank was thinking. That was not a possibility my brain could hold. "We put a stop to that. I just mean, he was in the water, right? I think." Key wasn't the only one with missing time. We were both apparently soaked and found on the edge of the Big Pond, but it had been raining and I didn't actually remember pulling him out.

"Well, he was very quiet last night. But give him time, Avery. This is real life, not a movie. Not everything goes back to normal in the very next scene. And please"—Frank waggled his fingers toward the front of the store as I got up—"take that five dollars."

"What should I do with it?" I took the little cup from the desk and downed the contents like a shot.

He shrugged elaborately. "Buy her a fancy coffee."

I held up the tiny cup and saucer, fine enough to see shadows through it. "This is the fanciest coffee I know."

"Avery, please." Frank pressed the fingers of one hand to his temple and waved me out with the other, so I went. There were already customers to deal with, a soothing caffeine buzz in my veins, and Frank seemed like he wanted to be alone.

SEVEN

BY LUNCHTIME, THERE'D BEEN ENOUGH CUStomers that I was the one who needed some alone time, so I took my sandwich and parked myself on the wooden bench in front of the store. People-watching and getting drowsy in the sun and humid air turned out to be the perfect accompaniment to my turkey on sprouted bread. By the time I finished my sandwich, my shoulders had dropped and the jaw I didn't know I'd been clenching relaxed. My break was almost over but I wanted to linger. All the parking meters were covered, every store had a display on the sidewalk, and the town square was full of lunchers, shoppers, and FallsFesters. If there was a perfect time of year in Crook's Falls, this was it. I held a slight preference for a slightly later version—when the sun was on its way down and the breeze picked up, but if the sunny, sweaty version was on offer, I'd take it.

Everyone looked so freaking *happy*. Maybe they were just full of sugar or endorphins from the sun, but their contentment was contagious. It had been a while since I'd put together a good stretch of happy, but I was on a roll recently. Key, my slightly less-fractured family, the end of the black water—everything that had happened made me feel like a new person, the person I should have been all along.

Across the street, a man walked hand in hand with a little girl of four or five, prime little-girl years. In his sandals, green cargo shorts, and ratty yellow Terry Fox shirt from three years ago, he could be an uncle or a babysitter, but the aura of sleep-deprived befuddlement that clung to him marked him as a dad. The little girl skipped beside him, her yellow balloon on a ribbon bobbing in the air with every movement of her wrist, and when she spied the fountain, she stomped her tiny sparkly sandals in excitement. Dad dug around in his pockets, came up with a coin, and put it into her little hand, where it rested for a fraction of a second before she launched it clear to the other side of the fountain rather than the traditional toss. I nodded, impressed. The kid had a good arm.

Coin thrown, she was ready to move on, but Dad remained staring into the basin of water, not responding to the tug on his hand. I watched her pull again, pointing to something she wanted to see, but dad stood motionless, his jaw slack.

I sat up straight, my skin going cold despite the hot sun. The girl tugged with no effect.

"Dada!" The shrill little voice finally seemed to wake him and he took two quick steps back, protectively pulling the girl with him before quickly leading her away, glancing over his shoulder at the fountain like he thought something might be following.

My lunch sat like lead in my stomach. My nails were biting into my palms, so I carefully spread my fingers out, flattening them on my thighs, making them still. I had experience fearing things crawling out of water, and seeing the dad brought it all back. It was most likely just an undercaffeinated, sleep-deprived dad moment. It didn't mean anything. I tried box-breathing like Stella had taught me but still felt my pulse racing and a rush of tension rising in my chest.

It's nothing. It's nothing.

I stood and brushed my hands off.

It's nothing.

A flash in my mind's eye of a colorless, ruined face sent a chill up my spine.

It's nothing.

I bent over the sidewalk sale table, busying my hands tidying the kids' books and manga on the table, but my mind wasn't buying it. All my contentment, all my optimism drained away and memories of falling, of cold rising water and faceless people lurching toward me flooded in.

Despite the heat, I shivered.

And jumped at a cold hand on my neck.

I whirled around, scattering alphabet board books on the sidewalk.

"Whoa!" Key backed out of range.

"Holy crap." I pressed one palm to my heart. "You scared me!" Not his fault, not even a little, but I gave his shoulder a light punch anyway.

"Hey!" He rubbed at the spot theatrically. "I brought you a coffee, but you seem kind of twitchy. Maybe more caffeine isn't the answer." He held the cup, dripping with condensation, out at arm's length in mock fear.

I took the cup and brought it to my nose, the ice cubes rattling gently. Iced coffee and vanilla cream. Not that I'd ever tell espresso-loving Frank this, but sometimes this icy sweetness really hit the spot. I gave Key a light apology hip bump. "Sorry. This is amazing."

I took a sip and used the moment to take a deep breath as well, not wanting to alarm Key with my twitchiness. If anyone should be taking care of anyone, it should be *me* taking care of *him*.

"This morning, Frank floated the idea of me being his partner someday." I knew he'd be interested in that little nugget.

"Well, look at you, little business owner!" He offered a fist bump.

"Not now, obviously." I accepted the bump, relieved to be back to our normal "us." "What do you think?"

"That's amazing!" He stood with one hand on his hip like his mom, listing all the reasons I should be excited. "You love working here. You love books. You love Frank."

True.

"Even Crook's Falls . . ." He waggled his hand: *so-so.* "It's not terrible. Sounds like a sweet deal to me."

He was correct—all true. But he'd left the biggest question unanswered—if I stayed and kept living my small-town life, snug in the bookstore, would Key be here?

It made me unreasonably nervous to breach the subject since he hadn't, but Key was now officially my "something," and I was New Avery, the brave one, the one who didn't hide.

"What about you?" I made my voice light. "What about staying in not-terrible Crook's Falls?"

"Yeah. Maybe. You never know." He smiled, but it wasn't his real smile.

Maybe? Pretty vague, which confused me because he'd always had dreams of photojournalism and travel, but those were plans he'd talked about before we became us. Was he suddenly being vague because of me, because he knew our plans weren't compatible? Or was it that thing happening again, the thing where Key dropped out of sight before popping up like he was bobbing on the surface of a vast ocean?

Future talk aside, even the now was still nagging at me.

"No camera?" I just didn't like it. Cameras were practically a part of Key, like another limb. But I hadn't seen him with one since he'd gotten out of the hospital. Not even the one that I'd given him as a gift, the one that had mysteriously turned up in my backyard after he went missing. The first day he'd come home, I'd returned it to him. He'd seemed relieved to have it back, but I hadn't seen it since.

He took his time answering, studying the crowd across the street. "It's summer," he said casually. "Just taking a break, you know."

But I didn't. He loved photography. Why would he take a break from something he loved? Would he someday take a break from me? The thought hit me like a thunderbolt and I had trouble keeping it off my face.

"Are you okay?" His eyebrows drew together in an expression of concern that got me every time. The sun made a warm halo around his dark curls, and the old t-shirt he had on showed off broad shoulders that I liked to rest my chin on when he held me.

"Fine." Another sip to stall. "Just hot and sleepy."

"Right." Key studied me for a moment, saw plain as day that I was lying, and mercifully decided not to call me on it, because until I figured out what exactly was bothering me, I couldn't talk about it. "Well." He bent to pick up the books strewn on the ground. "Maybe that should be your last one of the day." He pointed to the coffee in my hand and changed the subject, charting a conversational course away from what I obviously wanted to ignore.

But for the first time, I felt like Key wasn't keen on too many questions, either.

"Now, how did you have these set out?" He turned to the display table. "I know I'm not a professional, but..." He bent over the table, sticking his tongue out in exaggerated concentration as he carefully nudged the fan of books into perfect alignment, mocking my new attention to detail in all bookish things.

I sipped my coffee and watched this amazing person who knew me better than anyone, who'd chosen me as the one he wanted to spend his time with. I needed to calm down and just give things time to settle. We'd been through a lot and were navigating this new relationship. There were bound to be awkward moments.

Key's long brown fingers delicately adjusted the angle of *Baby's First Animals* into place while I stood with the same smile on my face that he always provoked—soft and adoring. I couldn't help it. I reached out and put one hand flat on his back, wanting to prove to myself that he was real.

"Don't distract me," he murmured, trying not to laugh. "I'm creating the perfect display. Songs will be sung about it."

Our reflection in the store window showed me what I'd always wanted but been too afraid to acknowledge—Key and me, connected and together—but as I watched, our reflection changed.

The Key in the window straightened up. His hands fell limp at his sides.

The sounds of the street receded, replaced by my pulse booming in my ears.

"I'm grouping them alphabetically. I hope that's acceptable to you," my Key teased, intent on arranging the books.

I pressed my palm firmly into his back, confirming that he was bent over the table, looking at the books.

But the Key in the window was looking at me, pleading with his eyes. The Key in the window was afraid.

The half-empty cup fell from my hand, split open, and bled sweetness onto the sidewalk.

Key straightened and turned. "Oh, man. That is a sad sight."

He was my Key, not dead-eyed, not frightened. "The cup was slippery," I said slowly, and when he bent to pick it up, his reflection copied him as it should have.

But it was too late. I'd seen what I'd seen and it had opened a door in me, one I'd kept shut and locked ever since I heard sirens in the forest, soaked to the skin and next to Key on a blanket of pine needles at the edge of the newly born Big Pond.

"I need to get back to work." I also needed time to think. We'd burned the Ragged Man out of existence, closed the black water, and created the Big Pond. We'd stopped that ancient cycle from repeating. But reflections didn't have lives of their own.

"Okay. I should go back to helping Mom at the office." Key gave me a quick kiss. "She gets tense lately if I'm out of her sight too long, anyway. It's like since I got out of the hospital, I've reverted to being a toddler or something." He shook his head at the mom-ness of his mom's reaction and waved as he went. He looked strong and relaxed as he walked, like nothing in his world had recently been shadowy and cold.

It's nothing.

I wanted it to be nothing. I had done my duty—I was the one who woke the black water by finding it in the forest and I had put it back to sleep. I was done, my debt repaid. The people the black water had taken because of me, the ones who'd never come back, unlike Key, I pushed them out of my mind. But I couldn't forget the look of fear I'd seen, not on Key's face, but his reflection's. His eyes had been asking for help. I stood and stared at the window, but now it was just me staring back, vacant-eyed and pale.

What I'd just seen couldn't have been real. Key was safe and he was fine. Maybe things weren't as over for me as I'd thought; it must have been something my subconscious conjured up. What else could it be? I hauled the door open and stepped into the store, closing my eyes against the shock of air conditioning that raised goose bumps on my skin. My heart went cold as the big wooden door swung shut behind me with a heavy *thunk*, solid like a verdict, a conclusion I had no choice but to accept.

What else could it be?

I'd thought my business with the black water was over, done and finished.

But maybe it wasn't finished with me.

EIGHT

THE WILLOWS RETIREMENT HOME WAS HUGE and ornate, a "you can't take it with you, so spend it here!" kind of deal. Where Aunt Lily had gotten Willows kind of money, I had no idea—her family certainly wasn't rich—but this was where she spent her days now, surrounded by deep jewel tones, plush chairs in the lobby that sucked you in like greedy marshmallows, and carpet so thick it turned even the most heavy-footed visitors into stealthy ninjas. Although Aunt Lily had always been elegant, the Willows veered more toward the snooty side of elegance, and for some reason, my mother bought into it. Sunday-night dinner with Lily was a monthly thing, and it matched up nicely with my run schedule. After a long run this morning, sitting and eating was pretty much all I could handle.

Tonight, Mom had traded in her jeans for a simple mauve maxi dress that made her skin glow. With a summer wardrobe dedicated to running, my only option was an A-line mini dress of sunset-colored stripes that Stella had picked out for me to wear to an end of the year party.

The dining room was peak Willows, decorated to look like an apartment in Paris. Tall, slender windows made up the whole west wall, with filmy white curtains extending floor to ceiling and framing a view of the massive old willow trees that gave the place its name.

Each table had elaborate place settings, far more spoons than I knew what to do with, and a glittering crystal vase of flowers, different varieties but all of them white. There were layers of linens on the table in shades of white and cream. Even the clink of silverware was muted and overly polite.

Like I said—money.

After Mom placed our usual order, we sat in silence at a table for four, waiting for Ru to bring Aunt Lily down. We spent a lot of time like that, actually. It wasn't uncomfortable, just the kind of silence you have with someone you know really well. And she made me; she'd known me before I was born, so I shouldn't be much of a mystery to her although I knew I sometimes was. I turned my fork end over end on the crisply folded napkin until Mom flicked her eyes at me to stop. I tried to entertain myself another way.

"Ru came to the store yesterday. She tried to pay Frank for some candy she stole from the store that was there when she was a kid."

Mom chuckled and shook her head. "That sounds about right."

I hesitated, reluctant to bring up Ru's real reason, but having her sister back was good for my mom, so I took every opportunity to talk up my auntie. "She apologized. For what she said." I didn't need to clarify what I was talking about.

Mom nodded, rotating her water glass slowly on the table, her own fidget coming out. "She was going through a rough time back then. Usually, I can tell. But I didn't know, so I took her words at face value."

Usually, Mom did know. She was a great reader of people, which had made keeping the few secrets I had pretty exhausting. Maybe Ru hadn't wanted Mom to know that she was having trouble and had gone to lengths to hide it. My dad, however—looking back, my dad had been suffering lately for the whole world to see. If Mom was so adept at reading me, at knowing when I was struggling, how could she have missed what was going on with my dad?

Maybe she hadn't.

The thought made me frown at my water glass, considering the possibility that Dad stepping up in my life might not be what Mom wanted.

Was no one who they seemed to be? "Dad's having a rough time, too," I blurted out.

Mom nodded and sipped her water.

Mind. Blown. "You knew?"

She sighed and raised her eyes to meet mine. "Yes, Avery. I knew." Like it was common knowledge.

"You could have said something!" It hadn't been obvious to me. I'd blamed him for not caring when really it had been a huge miscommunication between us. True, he was the adult and could have handled it better, but so could she.

"Keep your voice down, please," Mom said evenly.

Raising my voice was worse than letting me believe my dad just didn't care about me? "Mom!"

"Your dad isn't my business anymore," she said quietly.

True enough, but I was. She reminded me of that every day. I'd never been certain exactly what had led to my dad moving out, and now it was less clear than ever. Maybe he hadn't wanted to go.

"This is really complicated, and I'm tired." My body was worn out from running and my mind was just plain done. I threw up my hands and shoved a piece of bread in my mouth to keep from saying anything else, refusing to attempt to decipher any more adult nonsense tonight. I stared at the vase of white peonies on the table and fought the urge to rip them apart, shredding each bloom and leaving a mass of petals strewn over the table.

Mom looked up and I followed her eyes to Lily holding Ru's arm in the doorway. If any of us was out of place at the Willows, it was Ru. She was too loud, too brash for the snooty crowd, and fortunately, she couldn't have cared less. But even Ru had dressed for the Willows, toning down for my mom's sake to a purple T-shirt with the Haudenosaunee flag across her chest and wide white linen pants. Lily wore her long gray skirt, white blouse, and pale blue cardigan—perfectly put together as usual, the complete opposite of what was happening to her mind.

"Remember." Mom leaned forward and lowered her voice. "Happy talk."

Ever since Key had almost drowned in the Big Pond—which my mom insisted was all that had happened—Aunt Lily had seemed frailer, and Mom wanted to make sure that no mention of Key or the pond or me reached her ears. Especially me.

"Avery!" Lily cooed as she and Ru reached the table. "Don't you look—" She narrowed her eyes at me, seeming to sense something off, like my bad mood had a smell. "All my favorite girls." She smiled serenely and allowed Ru to push her chair in, her mind jumping to a happier track.

Sometimes Aunt Lily's thoughts were hard to follow, leaping from one topic to another, seemingly unrelated, but something in her eyes told me this had been a deliberate change of subject. Fine with me—I didn't want to talk about serious stuff anyway.

Eat dinner, talk to Key, crawl into bed—the only things left on my to-do list today.

"Isn't this nice." Lily smiled at us, then looked around the dining room. "What a ridiculous place." She pressed her lips together and gave her head a shake that sent her carefully set hair bobbing.

"You know you can always come live with me and Lance." Ru spread the napkin on her lap. "I've asked you a million times."

"And I'm sure I thank you every time." Lily leaned back as the waiter placed a steaming plate in front of her, far more food than she would eat in a whole day. Aunt Lily ate like a bird, pecking here and there, and she was becoming so light and delicate that I feared she was actually turning into a bird, getting ready to fly away from us.

"Oh, Ihstá," Ru chided playfully, dropping a healthy chunk of butter onto her potato. "You can't leave Crook's Falls."

"I know that," Lily snapped. "I know that very well."

Mom and Ru exchanged a glance, surprised at the uncharacteristic snark.

"You have your life to live. I had mine. Besides, everyone's safe with me here." Lily speared a piece of chicken with her fork and chewed placidly. "It'll stay asleep."

What was that supposed to mean? Ru glanced at me, and in that instant, I saw it. Whatever Mom had told herself to make the black water nothing but an urban legend, Ru had stuck to the unappealing truth. She was one of the few who knew.

"That stupid thing . . ." Lily frowned down at her plate, her chin quivering. "Causing trouble for everyone," she muttered to herself.

"How did you like FallsFest this year, Ihstá?" Mom said loudly.

"What?" Lily looked up as if she'd just awoken. "Well, I'd rather go to the powwow, but I guess it's better than nothing." She looked around the room, new disdain in her eyes. "This place is so boring."

"Powwow's not until July," Mom said, but now even she was watching Lily carefully. Lily had good days and not-so-good. It wasn't unusual to have to keep her on track, but the mention of staying in Crook's Falls seemed to have unleashed anger in her that I'd never seen before.

Lily jabbed the asparagus with her fork like she was trying to murder it.

Under the table, mom's foot tapped mine. She gave me a look, indicating I should say something. I was Lily's favorite subject. If anyone could pull her out of her funk, it was me, a talent I'd been born with. I cleared my throat.

"I'm working full-time at the bookstore, Ihstá."

"The bookstore?" She looked up at me, her eyes clearing, the hint of a smile hovering over her lips.

"Yeah. With Frank."

"Frank." Just like that, her face clouded again. "Useless twit," she muttered, moving food around on her plate.

Between having to remember to keep my elbows off the table and Lily's sour mood, I wasn't sorry when the dessert dishes were cleared away and we moved to the lobby to see Lily back upstairs.

"Don't trouble yourselves. I'm perfectly capable of finding my way." Lily waved us off irritably, like she couldn't wait for us to leave. She jabbed a manicured finger at the up button, then twice more for good measure.

So many glances had passed between Mom and Ru throughout dinner that I barely noticed the one they exchanged now.

"I'll see Miss Lily upstairs." A perky nurse in maroon scrubs and a sleek red ponytail joined us at the bank of elevators.

"Are you sure?" Mom turned toward her and lowered her voice. "She's a little off tonight."

Lily sighed, glowering at the elevator doors. Her mind may have been crumbling, but there was nothing wrong with her hearing.

"I'm doing med rounds on her floor," the nurse insisted. "It's no trouble."

"She's probably just tired." Ru sounded like she was apologizing for something.

They were so intent on explaining away Lily's behavior to a stranger that I was the only one who noticed Lily lean forward, closer to the door, peering at something in the gleaming metal.

The elevator doors weren't particularly shiny, but they were spotless, wiped down multiple times a day by one of the Willows' many unseen cleaners.

I moved forward, too, trying to see what Lily saw, when she started back, blinking, her eyes wide. She turned to me. "Well, that's not right, is it?" she whispered.

"What do you see, Ihstá?" I whispered back.

"Okay, Ihstá." Ru swooped in and smacked a kiss on Lily's cheek. "I'll see you on Tuesday."

"Bye, Ihstá." Mom's kiss was softer. "Sleep well."

My attempt to ask my great-aunt what she'd seen in the door was thwarted by Mom and Ru, and most likely, Lily had already forgotten about it. But as the doors closed on Lily and the nurse, I saw her face, her eyebrows knitted together, her mouth in a line. She hadn't forgotten.

In the parking lot, Mom and Ru walked ahead of me, heads together and murmuring, no doubt about Lily and some Very Important Business not fit for my ears. Behind us, the Willows loomed, the U-shaped building intended to be stately and elegant, but looking more like menacing arms that wanted to scoop us up and devour us. Although I loved Lily, I was always happy to leave that place, feeling like I'd dodged the monster's embrace one more time.

At the car, Mom got in and Ru gave me a tight hug. "See you, niece."

"Bye."

She released me, then unexpectedly gathered me in again, setting me off balance. "If you ever want to talk about it, I'm here," she whispered into my ear, then let me go and started walking quickly to her car with one final wave over her shoulder, leaving me staring after her.

Talk about . . . What did Ru know?

"Avery! Get in." Mom was always irritable after seeing Lily. It made her sad, and being sad made her cranky.

I got in the car and fastened my seatbelt, watching Ru start her little silver convertible and pull out ahead of us with a beep and a wave.

If you ever want to talk about it . . .

Ru had never said a word about the black water, but that didn't mean she didn't know anything, or believe. Maybe this was one more way that Mom and her sister were different people. If my mom hadn't been there, would Ru have said more?

Whatever Mom had to say about dinner tonight, I didn't want to hear it. I put down my window to escape the clammy heat that had been building in the car while we ate as well as the thoughts swirling around in my head. I hung my head out the window like a dog, gulping down the sweet, heavy evening air. Lily had been so strange tonight. Ru had me reading between the lines.

Was no one in this town what they seemed?

At home, Mom's bad mood continued.

"We need to see her more often," she groused as we took our shoes off inside the front door. "We can't take her for granted. She won't be here forever."

"How can we see her more often?" One of us saw Ihstá Lily every day, but I regretted the question as soon as it was out of my mouth. It only invited an enumeration of all the minutes in my day that I could be spending with my great-aunt but selfishly wasn't. My mom's mutterings weren't really about me—I knew she struggled knowing that there was nothing that we could do to stop what was happening to Lily's mind. I saw the envious glances she shot at other residents of the Willows who were bent and shriveled but perfectly sharp. No matter how many times a week we saw her, no matter how many photo albums we looked at, one day everything that Lily knew and felt and was would melt into nothing, while her body kept ticking away. I dreaded that day, and so did my mom.

When Mom paused her rant to take a breath, I made my escape, darting into the relative safety of my room. Buttons was out cold on my bed, not even cracking one eye open until I nudged him over and flopped down to call Key.

Our evening call—the tradition even if we'd just parted ways at the corner, now just as much a part of my evening routine as taking a shower and brushing my teeth. A nugget of tightness formed in my chest when he didn't pick up right away, remembering another time not long ago when he hadn't answered.

"Hey."

I sighed with relief at the sight of Key's face and the sound of his deep, smooth voice and told that nugget to take a hike. "Hey. What's up?"

"Nothing." Usually, I could hear witty dialogue or explosions from one of the superhero movies he'd watched a hundred times in the background, but tonight, there was just silence. He was lying on his bed, staring back at me.

"Well, dinner was weird."

"Dinner?"

The nugget was back. "Yeah. At the Willows."

Silence.

"With Ru and Lily." I sat up.

"Oh, yeah."

My turn for silence. Was he high? I was talking to Key, right? Key would have remembered it was Sunday dinner with Lily. He would want to know why it was weird; in what way. Key would want details. "Are you high?"

A soft chuckle and a slow smile that eased the nugget of tension, but not all the way. "Nope. Just . . . tired."

"Okay." Tired. That word again. This was weird, like I was talking to someone playing the part of Key. "I'll let you go, then. See you tomorrow."

"Yeah, sure." He nodded as if I'd asked a question, not made a statement.

"Okay. Night."

And he was gone. I held the phone away from my face to stare at it. WTF was that? Tired—yes, yes. Everyone kept reminding me that Key was tired. But he'd essentially just hung up on me after not seeming to know I was going to dinner when he knew my schedule as well as I did. Was he mad? Had I done something? Not done something? There was a little clunk and whirl as the anxiety machine started up in my head and I knew I wasn't going to sleep well that night.

Petting a cat is supposed to calm you, but maybe I wasn't doing it right. "What do you think, Buttons? Did he seem okay?"

Buttons looked up at me like I was working his last nerve.

Fair. I was getting on my own nerves. I dropped my phone onto the bed; I should have taken a lesson from Buttons—the sooner I was unconscious, the better. I changed into pj's, which were really just sleep shorts and a T-shirt too old to be worn in public, and hung my dress in the closet before peeking out into the hall. Mom's door was closed and the house was quiet, so I padded down to the bathroom at the end of the hall.

In the bathroom, I kicked at a towel on the floor, then sighed and bent to pick it up. Mom refused to set foot in here anymore, which was great because it was all mine, but that didn't stop her from commenting on how messy it was.

I folded the towel onto the rack and let my hair down from its eternal ponytail and brushed it, closing my eyes as the soft bristles moved over my scalp and down. My hair was getting really long. I never wore it down but also never cut it; maybe it was time for a trim. A new cut for a new me? I felt like I should do something—I looked the same as always on the outside, but inside had been recently and painfully renovated. Staring at myself, I pressed the silver turtle pendant between my fingers and worked the clasp around to the back of my neck where it belonged. I should probably take a shower, but right then, with so many thoughts swirling around in my head—Lily, Key—a shower seemed like too much work. All I wanted was to get in bed and not think for a while.

"Mreow." Buttons rubbed against my ankles.

"Yeah, okay."

While I brushed my teeth, I left the tap running a little so that Buttons could jump up onto the counter and get a drink; running water was apparently far superior to the filtered water in his dish. While I waited for the toothbrush to tell me I could stop, my mind veered straight back to Key and his odd behavior. So he hadn't felt like talking—maybe I was reading too much into it. Maybe I was being self-centered. Our relationship didn't mean I owned him.

Buttons finished his drink and started grooming himself.

Key *was* tired. He didn't owe me every single scrap of his attention twenty-four seven. Was I becoming one of those clingy girls? My nose wrinkled at the thought. "Am I?"

Buttons paused washing his face on the counter and went very still.

"What's worse, do you think—talking to myself or talking to a cat?"

As he stared into the mirror, Buttons's creamy-white fur began to rise, puffing him up to twice his size. "It's just you, you adorable idiot," I said around the toothbrush. It finally buzzed to let me know my two minutes were up. I rinsed and spat into the sink.

Buttons rose to his feet, arched his back, and hissed.

Not at his reflection.

At mine.

My eyes snapped to the mirror. I saw myself, Buttons with his bottlebrush tail and huge pupils, and the towel rack behind me. Nothing out of place. But I had the distinct impression of movement just stilled, that I had missed something by a fraction of a second. I wiped my mouth slowly, keeping my eyes on my eyes. I'd had this feeling ever since the fun house, this sense that I was missing something important—looking right at it but not seeing.

One thousand one.

One thousand two.

One thousand three.

The girl in the mirror stared back; she didn't move, didn't change. That fact should have been comforting, should have convinced me that I was just being silly. I turned off the water and watched it swirl down the drain. "Let's go, buddy," I said, forcing myself to turn, put the towel on the counter, and flick off the light without looking back.

Buttons jumped down and made a beeline for my room, beating me to the bed. It was too early for sleep, but I lay down and pulled the soft white sheet up to my chin. The fun house, Key's reflection, Lily's strange behavior—there was something I should know, some thought not quite fully formed enough to grasp. A flutter in the corner of my eye, a word on the tip of my tongue, that maddening feeling of *almost*. I turned on my side and curled up, fists tucked under my chin, staring into the darkness of my room. Something was itching at my brain, and when I finally caught hold of the thought, when I was able to hold it up to the light, I knew I wasn't going to like it.

NINE

MONDAY MORNING, I WAS A WHIRLWIND IN the bookstore. A dervish. A tornado of cleaning, organizing, and ringing up. Every second I was working was a second that I wasn't texting Key and every second counted. I was not a clingy girl. I refused to be.

Frank set a few new titles on the counter, watching me sweep for the second time this morning. "What exactly is up with you?" he asked carefully. In summer, Frank worked most of the day with me, which was generally nice, but I wasn't currently in the mood for talking.

"I'm being not-clingy," I said, gently nudging him out of my way to get under the edge of the New Releases shelf.

"Okay." Frank had no follow-up questions.

Questions. Exactly what I was trying to avoid. I was not going to text Key and ask if he was okay. I was not going to torture myself by scrutinizing everything I'd said and done to see if I could be responsible for his weirdness.

I was not going to do any of that, even if it took an entire day of sweeping.

My distraction ended as the early lunch crowd started to arrive, which was a shame. There was something about the back-and-forth

THE OTHERS

motion of sweeping that kept my mind pleasantly blank. A lot like running, actually. I added going for a run to my mental after-work list of not-clingy activities and then sighed at the realization that my brief period of sweeping-fueled contentment seemed to be over. Maybe this was just how I was meant to be—an anxious overthinker.

A man herded three little boys through the door, who promptly took off for the kids' section, while the man drifted over to a rack of fishing magazines. Boys that age plus FallsFest equaled sticky fingers or worse, and since a lot of my time yesterday had been spent tidying the kids' section, I headed to the back to stash my broom and then do damage control in the kids' section until I could go for a walk on my break.

But thinking of anything other than Key turned out to be challenging, even with sugared-up kids roaming the store, so the second Frank came to the front to relieve me, I was out the door like a shot, ready to let the sights and sounds of FallsFest distract me all over again.

It was already sweltering; no breeze, no clouds, just humid air heavy with the aroma of sugar and sunscreen. Instead of walking and getting all sweaty, I crossed the street to sit on the edge of the fountain and people watch—just to get a hit of vitamin D and then scurry back to hide out in air-conditioned comfort until the day got the worst of the heat out of its system.

The crowd in the square was pretty sparse, but later in the day I knew out-of-towners would start to trickle in and by the time I left work, FallsFest would be in full swing. Every summer, it was a draw—people love a cute town especially in the picturesque seasons, and FallsFest was Crook's Falls at its cutest.

I hadn't always loved living in a small town. Even here, in a bigger small town where we weren't in the middle of nowhere, everyone seemed to know too much about everyone else. It had always annoyed me that everyone was a little too informed about their neighbors. When Dad had moved out, my whole class had known the next day. Privacy in a small town was mostly an illusion. I was willing to admit that there was a sense of comfort in growing up surrounded by the same people, of ringing up a customer who'd babysat me years before, of knowing who people were, as much as anyone ever can. I'd always assumed that after school I'd leave Crook's Falls simply because that's what you did, but I had never been clear on exactly where I'd go. That had occupied a lot of brain space before, but since the black water and Key, that particular mental chatter had died down to almost nothing. I still wasn't sure what my post-school life would bring, but it didn't hold the same urgency as it had even a few weeks ago.

For now, my small-town self was content to watch some shoppers browse the vendor tables, listen to the midway music and water trickling behind me while I sat, pleasantly melting a little in the heat and wishing whoever was staring at me would stop. How bizarre that I could actually feel their gaze. Some evolutionary thing, no doubt, a need to be aware of camouflaged predators.

Stella plopped down beside me with a huff. "It's so hot." Her tongue hung out of her mouth like a dog, and she let her head loll back like she was on the verge of collapse. So much drama.

"What are you up to?"

"Being hot, mostly." She angled herself toward me and reached back to dip her hand in the water, swishing it around. "It's nice and cool; I wish I could climb in." She stuck out her bottom lip in an exaggerated pout. "I was so hot walking around."

She leaned way over, in the water up to her shoulder.

"Stell!" I grabbed her shoulder and pulled, afraid that Stella was planning on getting into the fountain.

She scooped up a quarter and held it up, smiling. "Lucky money."

"I think it's lucky going *in* to the water."

"Right." She considered this, clasped the coin to her chest, closed her eyes, and then tossed it. Problem solved.

"You made a wish." I smiled. "With a stolen coin."

"Does that affect my chances of it coming true?" She cocked her head but didn't wait for an answer.

"Is this how you're going to fund your summer—wishing on coins pilfered from the fountain? Must be nice not to have to work." I raised an eyebrow but cringed internally—that was so something my mom would say.

"I work!" Stella snorted, lifting her pale gold curls off her neck in an attempt to cool down. Technically true—every morning at six, she taught back-to-back water aerobics classes to the swim-cap ladies who favored joint-friendly exercise without any risk to their carefully set hair. After eight, her day was free. Since she left the pool today, Stella had been busy; it looked like she'd spent everything she'd earned at the vendors' booths at FallsFest.

"Look!" She modeled a white tote bag covered in bright blue sharks and then pulled out two hair scrunchies and insisted I feel them. "Silk. And these." She held up a pair of delicate beaded earrings—pale blue and purple—made by the same beader I'd bought mine from.

"Am I a fashion icon?" I tilted my head, teasing. Stella had never copied me before. Stella had never copied anyone.

"It's okay for me to wear these, right?" She frowned at me.

"You bought them. Why wouldn't you wear them? They're beautiful."

"Well," she said, reflecting. "I'm not Indigenous, and the earrings are."

"So is the woman who made them. Stell, it's fine."

"Ladies." I turned to find Foster walking over, his cane in one hand and beads of sweat on his temples.

"Foster!" Stella and I cheered, throwing up our hands. I loved it when Stella caught me up in a wave of Stella-ness. She had a gift for pulling me out of myself when I needed it most.

"Shé:kon." He flapped his hand at us, too hot for anything more. I made room for him to sit, and he eased himself down between us.

"It's fine for her to wear these, right?" I dangled the earrings in front of him.

Foster leaned in and peered at them. "You pay for them?" he asked Stella in a low voice.

Stella's mouth dropped open in indignation, but in fairness, she had just stolen a coin from the fountain.

"That's Terry Bomberry." He pointed at the earrings. "I know her work. I was just there. Why wouldn't you be able to wear them? They're pretty."

"She's worried because she's white," I said, giving him the short version.

"Oh, that's okay." Foster patted Stella's arm gently. "We like you anyway."

"Just checking." Stella took the earrings back and stroked the beads with her finger, smiling to herself. "Anyway, I should go. See you later for junk food and fun, Ave?"

"Sure." I'd wanted Stella's input on being not-clingy, but with Foster sitting there it wasn't something I was comfortable bringing up anymore. I could wait until later to ask for her perspective on Key. Stella wasn't an expert on relationships, but she did know Key almost as well as I did.

As I thought I did.

Off with two blown kisses, Stella went down the sidewalk doing her signature Stella-walk—unhurried and confident, like she never doubted that the next step would find solid ground.

Beside me, Foster cleared his throat loudly. In a navy T-shirt with a stretched-out collar and long olive shorts. If he'd ever looked cuter, I couldn't remember it. "I hear Ru and your mom are back to being sisterly."

The speed and the reach of news in Crook's Falls still surprised me sometimes. "Yeah." I nodded. "My mom is pretty happy about it."

She wasn't the only one.

Foster reached behind him, dipped his hand in the cool water of the fountain, and pressed it to the back of his neck with a sigh. I watched a single drop of water make its way slowly, meandering like it had all the time in the world before disappearing under the collar of his shirt. A shiver went down my spine like the droplet was traversing my skin, not his. If not water, something else was making my skin crawl. I looked around but still couldn't spot the stalkery eyes I could feel.

"Key's doing well?"

Foster was looking at me with a strange expression. I nodded, wrenching my focus back to him, unable to stop the smile that crept over my face at the sound of Key's name, despite my current doubts.

"You?" I asked. Foster had come to the hospital twice, and I'd been out with Mom to his house, but I hadn't seen much of him lately. I was glad that he was out and about; sometimes I wondered about the wisdom of him living in that little house all alone in the middle of nowhere, but none of the adults seemed to question it.

Foster shrugged. "Meh. Can't complain."

Too vague a response to quiet the tendril of worry in my stomach, but there were so many of those lately they were starting to cancel each other out. I twisted around on the ledge, trying to locate the idiot who just would not stop staring.

"And you?" He peered at me with his little brown eyes like he already mistrusted whatever answer I was going to give. "How you doing?"

"I'm fine," I said, immediately hearing an echo of Key. "I mean..." I shrugged.

Foster cleared his throat and looked up at the sky. "It's a lot, what you've been through," he said slowly. "It takes a long time to get over stuff like that. Look at me." Foster shook his head. He definitely had been stuck in the past before I met him; no doubt about that. "But I didn't have anyone to talk to. You'll be fine." He patted my hand. People kept offering to listen to me. I wasn't sure if this was a new thing or I just had never heard the offers before.

"Yeah." The word ended in a sigh. I wasn't sure what to say. Was he referring to the scary things we'd been through, or the scary things that seemed to be happening now?

"Living in the bad times will only get you so far." Foster reached back for another scoop of water to sprinkle over his head. "Stay there too long and you lose sight of the good times. Even the so-so times—hey, they're all right, too."

The good times... were now? Compared to the last few weeks, these were great times. Whatever was bothering me, Foster was right. If I focused on that, that's all there would be.

"Hey." I straightened up. "Could you teach me the thing you said? At the FallsFest opening?"

"The thing?"

"The Thanksgiving address. The short version, maybe?"

Foster's laugh was smoky and rasping. "The short version is still pretty long, but it's about intent, not speed."

"I get it. I just—"

"Have a lot to be thankful for," he finished for me, nodding. "Tough times really open your eyes, eh? They remind us what we've got, not just what we don't."

We both thought on that for a moment.

"So yeah," Foster said. "We say the words before all else."

I'd heard it before, the address, but had never really listened. I knew the basic structure—it was like a song, with verses and a refrain, but I didn't want to just recognize it. I wanted to be able to say it.

"Okay." Foster shifted on the ledge and leaned forward, his elbows on his knees. "First, we thank Mother Earth. Makes sense, no?"

Fact. Without your mother, you wouldn't exist. As mine often reminded me.

"Then we express gratitude for the things that nourish us—plants, animals, water, trees, and birds." Foster paused to cough into his hand and I noticed the bones of each finger standing out, tenting delicate skin that must have once been smooth and firm like mine. My eyes dropped down to my own hands.

"Now, some folks, they can go on. Like I just thank the birds as a group, but old Scotty Fraser . . ." Foster shook his head, remembering. "He'd thank the cardinal. The eagle. The sparrow. The bluejay . . ." He drifted off, lost in the past. "Claimed he just liked to be thorough. Really, I think he liked the sound of his own voice." Foster looked up at me with a mischievous twinkle in his eye. "Scotty was a good guy."

"I'll just stick with *birds*," I said.

"Good idea." He nodded. "The part that always stays the same, though, is the refrain, I guess you'd call it. After each thank-you, you say, 'Now our minds are one.'"

"Now our minds are one."

"So they are." He smiled, patted my hand, and was silent. "We'll work on it together."

"Is everything okay?" I asked softly. I wasn't even sure if I was asking about him or me, why tension was creeping into my back, why I felt eyes on me, eyes that didn't feel friendly.

"Eh?" Foster pulled a handkerchief out of his pocket and wiped his brow. "Oh, it's just so hot today. Melts my brain." He chuckled, but there had been a pause. He'd considered saying something and decided against it. I'd learned that silence can tell you just as much as words. Maybe more.

"Anyway, I was table-sitting for Terry while she nipped out. Sold some of her work. She doesn't charge nearly enough for it. I must have just missed our Stella." He gestured across the square

THE OTHERS

to where I knew Terry's table full of beautiful beadwork occupied prime territory. She was no newcomer. "Should have asked for the evening shift—it would have been cooler."

"You're going home now? Do you have a ride?"

Foster waved off my concern.

"I could bring you a bottle of water from the store. It's nice and cold." I stood, already determined to at least give him some protection from the heat.

"That'd be nice," he called after me.

The mini fridge in Frank's office was a treasure trove of goodies—the protein shakes I teased him about, bottles of water Stella rebuked him for buying ("Plastic!"), and on extra-hot days, cookies with a thin coating of chocolate that would otherwise melt in the heat.

I grabbed a bottle and went back out the door, only to stop two steps onto the sidewalk. Still sitting, Foster had turned and was leaning over the edge of the fountain, and for an instant, I thought he was fishing for coins like Stella. At the curb, I had a joke ready, but something in his posture stopped me. I stood on the sidewalk, the cold bottle sweating in my hands, watching as Foster leaned over farther, one hand on his knee for balance, staring down. His right hand slowly rose, drifting out and down toward the water. The bottle squeaked under the pressure of my fingers as I crossed the street, suddenly in a hurry.

Foster's arm dipped down toward the surface, his whole body tilting as if trying to get a better look at something when he suddenly jerked back and sat up, turned away, and blinked a few times.

I sat down next to him and silently offered the water. It took him a moment to register the bottle in front of him, but he accepted it with a nod, unscrewed the cap, and took a long swallow. Something had clearly happened, but I didn't know what to ask, so I said nothing. Was Foster also using every shred of self-control to not turn around, seeking the eyes that were clearly on us? Did he feel someone's gaze boring a hole into the back of his head, too?

I hoped not. I wanted to believe it was just me.

A little green hatchback pulled up, and the driver called something through the open passenger window. Foster waved in response and stood.

"Rideshares," he said. "Great invention."

"Yeah." I nodded, now more worried about him than ever. He settled himself in the back seat, and with one wave of his hand out the window, the car pulled away, leaving me on the sidewalk. An older man getting into a stranger's car to drive out to a house in the middle of nowhere. I wanted to call out, to run after them. It was a mistake to let him go. I scrubbed both hands over my face and forced out a long exhale. People took Ubers every day. There was nothing to worry about, nothing sinister and still waiting for him at home that would only come to life when he was well and truly alone.

TEN

ONE GLANCE AT MY PHONE TOLD ME IT WAS almost time to go back to the air-conditioned comfort of the bookstore. Fine with me, because there was no longer any comfort here. Another sweep of the square with the same negative result. No one was staring at me. It was unnerving, to feel someone so clearly but be unable to locate them. I dropped my eyes to the interlocked stones of the path, collected my awareness of my surroundings, drawing it in around me like a cloak and then sending it spinning out, seeking.

Ahead. Right. Left.

Behind.

I shifted on the ledge and slowly turned, the presence at my back now unmistakable, like my attention had fed it, given it mass.

I slowly scanned the other side of the fountain, seeing only people enjoying FallsFest or cutting through on their way somewhere else. A little girl in a green floral sundress pointed at an ice cream stand and begged. Two Asian women greeted each other with loud chatter and laughter. No one on the other side of the fountain was looking at me. Yet I felt it. I was being watched.

I couldn't get used to it, water flowing here. It felt out of place, like this fountain had been air-dropped from another dimension. I watched the cascade from the top, down the fluted sides and into the basin, the delicate music of the falling water overlapping with the cloying, artificial midway tunes that drifted through the air. I leaned over the edge of the basin and stared straight down. The merry ripples danced and sparkled in the sun, breaking up my reflection. I leaned farther, certain that there was something more to see, something else concealed in the fractured surface of the water, if I could just get close enough.

Suddenly my reflection was not alone.

"Fishing for coins from a public fountain is stealing," the sloucher said in a monotone, bored, like he'd been saying it all day.

This guy. One of Crook's Falls finest, sporting a uniform at least a full size too big as usual.

"I don't want coins," I scoffed, quickly righting myself. "I'm just amazed it has water. First time in my life." Good thing Stella wasn't still here.

"It's because the artesian well's back online." He sniffed and pulled at the uniform shirt sticking to his back.

"Huh?" I squinted up at him.

The sloucher hitched up his pants, and I knew I was in for some serious mansplaining. "You know what an artesian well is?"

I hated to give him the satisfaction but also had to admit I did not.

"A regular well, you dig it, hit water, and then use a pump to bring the water up. Right?" He mimed the whole operation with his hands. "But an artesian well is like a spring at the bottom of the well. It pumps the water up naturally, like you're setting that water free to go where it needs to go on its own." It sounded like something he'd looked up online and didn't fully understand but had memorized to impress the locals.

"Okay." It didn't explain why the fountain was suddenly flowing.

"This fountain was connected to the well decades ago." He jerked his thumb at the fountain and then hooked it in his belt loop. "Town didn't want to use the drinking water supply in case of drought, you know? When the spring kind of died down, the fountain got shut off. But now the Big Pond is back, so . . ." He waved his hands at the glory of the fountain.

What well?

The sweat on the back of my neck went cold.

"The Big Pond?" My voice was quiet, my brain sifting through what he was saying and not liking it one bit.

"Yup."

"What do you mean it's back? Nobody knew it was there." It hadn't been on any of the maps. No one had known about it until I stumbled on it, when it had been much smaller.

You only find it if it wants you.

He scratched his head. "I guess folks knew about it before and . . . forgot." His gaze drifted and his jaw slackened.

I swiveled back to the fountain. Still the same coins at the bottom, still my reflection—the sun so blinding over my shoulder now that I couldn't see my own face.

"This water is coming from the Big Pond." I needed to him to clarify that one fact. But an image of the cluster of pipes I'd seen at the waters' edge on Friday flashed into my mind.

"Only way it makes sense," the sloucher opined, getting back on track. "For a town this size to have a fountain this big going twenty-four seven. Local water source."

I was looking right at it, but once again, I just couldn't see. I stared down at my reflection rippling in the water, trying to focus on it until the motion made me a little seasick.

"Mind I don't catch you fishing in there." The sloucher pointed a warning finger and sloped off to his days' work of monitoring fun.

This water came from the Big Pond. I turned around and reluctantly leaned over the edge, half hoping to see what had transfixed Foster. This new knowledge changed things—but how? Peering over the edge, I saw only the surface of the water, fractured by droplets and the concrete bottom of the fountain littered with coins. Everything was as it should be. I drew in a lungful of warm, humid air. Summer was wasting no time. The air, the sun beating down on me, everything was so hot; it made my thoughts and my body soft and slow. The movement of the water falling into the fountain basin was hypnotic.

My mind drifted, as if the sun's rays were working their way into my head and untangling thoughts like yarn, drawing each one out long. Which Key would show up tonight? The one I knew or the one who made me worry? Foster had asked about him; was it just out of curiosity, or something else? The sound of the fountain intensified until I felt like I could hear each drop of water landing in the basin, each one sharp and distinct.

The Asian women sat on the bench on the other side of the fountain, knees turned toward each other and touching.

"He kept it to himself. No one knew until it was too late." The younger one tucked her long wavy hair behind one ear. She wore a red sundress and looked vaguely familiar.

I was still being watched. Through the sleepy, soupy haze, I could feel eyes on me like a physical weight.

THE OTHERS

The other woman wore a green sunhat and set a matching tote on the ground at her feet. She shook her head and scowled. "Selfish. Such a shock to Emily!"

Drops of water from the top tier of the fountain fell like drumbeats.

I turned and stared, watching the water pulse from the top of the fountain faster, the trickling turning into a torrent, sheets of water pouring into the basin, putting the women behind a shimmering veil. My eyes went soft.

"I brought that recipe you like." Sunhat dug in her bag and pulled out a folded piece of paper.

Wavy Hair laughed. "You're so old-school. Why not text a photo?"

"Recipes should be shared handwritten," Sunhat insisted.

"Well, we'll only be eating junk today. Should we have ice cream? Over there." Wavy Hair pointed to the Pink Unicorn. "It's the best place in town."

My shoulders sagged a bit, tension melting away as I watched the ripples that were somehow uniform but never the same twice. It was very relaxing and looked so cool, so refreshing. Suddenly, I wanted nothing more than to feel the cool kiss of the water on my skin. What had I been worrying about? I couldn't remember what had so unsettled me.

"Is it expensive? I want to be able to do a lot of shopping later." Sunhat chuckled. She picked up her bag and stood, her face clearly visible once again but her body still hazy and distorted behind the veil of water.

"Let's go." Wavy Hair motioned. "On a day like today, there's no time to waste."

I tried to follow the path of the water—out the spout at the top, streaming down to the first tier, trickling down to the second, becoming a series of droplets falling scattered into the basin. I stared down at the surface of the basin, alive with drops of water jumping like oil in a pan.

Then a ripple.

It spread from the center out to the edges, independent of the water falling, like it was layered underneath. I frowned and continued watching the surface.

There.

Again, a smooth, slow ripple, caused not by the falling water but by something else, a reverberation, the movement of something far below us. Not a lot of earthquakes in Crook's Falls—what could cause this?

I looked around but no one else seemed to have noticed anything. Sunhat and Wavy Hair were almost at the Pink Unicorn. The area around the fountain had emptied out, everyone's breaks from fun or work apparently over.

Then I felt it. In the pit of my stomach, a tremor.

I twisted back around on the ledge to see the ripple again but found something even stranger in the fountain. The coin-dotted concrete bottom was no longer visible; the water now seemed darker and impossibly deep, unfathomable depths with an indistinct shadow drifting far below me, something far too big to be in the fountain.

I gripped the ledge of the fountain, the sharp stone edge digging into my fingers keeping me tethered to reality. Each breath dragged in through my tight chest was a struggle. There was something down there, in this fountain that was now somehow deep as a lake. There was something huge—a graceful leviathan gliding through the depths—and I felt drawn to it. It pulled at me, a firm tug at the center of my chest like it was setting the hook in a fish.

Me.

Everything I was seeing in the fountain, the weird compulsion to get closer, should have alarmed me, but my mind was pleasantly fuzzy around the edges, like I was on the cusp of sleep. It was so hot. I bent over and stretched out my left hand, convinced that just trailing my fingers in the cool water would somehow soothe every feeling, every worry running hot in my mind.

All my concerns about Foster, my doubts about Key and what was going on with us—it all dropped away, fell from me like a discarded piece of clothing. The tension in my shoulders disappeared, relieved by the burden I no longer had to carry.

So much better.

My fingers drifted closer to the water and I watched with detached curiosity as the level of water rose to meet me. In the far recesses of my mind, an alarm rang, but I was too relaxed, too intent on seeing what was in the fountain to listen.

I leaned over the edge just a little farther, my hand hovering so close to the surface now that I could feel the coolness of the water on my skin. It would be so refreshing.

Come.

The water continued falling, but the surface stilled. My reflection coalesced and came into crystal-clear focus. How was this happening? I could hear the water trickling, but the surface of the basin was now like glass. I looked down at my own face like I was looking in a mirror. How interesting.

Fingers broke the surface, but they weren't mine. My reflection's hand darted out like a snake, latching on to my wrist and yanking me toward the water. I pulled back only for the dripping fingers to grip tighter and jerk me forward again. I was now submerged to my elbow. My right hand clung to the edge of the basin, the only anchor I had. My feet scrabbled against the ground as I tried to turn, get a better angle, get some leverage, but the hand was like a vise. Another sharp jerk and the inexorable pull drew my face closer and closer to the water. The warm fuzziness that had addled my mind was replaced with white-hot clarity. If I went under the surface here, I knew I wouldn't find myself in a fountain. I'd be back in the cold, lightless depths of the black water. At the thought, my heart rate shot up, and rational thought went offline, leaving only my animal brain to finally dig in my heels and throw my weight back so hard I lost my balance and toppled backward. My arm shot free of the water, instinctively folding close to my chest and pressing against my racing heart. I scrambled backward on the ground and pulled myself up, feeling nothing but the need to run, run, run.

I kept my eyes on the fountain as I backed away, stepping off the curb and into the street.

Beeeeep!

"Sorry, sorry." I held up one hand and crossed to the other side, got to the door of the bookstore, and gripped the handle tight, reassured by its solidity.

Had that really just happened?

I turned back toward the square. From this angle, I couldn't see the water in the fountain, but I could still hear it, dripping, trickling, taunting me. The water that came straight from the Big Pond. In town now, with access to whoever walked by.

The water. Even though I couldn't see it, I knew it was there, as it always had been, and now I feared it always would be. I thought I'd stopped the black water, but somehow, I'd made things worse.

The adrenaline that had made my fingers numb was slowly subsiding; my heart rate inched back toward normal. I let the door close, sealing me inside the bookstore, but remained looking at the fountain across the street, the glass of the big door between us.

As if that could keep me safe.

ELEVEN

"OKAY, LISTEN UP!" SIAN'S DAD STOOD AT THE side gate. He wasn't a big man, and he was perfectly nice, but he had this way of speaking to us as a group that made the only acceptable response "Yes, sir." He waited to make sure every one of the thirty people in his yard was listening before he continued, raising a finger for each point. "No moving the slide. No going into the house past the kitchen. No drinking on this property." He paused and let that one sink in.

In Sian's backyard, my entire class stood patiently, waiting while her dad went through his annual list of rules.

"Now"—he held up a clipboard—"has everyone signed?"

Attending Sian's Summer Slide required signing a waiver releasing her parents from all liability, in perpetuity, throughout the universe. They were both lawyers, and if they had their way, Sian would be, too.

He waited for everyone to nod. "All right. Enjoy!"

The water slide was a pretty epic summer tradition. While we shot down the hill in her backyard at unsafe speeds, Sian's parents went to FallsFest, intentionally ignorant of whatever happened in their backyard for the next few hours.

Parties had never really been my thing, but tonight was practically mandatory, partly because Sian was my friend, but also it was the end of the year. Even though I knew everyone there, I was always the party guest most likely to be found chatting with the dog or cat in a quiet corner or simply hanging out in the periphery, observing. I relied on Key or Stella to socialize for me—a vicarious partygoer. They both knew better than to ask me if I was having fun—I did, but in my own way. Just being at the party was enough—watching and listening to people having fun was fun for me. Key and Stella were both social butterflies but understood that I was not. One more reason to love them.

I'd been edgy all afternoon, going over what had happened at the fountain, trying to make sense of it, to come to some conclusion that didn't involve the black water. Finally, I'd gritted my teeth, told myself for the hundredth time that all that was over, and forced one more box of bad thoughts into the overstuffed closet of worry in my mind.

I was determined to get Perfect Summer back on track. I would have to tell Key and Stella about the fountain sooner or later, but maybe we could just have tonight. I would try to relax, have fun. It might be an unrealistic goal, but I was going to try. I refused to let the black water rule my life.

As I set up my folding chair next to Key's, I noticed that other people had obviously shopped for the occasion. Two girls I knew casually walked by in barely there bikinis, making Key turn to me with wide eyes, faux scandalized. I stepped out of my shorts and pulled off my T-shirt to reveal the same violet one-piece I'd had for three years. I was just never going to be a fashion girlie.

"Hey, Avery!" I was comforted to see that Sian was wearing

bikini bottoms with slightly sprung elastic and a T-shirt with a collar that looked like it had been ravaged by wolves. "We're counting for burgers—moo or veg?"

"We'll do two veg," I said. "Thanks for—"

"Actually." Key leaned in. "I think I'll take a moo."

"Sure thing!" Sian made a note on her phone. "There are a few coolers on their way in." She winked. "Could you help with those, Key?"

It was on the tip of my tongue to object. This time last week, Key had been in a hospital bed, and the entire football team was here and more than ready to show off. Key should be taking it easy. But in the name of his ego, I kept my mouth shut as he rose from his chair.

"Enjoy!" Sian hurried off to the next moo or veg, pointing Key toward the patio door.

Cheers and whoops drew my attention to the side gate, just in time to witness Stella's grand entry. Effortlessly cool—which was the only kind of cool—Stella scanned the yard, found me, and came straight over, her shark tote bag bursting with a change of clothes, hair-taming products, bug spray, a beach towel, and in the front pocket, the keys to Mimi, her precious red Mini. Under her white sundress, I knew she would be wearing a very sensible, slightly retro, but well-thought-out, water-slide-appropriate one-piece. I also knew it would be noticed and replicated later this summer by every other girl in the yard. The only thing I wasn't expecting was to see Derek, the somehow already-tan and bashful student council rep, trailing her into the yard, brushing back the dark hair that was always flopping over his eyes.

"Ave!" Stella dropped down into Key's chair, then registered my surprise. "What?"

I pointedly looked at Derek, and Stella followed my eyes. "Oh, he asked for a ride."

"Stell." I made my mom's disapproving face. "You know how he feels."

"How he feels is not my responsibility. Besides, we talked. It's fine." Stella breezily waved away Derek's inconvenient feelings for her, and honestly, as I watched him awkwardly flirting with the Bikini Girls, he did seem to have moved on.

"Huh."

"See?" Stella wrangled her mass of curls into one of her new scrunchies. "He's going to live, Ave." She patted my shoulder. "Now, are you going to slide with me or not?"

Every year, Stella was the one who dragged me to the slide, the crowning glory of Sian's Summer Slide. This latest iteration was laid out in a slightly curved track from the back of the yard and down a steep hill, ending on the grass where a tarp was strung like a hockey net. If you were really unlucky, you could theoretically go through the tarp, into the brush, and meet up with the chain link fence that marked the end of the yard. If that ever happened, the slide would be shut down for good, but so far, we were clear to slide for another year.

The slide wound down to the end of the yard like a giant yellow snake, with two garden hoses stationed at the top on full blast and a healthy dose of dish soap for extra slip. Every year, it was Stella who couldn't wait to try it, and then Stella who got cold feet once we were there, once the water was running, begging me to go first so I could be waiting for her at the bottom.

"You're a very complicated person, do you know that?" I shook my head, trading places with Stella at the head of the slide as usual.

"I'm not physically brave," Stella acknowledged, delicately twisting her fingers. "My therapist says it's a difference, not a weakness."

"Don't worry, Stell," I soothed. Stella was one of the strongest people I knew. I'd always admired her ability to know what was right for her and stick to it, regardless of what everyone else was doing.

Fortunately for Stella, I was her opposite in many ways. Some of those were not so good, like not always saying what I felt or wanted. I didn't trust the construction of the midway rides, but when it came to throwing my body off or into something, I had that covered.

The crew operating the hoses gave me the thumbs-up, and I glanced back to see Key standing next to our chairs, watching expressionless. I wondered if he was getting tired already and regretted that I hadn't said something about him carrying the coolers.

"Ready?" Des, who played first-chair clarinet but looked like a twenty-something bouncer, was tasked with making sure people went down spaced at a safe distance. He'd signed a separate waiver for Sian's dad and took his duty seriously. He stepped away from the head of the slide, making way for me.

"Remember to wait for me at the bottom!" Stella called.

I took three running steps and launched myself into the air just high enough to land belly first on the twin streams of water. I kept my feet together and arms outstretched and was carried away down the hill. This was not my first water slide. Over the years, I had perfected my form, getting characteristically and unnecessarily competitive about it. I had never actually shouted "Look at me!"—not out loud—but if Key wanted to notice how gracefully I slid, that would be great.

The first turn was fine, with everything on track, but then I picked up too much speed, rocketing down the second and third sections, barely staying on the plastic. The water pulled me along faster than it should have and definitely faster than I was comfortable with. Most people popped off the end of the slide and skidded to a stop on the few feet of grass, but I knew I was going to sail right over that. The last resort tarp strung up across the end might slow me down, but at this speed, I might just take it with me and crash into the wooded area beyond.

I hadn't survived the black water to get mangled in Sian's backyard right at the beginning of my perfect summer. Instinct kicked in, honed by years of avoiding obstacles on trails. In the space of a second, I pulled in my right shoulder, getting onto my back and spinning around, so my feet faced down, because better my feet than my head, right? I dug my heels down, hitting the grass and catapulting up and back down, skidding on my hands and knees before stopping with my nose almost touching the tarp. It was only then, with my heart thundering in my chest, that I acknowledged how much danger I'd really been in. I didn't move, trying to catch my breath.

"Holy shit!" Sian was the first to reach me. "Are you okay?"

"Ave?" Key grabbed my arm to help me up, at the same time leaning over to peer in my face for reassurance. It took only one careless step onto the plastic, and just as I'd gained my feet, Key went down, still holding on to me. This time, everyone laughed, but as I looked down at him, an image flashed into my mind—holding his arms, dragging him to safety and laying him down on the soft blanket of pine needles. The soft gurgle of the pond swelling. The splash of something behind me.

"Are your ankles okay?" Sian prodded my legs with long pale fingers, feeling for damage. "You really stuck that landing. Maybe a little too much slip," she mused, looking back at the slide. "Guys!" she called up to the top. "Less soap!"

"I'm fine." I rotated my ankles to assure her. "And anyway, I signed the waiver," I joked, rubbing my shoulder, which was actually what hurt.

"Yeah, Dad is *not* going to hear about this." Sian got up and started discussing shortening the slide with Des to leave a bigger stretch of grass at the bottom. "Maybe we should fold up some at the top."

Back at the house, Key draped my towel around my shoulders, and we sat down on our chairs, a little apart from the Bikini Girls taking selfies, the grill experts, and the unfazed daredevils lining up to slide even after what had just happened to me. Apparently, my close call hadn't scared anyone off, other than Stella. After testing my ankles to make sure I hadn't jammed anything, I accepted a hard cider from Stella, who was hovering.

"Stell. Please."

"I just feel so bad." Crouching beside my chair, it was written all over her face.

"For what? I'm fine. See?" I straightened out my legs and wriggled my toes, but she didn't look convinced. "If you don't have a good time tonight, *I'll* feel bad," I said, trying another tactic.

It was kind of a standoff at that point, me willing Stella to just go and be Stella, and her wrestling with imagined and unnecessary guilt. But all of that was pretty normal. What struck me as not normal was Key's silence. He should be rolling his eyes, accusing

Stella of being overdramatic while he covertly was just as much of a mother hen as she was. But he barely seemed to register the conversation, with his head tilted back, looking up at the stars like he'd never seen them before.

"Okay," Stella said doubtfully. "But I'm coming to check on you later. And no sliding at all for you." She pointed a preemptive disciplinary finger at Key, who'd already promised his still-overprotective mom that he wouldn't. Although given what had just happened to me, it was probably a good call. He gave Stella a finger gun and nod in return.

I pulled the towel tighter around myself, chilled by the slight breeze sending the aroma of charcoal swirling past. It wasn't that I wanted Key to fuss over me; I'd never been that kind of attention seeker. But Key wasn't just not fussing; he was oblivious. He looked blissfully content, sipping his drink and alternating between looking up at the sky and then turning to the slide when the squeals and cheers of those lined up attracted his attention, smiling quietly like an indulgent parent watching kids at the playground. I was glad that he seemed to be having a good time, but there was a quiet, insistent nagging in my gut that something was off.

Maybe my gut was right and there was some damage that had gone undetected by the doctors, who didn't know Key at all.

That was the best-case scenario running through my head. I couldn't even allow myself to connect his weirdness with the fountain that afternoon. I waved at something buzzing around the top of my drink and then took a sip of the cold, tart cider.

If Key weren't Key, how would I know?

A sympathetic groan came from the crowd around the top of

the slide as someone else wiped out at the bottom. Waiver or not, it sounded like Sian's parents were really pushing their luck this year.

"No camera?" I said, nudging Key's arm because this was getting too strange to ignore. My mom used to tease him about needing it to breathe, like audio-visual scuba equipment, and now he'd virtually abandoned it.

He shrugged. "I didn't think anyone would appreciate me documenting underage drinking."

Fair point.

"The stars are so clear," he marveled quietly, eyes on the sky, but I wasn't sure he was talking to me.

"Is your dad still golfing?" I couldn't believe what was coming out of my mouth and why. Was I seriously testing him?

Key hesitated, and my pulse sped up, always waiting for the other shoe, and here it was. He didn't know what I was talking about. He didn't remember. There was something wrong with him.

"Well, he plays," Key said thoughtfully. "And he's pretty good. But I don't think he's ever going to love it. It's just a work thing."

I was being ridiculous. The three seconds he'd taken to answer had sent me into a spiral, but there was nothing wrong here; he was just relaxed and I was looking for problems where they didn't exist. The buzzing was around my ears now, first the right, then the left. I swatted at it and noticed that my jaw was clenched. Old habits die hard. The fun house Friday night and the fountain today had gotten me all riled up; I needed to shut that down and just have a good night like everyone else.

But I couldn't let it go.

"Do you remember," I began slowly, eyes fixed on my fingers as I peeled off the label on my drink. If I was wrong, this was going to be hard to explain away. "When you got lost in the dark?"

His gaze didn't stray from the sky, but a slight frown creased his brow.

"In the forest," I clarified breezily, but my heart was thumping. "When your parents had to go looking—"

"With flashlights!" He turned to me with a grin and chuckled into his drink.

"Yeah," I said weakly, my stomach sinking. "With flashlights."

"You okay? You're shivering." He gave me the eyebrows of concern, but I drew back from the hand he laid on my shoulder.

"I'm actually getting kind of cold. I'm going to get changed." I grabbed my bag, wrapped the towel tightly around myself, and walked too quickly up to the house, slipping on the slick deck steps in my hurry to get away from everyone. I pulled the sliding patio door open and stepped into the freezing kitchen while Key sat on his chair, looking up at the sky, his face a mask.

It was my own fault. I'd given him silly little tests to prove that he was himself, to quiet the growing voice of alarm in my head. The tiles of the kitchen floor were icy under my bare feet, but I didn't move from the door, watching as people drifted by outside, greeting Key post-slide to rummage in one of the coolers.

Curiosity, my gnawing need to know—it always bit me in the ass, and this time was no different. I could have just ignored the little things, the moments when his eyes didn't look quite right or when he seemed to go away somewhere, the times when he felt like someone else entirely. I could have just enjoyed tonight with him, the start to our perfect summer. But I'd ruined it by testing him, not truly expecting him to fail.

But he had.

I had been the one who stayed in the forest too long and had gotten lost in the dark, not Key; my parents who'd come out with flashlights, not his. I slid the door shut, putting a thin pane of glass between us.

I pressed my fingers against the cold glass of the door, watching as they met my reflected fingertips on the other side. An image of those that had reached out from the fountain to grab me flashed through my mind and I quickly pulled my hand back. Out in the yard, I could see Sian and Derek gently nudging Stella into position at the head of the slide as she shrieked with excitement. Sitting low in his chair, Key had his head dropped back, face turned skyward.

And on top of everything, I could see myself looking back at me, eyes hard and cold, like seeing two worlds at once, two realities that were similar but not the same. On which side of the glass did I belong? I turned away from the door and took a deep breath, gripping the straps of my bag hard to stop the tremor in my fingers, alarmed at the thoughts running through my mind and the turn tonight had taken. I'd tried. I'd tried to forget it all for just a bit. I'd tried to make Perfect Summer a reality. But something wouldn't let me, and I was starting to reluctantly acknowledge what that something was.

After getting changed and returning to the yard, I put off going back to Key, uncharacteristically circulating, posing for some photos with Sian and our cross-country team members and checking on the progress at the grill where Stella caught up with me and recounted her incredible feat of bravery on the water slide and lamenting what it had done to her hair. I was chatty; I was social. If anyone was not acting like themselves, it was me.

Key was a mildly subdued version of himself for the rest of the night but definitely familiar enough to have me second-guessing myself, almost buying into the "he's tired" line of reasoning. Could he be tired enough to forget such a basic and well-known fact? He and Stella loved to bring up that lost-in-the-forest story anytime I had to navigate somewhere.

By the time Sian's parents returned, the sight of her dad at the gate making people start reaching for their bags and slipping on shoes, my denial had fully kicked in. I'd convinced myself that the problem was me—my brain and my tendency to go hunting for flaws in anything good that happened. It was anxiety rearing its head, and I was determined to slap it down.

Key and me—this was a good thing. It was almost unthinkably good.

Stella packed our folding chairs in Mimi's backseat and made sure Derek was buckled in the front before pulling away, sticking her whole arm out the window and waving like she'd never see us again as she drove down the street.

"Thanks, Sian." I turned to our host. "Sure you don't need help cleaning up?"

She waved me off. "The parents will want to comb the yard for any incriminating evidence. See you on the trails!" She gave me a one-armed hug. That should have been it, except then Key wrapped both arms around her.

"Thanks, Sian," he murmured.

Sian's eyes went wide at me over Key's shoulder before she stepped away, clapping him on the back. "Okay. You get him home, Ave," she said with an uncomfortable laugh.

I tried to laugh back, but it got stuck in my throat. Key was free to hug anyone he chose—that part didn't bother me. He'd just never hugged Sian before, and the single drink he'd nursed all night didn't explain it.

He took my hand, and we strolled down the sidewalk, only three blocks to go before we stopped at the corner of Maple and South, him going left and me going right. Our footsteps were muted, crickets were chirping, and the last partygoers' voices faded into the night. There were no other cars on the street and no one outside at this hour. Even with the streetlights, walking at night always made me feel like the only person on earth. It should have been scary, but with Key's hand in mine, it wasn't unwelcome.

At our corner, Key wrapped his arms around me and pulled me in close. He smelled of sunscreen and the ever-present vanilla, with a hint of something else, something new that I couldn't place. I dug my chin into the top of his shoulder, a little divot there that fit my chin perfectly.

"That was nice," he said, his voice low and just for me. "Seeing everybody."

"Mmm," I agreed. "A nice night."

Key sighed. "A nice night." Snugging up his arms around me.

This had to be the best part of any night, when we were alone and close enough to scandalize Key's dad. *A little daylight, please!* My mom had always said I was like a cat, that I liked to be swaddled, compressed, or squeezed, and she was right. Even Stella knew, which was how I'd scored a weighted blanket last Christmas.

I sighed in contentment, and Key held me tighter.

Then tighter still.

Bones in my shoulder ground together.

"Ow," I said quietly against him, expecting him to step back and make some quip about the pitfalls of superstrength. But he didn't let go, and suddenly I didn't know, wasn't sure who it was holding me there in the dark on a quiet street. Had I ever known? Was that even possible? "Hey." Louder this time, because now I was pissed off.

With no response from him, I went from pissed off to something else, a place in my mind that I couldn't consciously acknowledge. I tried to work a hand between us for leverage, but we were too close, and he wasn't giving at all. A dark shape fluttered in the windshield of the car parked next to us, but when I turned my head, nothing was there. Around us, the neighborhood was quiet, insects chirping like everything was normal, everything was fine, but it wasn't, not even a little. I made a fist, protecting my thumb like Mom had shown me, when suddenly Key's arms went slack. He released me and stepped back. There was an odd look in his eyes, like he'd just woken up but not from refreshing sleep.

He smiled and dropped a kiss on my forehead like nothing extremely weird and upsetting had just happened. "Night. Text me when you get home," he sang under his breath.

"Yeah, yeah." My response was automatic but weak. I was surprised he hadn't felt my heart pounding. Maybe he had.

At the curb, I turned back and watched him stroll down the street. Without missing a beat, he picked up a stick from the ground and savagely whacked at Mr. Patel's tiger lilies, sending deep orange petals falling to the sidewalk; the Stillmans' daisies were next. At the corner, Key flung the stick into the street, never once looking back.

Off the curb and across the street, I couldn't get home fast enough. I didn't notice the coolness of the air or the fresh scent of night. I didn't feel anything but the cold lump of dread in the pit of my stomach.

I ran up the porch steps and fumbled with the lock. Once inside, I stood there, both hands pressed against the cool door, panting.

"How was the party, Ave?" Mom called from the living room.

"Good." An automatic reply came out of me, a habit from years of trying to not make my mom worry. "The party was good."

Other things weren't.

I kicked off my shoes and flopped down on the sofa, a childlike desire to be close to my mom rising up sudden and strong. Buttons jumped up beside me and I scratched his neck absently while my mind buzzed.

There were so many questions swirling around in my head and not nearly enough answers. There was only one thing I knew for sure.

Two weeks ago, I'd gone into the black water and pulled someone from the pond.

But that someone wasn't Key.

TWELVE

BUTTONS MUST HAVE THOUGHT HE'D WON THE lottery the next morning when I stayed in bed, listening to Mom putter around—out of the shower and into the kitchen to get her prepacked lunch, then out the door and off to work, not disturbing me because I'd gotten in late last night. True enough, I didn't usually come home after the entire neighborhood was sleeping, but there was more. Buttons revved his purr up to maximum as I lay there scratching the top of his head, thinking about the real reason I'd stayed in bed. Mom would have had more questions about last night—innocent, well-meaning, "trying to be interested in my teenager's life" kind of questions—but I had my own questions, and I wasn't ready to talk about any of it.

For one, Mom wouldn't believe me. Not in an accusatory sort of way, but to think Key would step out of line with me was unthinkable, as impossible as if I stopped running to devote all my time to algebra. If he were anyone else, questionable behavior would send her straight to Mom Rage Level Five, but with Key, she was liable to talk to his parents, thinking as I had, that something was wrong with him.

Something was wrong, all right.

But Mom and his parents would go down the MRI/CT-scan-rabbit-hole variety of wrong, which would lead nowhere. I knew it was something else. How I knew, I couldn't say. But I did.

"Definitely something wrong," I whispered to Buttons, who knew all my secrets. He blinked at me slowly and purred.

While listening to Mom getting ready, I'd formulated a plan. Before I dragged everyone into my chaos—again—work was waiting for me. But if I was careful, if I phrased things just right, maybe I could get two things accomplished in one stop.

"Sorry, buddy." I checked the time, shifted Buttons off my chest, and got out of bed. I'd be very early to work, but I had to go before I chickened out.

It was a nice enough day—not too hot yet, the air fresh and sweet, still carrying the last bit of dawn. The sun cast a gentle golden glow over everything. I noticed very little of it. My mind was whirling with worries, what I'd say, how I'd phrase it.

I was so wrapped up in my head that the sight of him actually made me stop short. Key, waving at me from the corner of Maple, standing there like he'd been waiting for me. Usually, Key would only be up at this hour to meet me for an early breakfast, but I didn't remember us making plans for today.

"Morning!" He smiled and hugged me.

"Hey." I couldn't help it. Even as distracted as I was, as disturbing as the end to last night had been, the sight of him, the warm solidity and the scent of vanilla and soap made something unspool in my chest. Some small part of me went content and quiet.

He took my hand and we continued toward downtown.

"Neighbors got a puppy," he said. "So cute and wriggly. You'll love him. He's tiny now, but his paws are like this." He held up his fist.

"So he's not going to stay small for long." I smiled. Puppies were pretty great.

"Nope." Key raised his face to the sun, closed his eyes, and smiled, swinging my hand in his.

It felt so good. We were happy together and talking about puppies. Why would I ruin it by talking about last night?

Maybe Key knew he'd done something wrong last night, but it wasn't like him to not acknowledge it and apologize, to not want to talk about it.

I squeezed his hand, and he squeezed back, his other hand resting on the camera that hung around his neck.

"Your break is over?" I nodded at the camera.

"Hmm?" He looked down, as if surprised to see it there. "Oh! Yeah." He patted the camera fondly. "We're back on track."

Key and a camera. How much more normal could he get? But rather than reassure me, its presence unsettled me even more. This whole unscheduled walk downtown felt staged. It was almost like he wanted to make sure I saw the camera.

"You never know what you'll see that deserves immortalizing." He smiled. But he handled the camera like it was a stranger. He didn't shoot, didn't raise it, didn't even jokingly threaten to take a picture of me in my early-morning glory.

Does he know how? A bizarre thought that flew through my mind almost too fast to catch.

Key hummed as we walked, but I didn't recognize the tune.

I was almost relieved when we got to the bookstore, slowing to a halt and standing on the sidewalk in silence.

"Are you working for your mom again?" I asked, for lack of anything better to say. This was new, to feel like I had to fill the silence. I didn't care for it.

I caught a split-second hesitation. "Yeah. No rest for the wicked." Key shook his head mournfully.

More silence, with Key smiling at me expectantly like we were in a play and he was waiting for me to say my line.

"Getting a coffee first?" I asked. Because it hadn't been an apology walk. Why else was he here?

"You know it!" He pressed one finger to my chest, just above the silver turtle, and gave a delicate push and smiled. Suddenly I was certain that if I asked him if he would be walking down the sidewalk on his hands, he'd smile and agree to that, too.

"Okay." My mouth was bone-dry. This was just plain weird. "See you later?"

Key pressed both hands on my shoulders and looked into my eyes. "You will," he said quietly. One quick kiss and I was on my own.

And I wasn't sorry.

What the hell was that? I unlocked the big wooden door, no clearer on what I'd say to Frank, how I'd broach the idea that the nightmare we thought we'd put to bed might not be over. I would just gently ask if he'd noticed anything odd about Key, which I already knew he had because Key was now beyond "odd." Later today, I'd talk to Stella, who had a different skill set.

Open the door. Enter the store.

Act natural.

"Avery? You're early," Frank called from the back. "I'll be right out."

I put my bag on the counter and flexed my fingers. *Don't tell too much. Careful words.*

I stashed my bag under the counter, taking deep breaths and trying not to replay every moment of the walk here. It called up too many questions, and I didn't like any of the possible answers. The content, quiet feeling I'd had was long gone, morphed into a knot of squirrelly agitation that hummed just under my skin.

Foster walked through the door. "Frank!" he called. "You don't answer your phone?" he grumbled irritably, stopping short when he saw me behind the counter. "Oh. You're here."

I nodded. "I do work here."

"Yeah, but it's early." Foster cleared his throat and shifted from one foot to the other, eyes flitting around the store like he'd never seen it before.

Okaaaay. I frowned, scrutinizing Foster for clues. We were both here strangely early. I knew what my reason was, but why was he here?

"What's that?" I pointed at the thing he'd been trying to keep behind his back since the moment he walked in.

"Oh, this?" Foster looked down at the metal box in his hand like it had materialized just that second. "Fancy lunch box."

"It's a bento box, actually," I supplied, really curious now. "Frank uses one."

"Does he, now?" Apparently, this was news to Foster.

Like he'd been conjured by the sound of his name, Frank appeared at the end of the aisle and froze, the same way Foster had when he'd seen me. I looked from one to the other, trying to figure out what they were up to.

Foster sighed and held up the box. "You forgot your lunch."

Frank grimaced and joined us at the counter, where he took the box from Foster.

Why were they acting so sketchy? Foster had Frank's lunch—big deal.

Wait. Frank lived in town and Foster's little house was on the outskirts.

"Why did you have his lunch?" Once again, I knew something was happening right in front of me that I wasn't seeing, some puzzle I was slowly piecing together. "Did you come from Frank's?"

"Jeez, just tell her," Foster groused and waved his hand at Frank.

"Fine." Frank held the box in both hands and paused, lifting his chin like he was about to conduct an orchestra or—

"Foster is staying with me."

—officiate a wedding.

I blinked. Foster was living with Frank?

Why?

My brain ticked through the possibilities.

No.

NO.

"Oh my God." My mind was blown open, vaporized into a slack-jawed wasteland by the possibility of romance. "Oh my God. So, the other night, at FallsFest, when you said Foster had gone home . . ." I tucked both fists under my chin and bounced on the balls of my feet, channeling Stella. The thought had never entered my mind before, but now that it had, it was all I wanted. Oh my God. The cuteness.

"Home." Frank nodded. His tidy little bungalow on the corner of Market and Matilda, surrounded by hydrangeas and an actual white picket fence. Could they be more adorable?

"And you didn't tell me this because . . . ?" This was the most fantastic thing to happen—ever.

Frank huffed. "You, my dear, are not the center of the universe."

Ouch.

"And we didn't want to worry you."

Worry? That stopped me cold. Why would I worry? If not romance, what possible reason would Foster have for bunking with Frank and keeping it from me?

"What do you mean?" The anxiety-powered squirrel in my chest woke up as the only other answer presented itself. "What do you mean? Are you sick?" I scanned Foster for signs.

"What?" he barked irritably. "What are you looking at?"

"Did you have a heart attack?"

"Wh—why would you think that? Do I look like—"

"Just tell her." Frank sighed.

Foster turned to him, raising a finger. "We discussed this, and—"

"She's just going to worry."

"Yes." Foster dropped the word like a stone and fixed Frank with a stony gaze. "She will."

They stared each other down while I stood there, twisting my fingers together. More people I loved were changing and acting weird. I didn't know how much more I could take. I couldn't yell at them, couldn't say anything snarky to break it up the way I did when Stella and Key took things too far. But whatever was going on here, I wanted it to stop.

Frank placed the box on the counter like he expected it to explode and let out a dramatic sigh. "Okay."

"It's probably nothing," Foster assured me in a low voice.

How many times had I said that myself, when the nothing turned out to be a huge, scary something? I was not comforted.

"Foster is staying with me because he had . . ." Frank pursed his lips, searching for the words. "A scare."

I waited. This could mean many things. "And . . . ?"

Frank took both of my hands in his. "Sweetheart, after everything—we just wanted you to relax and enjoy the summer."

I felt an expanding lightness, like the top of my head might pop off at any second. "There's nothing wrong with Foster?"

They both shook their heads.

So it was something worse.

"I've seen some things," Foster confessed like a guilty secret.

And there it was. The other shoe. A tight knot of "I told you so" cinched in my gut.

"Seen things like what?" I asked numbly, images of faceless people flashing through my mind.

"Just . . . reflections." Foster rubbed his face, suddenly sounding weary. "Probably stress." He tapped his temple with one finger.

A shot of adrenaline zinged through me, and I was suddenly exquisitely alert.

"Reflections." The fun house. The store window. The fountain.

I should just shut up, wish them a happy slumber party, and do exactly as Frank suggested and enjoy the summer.

But I couldn't. "In your house?"

Foster made some noncommittal noises in his throat and waved his hand vaguely. "You know, when you're alone . . ."

We stood in silence as I processed everything. The store was now uncomfortably cold and the air felt too thin to breathe, like we were standing on the peak of a mountain with nothing on either side but a sheer drop.

"Is that why you put up curtains in your office? To cover the window?" I turned to Frank, the thought just occurring to me. Frank was always updating things in the store—HVAC, security, lighting—but he'd never redecorated, claiming he'd reached peak "bookstore" on the first try.

He pursed his lips and shrugged, smoothing one hand over his silver hair.

I leaned back against the counter, my legs suddenly weak. I wasn't the only one who'd been seeing things. But why reflections? That was new, and that fact disturbed me more than anything—the idea that the black water still had new tricks up its sleeve.

"I . . ." There was still time. I could end this conversation and walk away to sweep and shelve books. "I saw something in the front window," I said, defeated. "It really freaked me out. And . . . the fountain." I had seen a strange reflection once before, one that didn't copy me exactly. In the pond in the forest. When this all started. "It's gone, right? We closed the black water. We burned the bones, the Ragged Man went *poof*, it's over." I stared at them. "Right?"

"We did." Foster nodded.

And yet.

There weren't any zombie-like Unfinished wandering around like before, but reflections weren't supposed to act independently. They didn't have lives of their own and certainly couldn't reach out and grab you.

As long as they were reflections and not something else.

"I mean . . ." Foster spread his hands open, palms up.

"What?" I'd done my bit—I'd woken the black water, and I'd closed it. Done. I'd thought I was permanently off the clock in terms of creepy Crook's Falls happenings.

"We know the black water is a door," Foster said quietly, talking himself through it.

I nodded. "And we closed it. The Ragged Man is gone."

Foster licked his lips, looking nervous. "What if he wasn't what was keeping the door open?"

I didn't have anything to say to that.

"Sit down, Uncle." I dragged my stool to the other side of the counter and then stayed there like a spent windup toy.

"Avery." Frank's voice was low. "You're right—we did take care of things, but—"

"But you and Foster thought you'd 'taken care of things' the first time, years ago," I pointed out gently. A few puzzle pieces were coming together, and I didn't like what I was seeing.

Frank took a breath and opened his mouth to defend their actions, but I cut him off.

"Was the fountain running back then?"

"The fountain?" Frank cocked his head.

"Yeah." I kept my voice steady even as my heart sped up and the tangle of thoughts in my head started to work themselves free. "Was there water in the fountain the last time the black water woke?"

Because the black water, the Ragged Man—all of that had happened before, over and over. Maybe the past could help me now.

Frank blinked at me like an owl. "Avery, this is the first time that thing has had water since I was born. Why are you asking about the fountain?" He looked at Foster, who shook his head and shrugged.

"When was it built?" My mind was tripping over itself, going so fast that I had to just trust it.

"Avery—"

"You're Mr. Local History; when was it built?"

Frank raised his eyes to the ceiling, seeking answers there. "I don't know, around 1900. Foster?"

"Ish," Foster agreed, seesawing his hand.

The pond must have been big enough back then to feed the fountain, to connect to the water system in town. Then something had happened and the source dried up to little more than a puddle for decades, until it had filled it back up once more. Now it was flowing right into town again.

Who had filled it up?

Me.

But how? What had I done?

Frank was doing the math in his head, matching what he knew of the black water to the dry fountain.

"The fountain?" Foster mused under his breath, eyes on the floorboards, connecting his own dots.

I slumped back against the counter and stared down at the floor, too, trying to absorb everything I'd just learned. The black water's connection to the fountain changed everything. But how?

We'd done everything right.

Foster shifted on the stool uncomfortably.

"Why don't I drive you home?" Frank stood, patting his pockets for keys.

"I'm not helpless," Foster snapped.

Instead of being gone, the black water had grown.

"No, but we can . . . talk," Frank said tightly, not-subtly dipping his head toward me. "In the car."

"Oh!" Foster nodded. "Right."

We knew the black water slept and woke in a cycle. The Ragged

Man came, people went missing and were transformed into the Unfinished until the black water was put back to sleep. We'd assumed the cycle was complete.

Maybe we'd been wrong.

The air conditioning kicked on, and the skin on the back of my neck prickled. Maybe the cycle was bigger; maybe the Ragged Man wasn't the end. But if so, why was it different now? What changed this time?

Me. I was the difference.

Foster stepped through the back door, turning to speak over his shoulder. "Why didn't you tell me—"

"In the car!" Frank jabbed Foster in the back, following him out. "I'll be just fifteen minutes, Avery!"

"There's something wrong with Key," I said dully, but there was no one left to hear.

Fifteen minutes, fifteen years—what did it matter? We always seemed to be in the same place, right where the black water wanted us.

The bento box sat forgotten on the counter, gleaming like it was in a spotlight. I hauled myself vertical and took it into the office to stash in the little fridge under the espresso machine. If I knew how to use that thing, I'd make myself one—I'd make a bucket. My body felt leaden and slow. The doorbell jingled as the mail carrier came in, dropped mail on the counter, turned, and left before the door had swung shut, sealing me in with my thoughts.

The black water had gone to sleep in Foster and Frank's day and stayed small; it hadn't grown into a pond big enough to supply the fountain. But something about the cycle that I started was different. Something—

I drew in a sharp breath.

Key.

Frank and Foster hadn't brought anyone out of the black water. I had.

My body strolled back to the counter, and my brain tagged along, trying to fathom how I'd spend the day selling books like my life wasn't falling apart again. I thought we were done, that the horror movie credits had rolled, but I was back in it, right where I'd left off. That there was more to come was bad enough, but what really worried me was that the second half of the movie was always the scariest. Whatever Frank and Foster were bickering about in the car, I knew they wouldn't be able to help me this time. None of us had any experience with whatever was happening now. The dread of what was coming settled over me like a cloak.

THIRTEEN

FRANK WAS GONE A LOT LONGER THAN FIFTEEN minutes. He still wasn't back by lunch, so I snuck bites of my sandwich at the counter. I actually didn't mind being in the store alone, except that it gave me a lot of time to think that I didn't want. I tried to keep busy, physical activity my usual method of distraction, but this time, it failed me.

In the early afternoon, a woman came in with her kid, whose favorite color was obviously orange, hyped to pick out a book as a reward for not biting the dentist.

"I'm getting this!" The kid held up a book at the counter for me to see, one of a series about ponies who are besties.

I gave a thumbs-up. "Looks good!" I smiled but knew my eyes were dead.

On the way out the door, the mother gave me a look, like I hadn't put enough effort into my performance with her kid, probably thinking I was bored with my job, just in it for money to blow on bags and clothes, that I didn't care.

The truth was I cared too much. I sat on the stool, staring at the counter, reclaimed wood from an old barn in the area that had been sanded and stained a rich dark brown, covered with a lacquer perfect as new ice. My fingers trailed over the grain, the lines that flowed from one end of the plank to the other. The tree had died long ago, yet here it was, under my fingers. Still beautiful. Still here.

The bell over the door jangled, giving me a whole-body startle like Buttons.

"Twice this week!" Ru sauntered up to the counter with a cup of coffee in one hand and surveyed the store like a queen. "Feels like freedom, being able to come in here whenever I want after all those years of staying away."

I had to smile at the thought of anyone trying to keep Ru out of anywhere, like holding back the rain.

"How you been?" Ru looked at me shrewdly.

When this many people ask you this many times if you're okay, the answer becomes kind of obvious.

"We never had much of a chance to talk"—Ru leaned forward, settling her elbows on the counter—"about what happened out there."

"Out there?"

"The Big Pond."

The way she phrased it, lack of opportunity was the only reason I hadn't spilled every last detail to her. Yet even if I'd wanted to, Ru hadn't been in my life to tell.

But she was now.

"I mean"—she docked her chin on her hand like she was settling in for a long one—"I've never, you know, experienced anything. But there's no way that a legend like that, surviving for so long, is just a story. A pond in the forest that doesn't exist." She leaned in and spoke in a hushed voice. "Did Key really fall into the pond?"

I blinked. Ru was the first person to ask that question. The old me would have sidestepped it and given some vague answer, keeping the burden all to myself. New Avery knew better. I decided to trust my auntie.

"I don't remember very clearly," I said quietly, answering as honestly as I could. "As time passes, I remember less and less. Like a dream."

"But it wasn't," Ru said firmly, looking into my eyes. "Whether you remember or not, it wasn't a dream."

Was it too much to ask that it stay a dream this time?

"I think Lily would have been the one for you to talk to about all this." Ru straightened up and cracked her back. "But . . ." She waved her hand in the air, not needing to detail the reasons why my great-aunt was no longer a reliable source of information.

I nodded. There were so many people who *wanted* to help me but so few who actually could.

"Why are you so certain something weird happened?" I asked her.

Ru gave a massive shrug. "Crook's Falls is a weird place. It has a long history of weirdness. You didn't know?"

I had not, although I could tell a few stories now.

"I've never heard—"

"Exactly!" Ru jabbed her finger in my face. "Weird things happen, and people don't talk about it. Or it's like they *can't*." She tilted her head, trying to find just the right words to explain it to me.

Totally unnecessary.

I looked down at the counter, pressing each of my fingertips onto the smooth, shiny surface, trying to ground myself for what might come next. "But you've never seen any . . . weirdness?"

She shook her head. "Not personally, which is honestly kind of disappointing. The closest I got to weird was Bee."

"Bee?" My heart sped up.

"I had an imaginary friend when I was a kid." Ru laughed and patted my hand. "One day Dad and I went fishing, and while I was staring into the water, waiting for a fish to bite, I felt like my reflection was watching me, like there was a whole other world under the surface of the water and she was looking up at me. I thought she must be a mermaid."

Icy fingers skittered down my back.

"What water? Where?" I tried to keep my voice steady.

"Oh." Ru waved, taking a sip of her coffee. "I don't remember. I was that little. I'd almost forgotten about her." She chuckled softly. "Bee. My mermaid friend, Bee. I was always leaving Bee secret messages on the bathroom mirror. You know, fogging it up and drawing a smiley face." Ru sketched in the air with her finger.

My heart wanted to race and stop all at once.

"Lily didn't seem to like it, but everyone else just laughed when I talked about her. My mermaid friend."

Ru didn't think she'd ever experienced any Crook's Falls weirdness, but I wasn't so sure about that.

"Ru-by," she said, in case I hadn't gotten it.

"Huh." I nodded, not trusting any other words.

"Anyway." Ru pushed back from the counter and glanced up at the big clock on the wall. "My coffee break's about done. Like I said before, if you ever do want to talk about anything, I'm here. I won't tell anybody—not Pearl, not your mom."

For someone who was the prime source of gossip in town, that was quite a statement, but my gut believed it.

"Every person your age needs that—a good listener." She patted my hand, each of her silver rings carrying the warmth of her skin.

At the door, she breathed on the glass and drew a quick smiley face. "For old times' sake." She blew me a kiss and left. As soon as she was out of sight, I hopped off my stool and darted to the door. I leaned forward and exhaled. Ru's smiley face appeared in the patch of condensation like something reanimated. I swiped the side of my hand through it, obliterating the face. I didn't want it there but didn't know why.

I made my way slowly back behind the counter, wiping my hand on my shorts. Ru knew a lot more about this town than I did, that was for sure. The back door clanked shut.

"You know what?" Frank strode in, looking refreshed. He slapped his hand on the counter. "Why don't you take off? I left you alone all day."

"I don't mind." I shrugged. "Foster okay?" My shift wasn't over, but maybe Frank felt the same way I did. There would be no idle chatter between us for the rest of the shift, not with this hulking nightmare sitting between us. With what we now knew, how could we talk of anything else? Even though I was desperate to talk about *anything* else. I picked up a book I'd found misplaced and walked past Frank, taking it back to its rightful home in the fiction section.

"Oh, he's fine." Frank waved that away. I felt his eyes follow me. "Seriously, Avery. It gets quiet this time of day. I'll be fine."

"Did you and Foster talk?" I jammed the book back between its neighbors, not quite ready to let that go. "In the car?" Unnecessarily snippy, maybe. But Frank and I had been here before, with him keeping things from me, and I needed to know that this wasn't going to be like last time.

Frank understood exactly what I meant, and had the grace to

look chastened. He folded his hands on the counter and lowered his eyes. "We did. But, Avery, you know everything we do, I swear." He laid one hand over his heart. "This is all new to us, too, this business with the fountain. If we—"

"It's okay, Frank." I came back behind the counter and rested both hands beside his on the dark wood, drawing his eyes up to mine. "I believe you. I understand."

And I did. I'd lied to my mom to keep her safe. I'd lied to Stella and Key in the beginning for the same reason.

Key. He hadn't been by all day, hadn't texted, nothing, and I hated that I was fine with that.

"Has your beau been around?" Frank asked carefully, like he was reading my mind. I shook my head and Frank bit his lip and looked down. I knew we were thinking the same thing. Key being weird could be explained away. Foster could be overreacting. The things I'd seen could be written off as residual stress. But all of those things together . . . Frank and I both looked out the window at the fountain, barely visible through the crowd, and then at each other.

"It's possible we may have a problem," he said softly.

I nodded and felt my breath leave me. Honestly, it was a relief to hear him say it, but neither of us wanted to say what came next. We stood in silence, the quiet click of the air vents high above us louder than the muted sounds of FallsFest across the street.

I met Frank's eyes and saw sadness there, the same look he got sometimes when I knew he was thinking of his late wife, Louisa, and the things they never got to do. It was all so unfair, the opportunities some people got and others were denied.

Frank laid his hand on my shoulder and pressed down, a gentle anchor. It was the calmest I'd felt all day. "Let things percolate," he said softly. "We'll talk later."

Just knowing I wasn't alone sent a wave of—not relief, but it took my stress level down a notch.

Frank lifted his chin toward the window, and I followed his eyes.

A block away, my dad was walking down the sidewalk, trying to pocket a folded piece of paper too big to fit with one hand and maintain control of a paper cup of coffee with the other.

"Excuse me." An older white man tapped his fingertips on the counter to get our attention. "Do you have this book?" He tilted his phone toward Frank, ignoring me.

"Of course we do." Frank nodded and waved to the right back corner of the store. "I'll show you." He edged out from behind the counter but then turned back to me. "You go on, now," he said, pointing to my dad, before heading back between the shelves, listening to the customer name all the stores he'd been to that had failed by not stocking the book and how he hated to order things online.

Everyone was so interested in getting me and my dad back together. He'd successfully pocketed the paper, and the closer he got to the store, the more I became aware of tension in my shoulders. Would he stop in, or would he keep going? How much had he really changed?

I could stay where I was and find out, but I'd waited for him to text, to show up or not for so long, and look where it had gotten us. If I wanted a real relationship with my dad—which I did—it was time for me to be brave and do something about it. It looked like I was leaving early, after all.

THE OTHERS

I grabbed my backpack from under the counter and hurried out the door, making it to the sidewalk just as my dad arrived, his trajectory already angling toward the store.

He would have stopped in.

I conjured up a smile and waved. "Hi, Dad."

FOURTEEN

DAD LOOKED AT HIS WATCH AS I LET THE BIG door swing shut behind me and stepped out onto the sidewalk, the accumulated heat of the day hitting me like a wall. "I know you're not quite finished for the day."

He knew my work schedule now? After three years of failing to show up for anything? Out of habit, I tidied the sidewalk sale display table with my back to my dad. Also habit. A little spark of resentment flared but dimmed just as quickly. There was only one way he could know my work hours.

He'd talked to Mom.

Wow. He really was trying.

"Frank gave his blessing because I was on my own in the store for so long today," I assured him and slipped my backpack over one shoulder. He didn't need to know that my leaving early had been Frank's idea, not mine.

"Good boss," Dad said. "Do you want to . . . ?" He gestured across the street, where the vendors were starting to refill their tables in preparation for the evening crowd.

I hadn't done FallsFest with my parents since I was little. FallsFest was a friend thing now, but Dad really seemed to need this. "Sure." I nodded. "Let's go."

THE OTHERS

We wandered through the vendor area, strolling by tables selling jewelry and T-shirts and the booth where Stella bought her shark tote bag and silk scrunchies. I recognized some longtime vendors, but this year there seemed to be an influx of new blood. One sold intricate wood carvings—animals, miniature trees, and delicately painted dragonflies. There was a booth making customized kites of vibrant colors, which fluttered softly in the breeze, reaching out to brush against my cheek as we passed. We walked the perimeter in a silence almost as uncomfortable as I'd been with Key that morning. It was like a bad first date.

"I guess you're too old for the fishy game," Dad said wistfully, gazing down toward the games and rides. It had been my favorite game when I was a kid—standing with a little net and waiting to scoop up the plastic fish that would win me a prize. The different colored fish corresponded with different levels of prizes, but I'd always tried to get the blue ones. They meant a medium-level prize, but I didn't care. I just liked blue.

"Ice cream?" I suggested, because that was one thing we used to do that I still liked, and there was no water or glass there to freak me out. Business at the Pink Unicorn was just starting to pick up, not as busy as it would be later in the evening, but during the summer, ice cream became an acceptable dinner option for some. So I grabbed a table while Dad went up to order.

While I waited, I traced my finger over the carved initials in the table that had been painted over with the Pink Unicorn's signature bubblegum pink. I'd never really understood it, the desire to cut up a table or tree to leave a message meaningful to no one but yourself.

"One mint chocolate chip." Dad handed me the cup.

"What did you get?" I peered into his cup, more to make conversation than out of real curiosity. He was trying, so I felt like I should, too.

"Peach pie." He tilted the cup to show me. "Actual chunks of peach pie mixed in with vanilla. Want to try? It's good."

I did. It was. Dad kept glancing up at me with a smile at once unsure yet hopeful, like he was interviewing for a job he didn't really think he had a shot at. It broke my heart a little, because if he didn't think he could do this job, who could? I noticed he'd cut his hair short and was wearing a pale green short-sleeved cotton shirt with buttons and green cargo shorts that looked either brand new or pressed. Dad had always been a T-shirt-and-whatever-was-on-the-floor kind of guy, but I didn't know who he was now.

An extra-big scoop of my mint chip gave me a few seconds where I didn't have to say anything. Maybe he'd dressed up to come and see me; maybe wearing tidy grown-up clothes was just something he did now.

"This is nice," I said, and the look in his eyes, the gratitude for that tiny bit of effort from me, made my throat tighten a little.

"It's really nice," Dad said. "I've missed you so much, Ave."

Weeping into my mint chip in public—did not have that on my bingo card for today, and to stop it from happening, I scrutinized the cryptic tabletop messages. All I could manage without losing it was some quick nodding and a smile, but Dad seemed satisfied with that, more settled as he went to work on his ice cream. Just like that, some little bit of tension, a tiny muscle that had been held taut for so long it no longer registered, let go. I took in a long breath, my lungs newly deep.

When my phone dinged the habit was so strong it was out of my pocket before I realized it. It was Stella, asking if I'd seen a documentary about a man and an octopus followed by the crying emoji.

Dad started eating his ice cream faster.

I sent Stella a heart, because she'd already made me watch it. "Sorry." I put my phone facedown on the table. Dad shook his head quickly, dismissing the need for an apology. He was really going to town on his peach pie.

"I should have turned it off."

"It's okay, Ave." Dad smiled but didn't look at me. "You've got a life. I know that."

I'd hurt his feelings. He thought I couldn't wait to leave.

"It's just Stella." I swirled the little pink plastic spoon in my mint chip. "Dad."

He looked up, and if I still had any doubts, they vanished the second I saw his eyes. He was desperate for this, to make this work. I smiled to let him know that this was fine. We were on the way to fine.

"There was a party last night. Summer kickoff kind of thing," I told him, ready to share something of my life, one of the good parts. Well, it had been good. Until . . . "Stella, Sian, everyone."

Dad smiled back and relaxed a little. "What's Stella up to?"

I shook my head. "Oh, you know. Stella Stellas pretty hard."

In our "before," Dad had always made special weekend breakfasts when Mom had shifts at the hospital. I'd wait at the table while Dad stood at the stove in a ratty old T-shirt and joggers he wore as pajamas, pouring pancakes into shapes that never looked like what he claimed they were and dotting them with blueberries or chocolate chips before flipping them. The whole operation—making and consuming—was done in near silence, peppered only by suggestions of activities for the day. Those mornings had been soothing and snug; they'd warmed me from the inside. Sitting at the picnic table with him now, this wasn't that, but it was as close to it as we'd gotten in a very long time. Maybe we really could bring back "before." Maybe just some of it would be enough.

Dad smiled and touched the back of my hand. "I'm glad you're going out with your friends. You deserve to have fun, Ave. You deserve to be happy."

I did. So did he.

Dad and I had gotten lost somehow, but maybe we could find our way back together.

I dug into my mint chip, wanting to draw out the best moment with my dad in a long time. But even here, even now, part of my mind was focused on the trickling of water in the fountain, a sound that seemed to follow me everywhere.

I chose my words carefully.

"Dad, do you know why the fountain's running again?"

He glanced over his shoulder toward it, like he'd forgotten it was there. "Huh."

"The water comes from the pond. That Key . . . fell into."

"Huh." He scraped the inside of his cup with the pink spoon, seemingly uninterested in this change of topic.

"Some people say . . ." I so wanted to not be alone in this. If Ru at least suspected the truth, could he? "That the pond is the black water."

Dad shook his head. "The black water. That's just a story."

Yes, just a story. I bit back my bitterness. A story about a pond that only showed itself to those it wanted. A pond that spawned the Ragged Man, who stole people and turned them into mindless drones. Just a story that had almost destroyed me.

Exhausted, I turned to watch people strolling by on the sidewalk. My dad wasn't going to be any different than Key's parents or Mom, believing that anyone who went missing in the forest just got lost or ran away. The black water had a firm grip on the mind of almost everyone in town.

"I mean, isn't it?" Dad mused, his spoon stilling. "People do . . . leave a lot, don't they?"

Something in his voice made me slowly turn to face him, watching his brow crease in concentration. The way the sunlight hit his face changed the color of his eyes, making them a brighter green.

"There was another one, a girl. . . . ," he said.

"Jackie," I supplied quietly, not wanting to break the spell.

"Yeah. They said she ran off. To a music festival."

But she hadn't. I'd seen what had happened to her, one of the black water's first victims. I held my breath, watching the wheels turn in my dad's mind, seeing in real time the black water's grasp falter and slip.

"She didn't?" He frowned at me, confused like a sleeper just wakened from a dream.

I shook my head. "No, Dad. She didn't."

Go! You can do it! I cheered him on in my head.

But he couldn't.

"Well, all the more reason for you to stay away." Just like that, it was over. His face cleared, and it was business as usual. "Swimming was never your thing anyway." He smiled.

I sighed. He'd been so close. It was beyond disappointing to see him sink back into the fog the black water created; the tendrils it sent into the minds in town regain control. But it was intriguing that he'd managed to clear his vision even for those few moments. If he could do it, could others?

"So . . . Frank left you on your own today? That doesn't seem like him." He licked the last sweet remnants from the spoon.

I shrugged. Where to begin? "He's got Foster staying with him."

"Hmm." Dad nodded. "In town for FallsFest?"

"No, Foster lives here. He's a Miller."

Foster had seen things in his house. What, exactly, he hadn't said. But I could guess.

"Dad, can I ask you a favor?" The question was just a formality. A ride, a kidney, I knew my dad would give me whatever I asked for. He'd never been any different, but I hadn't realized that. I'd misinterpreted his behavior, thinking his feelings for me had changed. Nothing had changed—my dad was still my dad.

Frank said he was telling me everything he knew, and I didn't disbelieve him. But I hadn't returned the favor—not quite, and I had a feeling that Foster's house might offer something that would help me grasp the last puzzle piece that was just out of reach.

"Can you give me a ride?"

Dad's fingers tightened on his cup, sending melted ice cream dribbling over the top. He was so hyped to be of use to me, it made my heart clench. "Of course!" He launched the cup into the nearest trash can in a pretty impressive free throw and stood. "Where do you want to go?"

***

The little blue house looked the same as the last time I'd seen it, out to visit Foster for tea and a story. We bumped up the skinny dirt driveway.

"Sorry about the potholes." I held on to the window as the car lurched through one.

"Ave, this car is so old, nothing can hurt it." But he crept along carefully anyway.

Once we stopped with a squeal of the brakes, I got out and stood for a moment, hearing the driver's-side door creak and not much else. The trees here were silent, the grassy hill behind the house still and expectant.

"You don't have to come." My dad had appeared at my shoulder.

"Oh. Okay." He immediately turned around, and I backtracked, afraid I'd hurt his feelings.

"I mean, I'm not telling you *not* to come."

"It's okay." He shook his head.

"I just meant you don't *have* to—"

"Ave." Dad stopped. "It's okay. I know this is . . ."

"Weird," I supplied.

"Different," Dad amended.

True enough. This careful dance we were doing with all our old lines of communication cut was exhausting.

"Besides . . ." Dad gestured to the house. "It doesn't look like anyone's home."

"Nope." I mounted the porch slowly, trying to see in the living room window but foiled by the drawn curtains.

The front door was closed but not locked, which made me frown. Crook's Falls was a pretty friendly town—aside from the obvious—but we still locked our doors. Foster hadn't taken the time to do that, and he'd been at Frank's a while. Going inside without Foster there felt like crossing a line, but what I could see through the little window in the door felt like enough of a justification to go inside.

I cautiously pulled the screen door open the rest of the way.

"Ah, Ave?" Dad quickly mounted the steps behind me. "You said he's not here?"

"I told you, he's staying with Frank." I took one cautious step inside. I needed to know what Foster had seen; it must have been pretty bad to drive him from his beloved granny's house. The air in the house was hot and still.

"Not sure we should be going in if he's not home," Dad said, tension in his voice.

"I just need to see. He won't mind. I'm worried about him."

Dad reluctantly followed me. "Okay." He breathed the word like a question.

I stood in the foyer of the little house, aware of my heart rate picking up. Whatever I'd been expecting, it wasn't this.

Foster's tidy little house looked like it had been ransacked or hit by a tornado. The TV was on the floor and turned to face the wall. Most of the many framed photos were facedown on tables, and the few that weren't were freed of their glass. The mirror over the fireplace was just gone, now nothing more than a thousand glittering shards. I'd been here quite a bit since my first visit with Stella and Key. It seemed like a lifetime ago that we'd sat on the love seat, when Foster was still a stranger. Since then, I'd spent afternoons curled up on the same love seat, listening to stories, but the room felt alien to me now, like I'd never been here before.

I took another step and startled at the loud *snap!* of a piece of glass the size of my hand giving under my shoe. How could Frank and Foster not have mentioned this? Foster hadn't "had a scare"; that's not what this looked like. This looked like terror, panic, abject fear. This wasn't the explanation I'd been looking for and it was making me feel worse, not better.

Dad slowly crunched through glass across the living room. "How do you know this guy again?" I could practically hear the disapproval and parental concern meter rapidly ticking upward.

I continued down the hall, past the living room and deeper into the house. "Dad, he's like one hundred years old. He's staying with Frank and he's an old friend of Lily."

This part of the hall was shadowy and cooler. From here, I could see the kitchen doorway, where the toaster lay on the floor like a shiny silver beetle, still and resting on its side. Something about it made me wary of looking away, like it might suddenly jump up and scuttle off.

"Hmm." Dad came into the hall and picked up a picture frame that no longer had any glass from the floor, only a blurry black and white image of a little boy on the knee of an old lady. I wished he would put it down. I hoped he would be quiet. Just being there, walking through the room, I had the sense that an eye had turned toward us, that we'd tripped some perimeter wire and now were being watched by something very old and patient. Coming here had been a mistake.

"What happened here?" Dad wondered.

"I don't know." Which was partly true.

"Maybe this guy is going like Lily." Dad put the photo down, slid both hands into his pockets, and looked around at the debris covering every inch of the room.

I spun to face him. "What?"

"Well," Dad shrugged. "This looks kind of . . . Lily did some odd things, back when it started with her; talking to people who weren't there, keeping the windows covered. Just acting strange."

This was news to me. "I don't remember that."

"Oh, this was before you were born." Dad scuffed his shoe on the floor, clearing a small patch free of glass. "Then she did the complete opposite—curtains were always open and she put up mirrors everywhere. That seemed to settle her. She was fine for a long time. Before her memory started to go, that is."

So the Lily I'd known most of my early life had been the eye of the storm—there'd been something wrong with her before I was born; then she'd had a period of tranquility before her memory had started to slip away for good. I put this piece of information in my mental pocket, not sure of what it meant but uneasily certain that it was going to fit somewhere in my puzzle.

A current of fresh air swirled in through the front door, circled me like a curious animal, and swept off farther into the house, which meant a window was open somewhere. The screen door clapped gently, lifting open and falling closed as the breeze picked up and then dropped, each time opening the door just a sliver. Not far enough for anything big to get inside. Not yet.

I stood rooted to the spot, with the hall to Foster's bedroom stretching out to my right. I'd only ever gone as far as the cornflower-blue bathroom with its tarnished but sparkling clean faucet and a medicine cabinet over the sink that I'd been tempted to open but never had. It was the kitchen straight ahead that had me transfixed now. Everything else faded away, my vision extra sharp on the doorway and what lay beyond.

I stared at the doorway, only the far wall and half of the back door visible, but it wasn't what I could see that had my skin crawling. I had the creeping feeling that something was waiting in the kitchen, crouched just out of sight on the other side. I knew the kitchen well; lately, it had been me on tea duty when I came to visit Foster, even when Mom tagged along. The kitchen was small and bright and mostly white, with wooden cupboard doors that didn't all close properly, the Formica in front of the sink worn almost down to the wood by generations of hands, but everything always clean and neat. There wasn't room for much in there, and the toaster on its side on the floor reflected a dark shape that I couldn't account for. It wasn't the old stove or the relatively new fridge.

So what was it?

An image flashed through my mind—a dark, dripping, hulking figure—and a shiver followed in its wake.

There was something in the kitchen. A metallic taste flooded my mouth, a bitterness in the air here, undetectable until it caused a reaction.

Dad followed my eyes to the kitchen, but I knew he wouldn't see anything there. Ru might. "There's a lot of glass in here, Ave."

Glass, if we were lucky.

"And we really shouldn't be here," he added gently.

He didn't know how right he was.

I felt the presence in the kitchen swell and grow denser, gaining strength with every passing second that I stood there like a patient animal waiting for the farmer's knife.

"Yeah." I nodded. My body was singing with tension, but

my voice sounded breezy and normal, a dissonance that my dad shouldn't have missed but did. I took a careful step back toward the door, shards of glass crunching delicately under my shoes like tiny bones. "Let's go."

I waved one hand behind me for my dad to go, desperate to get out but not wanting to turn my back on the kitchen. A larger piece of glass broke in two under my foot with a sharp, brittle sound, and suddenly I could only think of the doorway as a gaping maw, jaws that would slam shut before we could escape, and then it would be our bones snapping.

There might be more to see in the kitchen, but just being here was enough to tell me that Foster wasn't overreacting. Something had been here, and it wasn't completely gone.

"Let's go." I forced myself to turn calmly to my dad, trying to keep my face neutral. I couldn't protect my dad from a threat he wasn't even aware of.

"That's it?" Dad opened the door and I hurried him out onto the porch.

"That's it."

Back in the car, I turned my face to the window and kept it there, confusing my dad, no doubt, but I couldn't worry about him and his feelings just now. The thoughts running through my head now weren't anything I could share with him. Coming out here had confirmed everything I had feared in the vaguest way possible.

My dad's theory about Foster going like Lily dominated my mind, but slightly smaller, in its shadow, was another thought—what if that's what was happening to Key?

As we went back down the skinny driveway, I twisted around

in my seat to look back at the little blue house. The front door was still unlocked, but I wasn't worried. There was a very good chance that anyone who went in there wasn't going to come out. I slumped back in the seat, staring out the windshield and barely registering the potholes.

"Wow, this is rough, right?" Dad grimaced at the biggest pothole yet.

"Yup." I sighed, all my hopes for a perfect summer leaving with my breath, out the window and up into the sky, stirred by the breeze.

Gone.

FIFTEEN

AFTER DAD DROPPED ME OFF, I STOOD ON THE sidewalk for a moment, watching his taillights slow at the stop sign before he turned and left my sight. What I'd seen at Foster's had started a dull ache in the pit of my stomach, the way it felt after cruising FallsFest with Stella and Key, but for the absolute opposite reason. This wasn't sugar; it was pure dread, like I was standing watching a storm roll in, knowing that it was going to be nothing but ferocious wind and pelting rain, and not being able to do anything to stop it.

My shoulders sagged as I turned and plodded up the driveway. The little house was dark except for a blue-tinted light flickering in the living room, which meant Mom was having a self-care evening of popcorn and TV, curled up on the sofa with a blanket tucked around her legs. I wished for the millionth time that I could talk to her and that she would *hear*. But I knew she couldn't, and it made me feel completely alone. I took a few breaths, hoping that Mom wouldn't sense anything was wrong, and walked in the front door to find her as expected on the sofa. Buttons was curled up next to her, but when he saw me, he jumped down and made a beeline for my bedroom, stopping in the doorway to turn back and give me a pointed look. He'd hang out with Mom if I wasn't around, but I was his person.

"Want to watch with me?" Mom asked, patting the sofa next to her.

"I'm kind of tired." Which wasn't true. If anything, I was wired, my body buzzing with adrenaline. Besides, unless she was super invested in whatever she was watching, Mom would know in two seconds flat that I was hiding something. Halfway down the hall to my room, though, I stopped and reconsidered.

A moment of normalcy was all I wanted, so I turned back to the living room, lifted up Mom's feet, and plopped down on the sofa. Sometimes, you just need your mom. Even if there wasn't anything she could do for me, just being there with her was comforting because it reminded me of a time when she could fix any problem. The movie she'd chosen was one of those thrillers where a nosy neighbor witnessed some dark business while pruning her roses and unleashed her inner detective.

"Good talk with your dad?" Mom asked absently.

Seeing Dad today had been a surprise, so either my mom was psychic or she'd been peeking out the front window seconds ago. I could make a guess as to which one.

"Hmm." I nodded.

"That's good. We should all try," she said absently, eyes on the screen as the neighbor crept down into someone else's basement.

The neighbor's cautious, hunched-over posture reminded me that soon I'd have to call Key for our good night chat. *I'd have to.* Nothing related to Key had ever felt like a chore before. The thought sent something squirming in my stomach, wondering which Key would pick up. I snuggled in beside Mom.

Realizing I wasn't headed to bed yet, Buttons hopped up on the sofa and settled into a contented sphere on my lap, grumbling softly.

The movie was what I'd expected, a thriller so predictable it contained very few thrills.

"I don't know why I watch these. They're all the same," Mom admitted. But I tried to get into the story, tried to focus on a dark scenario that didn't star me for once.

The main character was so bland, a middle-class white lady who I couldn't relate to, so inevitably my attention drifted. The TV cast the only light in the living room, creating hypnotic flickering shapes on the wall; the drapes behind the TV hung heavy to the floor where the curves of the dark gray fabric, made darker in the dim light, pooled into shapes that looked like feet.

"Look at that kitchen." Mom tapped my leg. "All those bare surfaces. Who lives like that?"

Now that I'd thought it, the idea grabbed onto me and wouldn't let go—that there was someone standing concealed in the shadows against the wall. There wasn't; there shouldn't have been, anyway. But Foster's house should have been empty, too. I clenched my jaw and wrenched my gaze back to the screen, where the nosy neighbor was now searching records at a library. What kind of records? I couldn't recall and I didn't care.

But I had to. I had to focus on the movie to avoid what was really drawing my attention. Icy fingers walked slowly up my spine.

Movie. Watch the movie.

I became aware of my breathing, even but deep and speeding up.

Don't look.

But I couldn't resist.

I let my eyes shift to the left, took a sharp breath in, and froze. It was there. A deeper shade of shadow, the darkness coalescing into something denser, something with an outline. Something in front of the drapes.

"Just you watch," Mom said around a mouth full of popcorn, oblivious. "It's going to be the hot neighbor."

Sitting right beside her, I was caught up in a totally different horror show.

The last time something strange had happened with this TV, it had been Foster's long-gone granny Maxine trying to help me fight the black water. Whatever was there now, I could feel it seething with malice. It was not Maxine, and it was not here to help.

The thing by the wall moved, swaying slightly. Not the drapes, not the shadows, but whatever else was lurking there. My breath caught in my throat.

"Why would you go to a remote crime scene in the dead of night? That's just stupid." Mom shook her head.

Was this what had driven Foster from his house? The little kid in me wanted to close her eyes and count to ten when the monster would disappear. But I couldn't close my eyes, not while my mom was sitting right there, defenseless. I took a deep, slow breath in.

There was nothing there. It wasn't real.

But then it proved me wrong.

The thing stepped forward, and an actual foot with long, clawlike toes broke into the circle of light cast by the TV. Heart pounding, mouth gone dry, involuntarily shrinking beside my mom, every instinct told me to make myself small even as I felt Buttons puff up under my hands.

"Mom." But it came out as nothing more than an unintelligible sound, a sigh. Fear bolted me to the spot, had taken my ability to move, to speak, to think.

"I know, right?" Mom nodded, eyes riveted to the screen. "Going up the stairs? Is she actively trying to get murdered?"

I watched helplessly as the thing moved again, revealing a rail-thin figure, gray like the paint on the wall, limbs spindly and disjointed, eyes huge and beetle black. My heart wanted out of my chest.

"Oooh, here it comes. . . ." Mom pressed her hand to her mouth, watching the housewife slowly turn a door handle.

The thing stepped out, fully revealed by the flickering light of the screen.

I yelped and squeezed my eyes shut tight, grabbing Mom's arm, making her laugh and tease me. "You never used to scare so easy." She wrapped her arm around me and folded me into her.

When I raised my face from her shoulder, the nosy neighbor was talking to a cop in a sea of flashing red and blue lights.

"Well, that's that." Mom raised her arm to turn on the standing lamp.

"Mom!"

The room flooded with light. Mom turned to me with a frown. Buttons looked up and blinked.

"Ave, are you okay? It's just a movie."

There had been something standing in the corner, watching us watch the movie, but it wasn't the Ragged Man or one of the Unfinished. Something had been there, but it was something new.

Whatever it was, it had been wearing my face.

The light from the lamp was backlighting Mom, casting her features into shadow. She hadn't been able to break through the black water's hold like my dad. I'd already tried when Key was missing. It was strange, because she'd always been the stronger of the two, but here was something my dad could do that my mom couldn't. And I had no idea why.

"Is this about your dad? Or Key?"

There were so many things in my life to choose from, so many possible reasons I could be acting weird, she couldn't choose just one. Mom opened her mouth and I saw a lecture coming, but then she pressed her lips together, swallowed her mom-advice and gave me the independence I'd asked for so many times and suddenly no longer wanted.

"You let me know if I can help." Mom tapped my fingertips with hers, clicking off the TV.

I tapped her fingers back, wishing she could. "Yeah." She was talking about my dad, but that wasn't the only thing I needed help with. I was seeing things again that might not be in my head, something had happened at Foster's house, and then there was Key.

One last wary look at the drapes and I headed to my room to change into pj's. I took my time brushing my teeth and settled on my bed with my phone until there was finally nothing left to do.

"Hey." Key rubbed his eyes like he'd been sleeping or staring at a screen for too long.

"Hey." I fluffed the pillow under my head and lay back.

"So how was your day?" He smiled and patted his hair, checking on its perfection.

My fingers wrapped a little tighter around the phone like it was his hand. "It was . . . long."

"Mm." He nodded. "I hear that. I was at Mom's office all day, clearing out that storeroom in the back—where they toss all the old brochures and stuff?" He rolled his eyes. "There was so much dust, it was like airborne paper. Paper particles. Why would she want her precious baby breathing that in all day?" He huffed. "Hoarding behavior in that office, let me tell you."

I chuckled, mildly disturbing Buttons, and everything I'd been worried about, all the bad thoughts hanging out in my brain all day, they started to melt away, just a bit. I listened to Key rant about the horrors of boxes upon boxes of open-house brochures for houses long since sold and then segue into the truly amazing kebab salad he'd had for lunch.

"Salad!" My jaw dropped in mock horror.

"I know." Key smiled, the bright ear-to-ear kind that always drew the same out of me. "Mehmet can make anything taste incredible."

"You want incredible?" I kept my eyes locked on his because I wanted to savor his reaction to this. "Foster is living at Frank's."

Cue the incredulous shriek.

But what I got was silence and a blank stare. "Oh yeah? Since when?"

Where was the excitement? He should have instantly jumped to the same wild conclusion that I had.

"Um, I don't know, exactly." My voice was quiet and small.

"Huh."

Silence in our conversations wasn't new, but this one was different. This was like this morning. Key yawned and everything else I'd wanted to tell him—the fountain, Foster's house, the TV girl—I wasn't going to share any of it.

Because I was no longer certain who I was talking to.

"Well, I've got another long day of hoard-busting in front of me." Key stretched languidly.

"Okay." To be honest, I was not sorry to end the conversation, and how wrong was that? "Night."

"Mwah." Key blew a loud kiss and was gone.

Usually, I hung up with Key feeling warm and content, but tonight was pretty much the opposite. I put my phone facedown on the nightstand and lay in the dark with Buttons curled up at my shoulder.

I thought I'd run a race and finished, but now the course stretched out in front of me, still miles left to go. So many people wanted to help me, but so few were actually able, and now, with Key not being Key, it seemed like there might be one less. Wherever the next leg of this race went, I'd have to run it on my own.

SIXTEEN

THE SOFT PINK SUNLIGHT OF A NEWBORN DAY had crept into my room and over the wall, no doubt beautiful but unappreciated on this particular morning. I'd lain in bed, listening to the quiet noises of Mom packing her lunch and shutting the front door softly. Then I was left in the warm tangle of sheets with Buttons curled against my shoulder, breathing slow and deep in the quiet of the early morning. It should have been soothing and peaceful.

But I was already wide-eyed and staring—had been for hours. I'd been awake to watch the moonlight turn to sunrise, to hear Mom get into the shower and out, to think about what I had to do today, and it all seemed impossible, which is why I'd been lying there so long, trying to put it off. Wednesday was a heavy day at work, so Frank would be with me the whole time. Normally this would be good news—I genuinely enjoyed chatting with Frank and listening to his stories, but today I knew it would be tense and awkward, both of us holding back, swallowing things we didn't want to acknowledge. The fountain, Foster, Key, last night . . . I already felt like I was fraying around the edges just lying in bed—the pressure of pretending to be okay was likely to push me over the edge.

But not going in would just make things worse, and there was still a slim chance that it could make things better. I nudged Buttons with my shoulder and got a cranky *mrrr* in response.

"I have to get up," I whispered.

"Mrrr." He didn't even open his eyes.

I slid my shoulder out from under his paws and sat up, letting my feet hit the floor with a thump. Buttons yawned, stretched and then curled up again in the still-warm spot I'd just vacated.

My body felt heavy and sluggish. I wanted nothing more than to get back into bed and rewind to a few days ago when everything had been good.

But there was no going back, only forward, even if I didn't know where that would take me. "I have to get up."

On my feet, I raised my hands over head, reaching for the ceiling, trying to get out of my head and back into my body. Brush my teeth, get dressed, go to work, be normal.

I could do this.

My nerves were so taut that my reflection stepping into view in the bathroom mirror startled me. I splashed water over my face and watched as it beaded on my skin, staring into my own eyes. I looked different. Which would be understandable, especially after going to Foster's house yesterday and whatever I'd seen in the living room last night. None of it was good, but Key was what really worried me. He was definitely not himself, and the possible reasons why were numerous and terrifying.

I squinted at myself in the mirror, smoothing back my hair, wild from sleep. My eyes didn't look right, but I couldn't decide what was wrong. Leaning a little closer, I turned my head to get a different angle. My whole face was tighter; it had a pinched quality that hadn't been there before.

But it was more than that. I searched my face in the mirror. I didn't just look different; there was some fundamental change in the reflection that made it look really similar to me but not, another person entirely staring at me across the counter. Another girl in another bathroom. Someone whose life was teetering on the edge—again—looking into her mirror and seeing me. An accidental intersection to another dimension, Key would say. Assuming it was an accident. Assuming this other Avery had nothing to tell me. I stood there, listening to the air conditioning tick and staring at this almost-me. Every second that passed, I felt more and more disconnected from her. The fun house popped into my mind, making my fingers grip the toothbrush tightly.

We brushed our teeth together, watching each other warily.

"I'm stressed," I finally said to the other girl.

The other girl nodded.

I shoved back from the counter, dropped my toothbrush into the sink, and backed up to the door, staring wide-eyed at the girl in the mirror before squeezing my eyes shut.

"I'm super stressed," I said loudly. Hopefully I was much more stressed than I'd realized, enough for it to manifest in strange things in the mirror over the sink, because the alternative was nightmarish. I felt along the wall behind me, felt the towel on the rack and reached out for the door on my left. I took a deep breath in and opened my eyes.

The other girl was back at the counter, leaning forward, brows drawn together in concern but the ghost of a smirk playing around her lips. She hopped up on the counter and drew closer to the glass, peering out at me and tilting her head like a bird.

Peering out. Not back, but out of somewhere else, like there was something on the other side of this mirror, someplace hidden and yet right in front of me.

I brushed my fingertips against the door to remind myself that I was here, and this other girl was . . . somewhere else. This girl looked like me but was clearly not just a reflection of me; she was a different being altogether. She'd been on the other side all this time, watching.

I tried to move and found I couldn't. It occurred to me as the girl extended her index finger, that if the mirror was the only barrier between us, I might be in trouble because she didn't look like she wanted to be my friend. Her face was calculating. She had plans. An image came into my mind, of standing in front of a tiger at the zoo, putting all my faith in the strength of the glass, assuming it would hold against the tiger's weight.

But what if it didn't?

The girl pressed her finger to the center of the mirror, and I watched with eyes wide as the glass cracked, a sharp-edged star with one fine splinter racing to the edge. The girl laid her palm on the crack and pushed so hard her skin went white. She smiled in satisfaction. Buttons had seen enough, just a blur of white out the door and down the hall.

My heart sped up, fingers gripping the door handle like it was my only anchor to reality. I felt lightheaded, and my body seemed far away. The girl in the mirror was just a reflection. She couldn't hurt me. I repeated the words in my head, wanting to believe and failing. There had been so much glass in Foster's house.

The mirror creaked under the relentless pressure of her hand, and more tiny splinters appeared, like a spider egg opening. I pressed my back to the wall. This girl, Key's reflection in the window, the things I'd seen in the water—what if they weren't just images? What if they were something else?

What if they wanted out?

The girl held my eyes, a slight sneer on her lips, the darkest, basest version of me.

Craaack!

I jumped at the sound like a shot, twisted the doorknob, and prepared to run. Whoever she was, whatever she wanted, the girl was coming through.

I lurched out into the hallway and slammed the bathroom door behind me as the mirror shattered, heart thumping hard like I'd just sprinted. I backed up down the hallway, fingers trailing on the wall on either side, keeping my eyes on the door, afraid to look away.

Two more steps back got me to my bedroom, where Buttons crouched on the bed, puffed up to twice his size as I circled like a dog that couldn't settle, pacing from the closet to the bed and back, shaking my hands out to get rid of the adrenaline tingles. The tinkle of glass hitting the floor followed by a thud came down the hall from the bathroom. This wasn't good. She'd broken through the mirror.

The tiger was loose in the zoo.

I came to a stop in the middle of my room, trying to slow down my racing mind and think. This had happened before—I'd seen things, panicked, and tried to handle it on my own with disastrous results.

I knew better than that now.

I took in a breath so deep my lungs felt bottomless and looked around. Buttons watched me with huge pupils.

"You'll be fine," I told him, pulling on a T-shirt and plucking a pair of shorts from the floor. Whatever was in the bathroom wanted me, not him.

Rustling came from the bathroom, the soft sound of something trying to be sneaky.

My head snapped up. Still as a stone, blood pounding in my ears, I kept my eyes on the doorway, half expecting a darker, nastier version of me to appear.

Maybe more than half.

"Buttons!" I whispered, pulling up the shorts and turning just in time to see a fluffy white tail disappear under my bed.

My gaze fixed on the oval mirror hanging over my desk, photos of Key and me and Stella tucked along the edges. Key loved that old-school Polaroid stuff. I approached the mirror slowly from the side, crouched like I was on the starting line. I bent without stopping, picked up a T-shirt, and tossed it. The shirt covered only half of the mirror, but it would have to be good enough. At least now I didn't feel like there was someone at my back sneaking up on me, but I was struck by a sudden and intense desire for my mom.

"Buttons," I whisper-called, but there was no movement under my bed.

I crept to the door and cautiously poked my head out, relieved to see the bathroom door still closed. There was no nightmare version of me waiting in the hall, but the house didn't feel empty, either.

I stared at the door, convinced that if I kept my eyes on it, it wouldn't open, a grinning gray me wouldn't lurch out. The only thing I could hear was my ragged breath as I stood motionless, unable to move, scared to stay and afraid to go.

In the bathroom, I heard the soft *clink!* of metal hitting tile.

And that did it. I fled down the hall, scooped up my shoes, flew off the porch, touching not a step, and tore down the sidewalk, my heart rate spiking like I'd never run a day in my life.

Where to go? Frank.

My body knew that route by heart; I wouldn't even have to think, which was good because my mind was a white, screaming blank. There had been a girl in the mirror, it wasn't me and she wasn't in the mirror anymore.

I sped along the sidewalk registering nothing around me, then noticed that I wasn't where I should be. My body wanted to keep going but I forced my feet to stop. The street ahead should be Maple, but it wasn't.

Meadowbrook Lane. I was headed in the wrong direction.

I turned around and ran back the way I'd come. Frank would be at the bookstore already. I'd tell him about the girl, and if he didn't know what to do, Foster would be my next stop—

Meadowbrook Lane. I stood on the corner, my head swiveling in all directions. *What*—

My heart was thundering, my breath coming in short, hard gasps. I could feel the muscles in my body itching to go, to keep running, but now I didn't trust them either. What was happening?

I turned carefully, putting my back to Meadowbrook Lane and walking deliberately, eyes focused on each step, toward Maple, toward the bookstore. Toward help.

At the end of the block, I looked up and froze.

Meadowbrook Lane.

"What?" I rubbed my hands over my eyes, on the verge of tears. I didn't want to go this way, but something was pulling me on, and the knot of dread in my stomach told me where I was being led.

This had happened before, the black water messing with my mind. But we'd put it to sleep; how could it still be affecting me?

Unless. My heart stuttered at the thought. It couldn't be. But the fountain, Foster's house, and the girl in the mirror told me it might. More than might. Everything I hadn't wanted to believe was true.

I stared up at the street sign, weighing my options, which seemed few and unappealing. Something didn't want me to go to the bookstore and had the power to stop me. One deep breath and a glance over my shoulder to make sure the other me wasn't on her way, and the breath stuck in my chest.

Because she was.

Everything else fell out of focus and faded away. My vision narrowed to a single point—the impossible thing coming toward me. It couldn't be, but there it was—another me, solid and real, still in the T-shirt and sleep shorts I'd changed out of, striding down the sidewalk, steady and unconcerned. Almost as if she knew where to look for me. Almost as if she knew I had nowhere to go except where I was being herded.

Against the panic rising in my chest, I looked around in every direction but saw no one to help me. Help me how?

The other me continued at her leisurely pace, stretching her arm out and letting her fingers brush through the knee-high daisies in my neighbor's yard, wearing the same smirk she'd had in the mirror, like she already knew how this was going to end. And maybe she did. I felt like I had no choice but to continue, being herded somewhere against my will, going where the black water wanted me to, just like before. I seemed to be a character in a story, doomed to repeat her mistakes over and over.

But I couldn't accept that.

Without taking my eyes off her, I took a few steps backward, blinking away the tears that would do me no good. She picked up her pace a little, and that triggered something in me, more motivating than any starter's pistol had ever been. Whoever this was, I did not want to meet her. I turned on my heel and took off like a shot.

Meadowbrook Lane it was.

Before I knew it, I was passing the big white-and-green sign that read *Crook's Falls Conservation Area*, the wooden posts carved up with initials and messages just like the Pink Unicorn tables.

I followed the pull in my stomach and made a hard left, turning up the driveway where asphalt turned to gravel. At the gatehouse, the summer staff—an eternally bored scrawny white guy with hair like straw—waved me in, used to seeing me every day on my runs, although usually earlier in the morning and generally not tearing along in wide-eyed panic. There was only one place the girl in the mirror could have come from and whether I wanted to or not, I was about to see it.

Instead of going up to the trail head, something in my chest pulled hard to the left, leading me to where the bushes had been ripped, the forest torn open to create a new trail, a shortcut to the Big Pond.

Alone on the gravel path, the crunching under my feet reminded me of a video I'd seen, saying that cats liked crunchy food because it was reminiscent of tiny bones snapping between their jaws. Which made me think of Buttons, who I'd left at the mercy of the girl in the mirror. If he was okay, I'd give him all the treats in the kitchen cupboard, every single one. The girl herself was a problem because even if she hadn't hurt my cat, she was up to no good. I'd seen the calculating look on her face, the slight sneer wrinkling her lip, and honestly, no one who crawls out of a mirror uninvited has good intentions.

The heat of the sun beat down on the back of my neck, a physical weight slowing me down, like nature itself was trying to stop me. Despite my desire to never, ever go back to the pond, something was pulling me there and I couldn't fight against it. But a part of me did want to go, needed to see—to confirm that it looked the same. I wanted to see that it hadn't grown, hadn't darkened, that there was nothing dark and dripping crawling out or lurking on the banks. Knowing where the water in the fountain was coming from had changed everything; whether I liked it or not, I was about to see it again. My mind was a tangled swirl of thoughts, different feelings and ideas overlapping, like a signal that wouldn't come in clearly.

Around a slight bend, the gravel trailed off into dirt, then a narrow ring of scrubby grass and the pull in my chest was suddenly gone, the black water's leash released. The Big Pond waited ahead, looking same as the last time I'd been here, with one exception that stopped me short. A floating dock had been added, anchored to the bank with two metal stakes driven into the ground and guardrails attached to a set of metal steps. The steps were blocked off with a thin chain bearing a sign reading *Water Testing Only—No Fishing*.

So it was true. This water—and what it contained—was being pumped into town to feed the rejuvenated fountain. The danger in this water wasn't going to show up on whatever tests they were doing. The breeze rustled through the birch trees on either side of me. A blackbird trilled and then went quiet.

A quick glance behind showed me the empty path. The girl

from the mirror was nowhere to be seen. That should have been comforting. It was not. The pond itself seemed normal. Everything was as it should be.

Except.

I took a few steps closer to the pond. Maybe it was the angle. The sky was cloudless and bright, the breeze stiff, transforming the surface of the water into a glittering field of diamonds, each tiny wave capped with a glint of light.

Was it . . . bigger? Maybe not noticeable to someone who wasn't so wary, but the longer I looked, the more I was sure of it. Definitely bigger, the waves lapping closer to the end of the gravel path than the last time I'd been here.

When I'd found the black water, it had barely been big enough to skip a rock, surrounded by small mounds of earth like tiny graves and long grass that now moved, weightless under the surface. I went cold in the center, like a core of ice gleaming faintly in the dark.

Mounds formed by waves and current.

Which meant the black water hadn't always been small. The fountain may not have flowed in Frank's life, but it had at some point. And some time, far in the past, those little mounds of earth had been formed and the grass had swayed free underwater. The core of ice gathered strength, branching out through my whole body until my entire being was consumed with one cold thought:

The black water had been this big before.

I hadn't woken it by stumbling on it in the forest, but I had gotten its attention. It had stretched and yawned, and the Ragged Man had emerged. It was only now that it had truly opened its eyes, swollen in size, and worked its way back into town.

If the pond continued to grow, would they use it to feed more places in town? Would there be a day when this water flowed into homes? When people drank it? What did this have to do with the other me? They had to be connected. I shuddered, wishing now for the sun on my neck but not feeling it.

Ducking under the chain that was never going to keep anyone out, I gripped the rail and climbed the three steps onto the dock. It was surprisingly solid under my feet, not the swaying, unstable fun house floor I expected. It felt like it wasn't sitting on water at all.

On the dock itself there was no railing, so I crept toward the edge, wanting to see; if I looked down, would the water still be clear? Could I gauge the size by seeing the depth? Two more shuffling steps to the end was as far as I was willing to go. The little voice in my head warned I was already too close.

Keeping my weight in my back leg, I leaned forward, peering over the edge, into the water that rippled gently in the breeze. Would I see my reflection? Because there was already one of those after me. The breeze picked up again, sweeping over the bead of sweat slipping down my neck, leaving an icy trail in its wake.

Shifting forward a little more with my arms extended to either side to steady me, I steeled myself to peek over the end of the dock. Whatever I saw there, I had to know how bad this was. Sudden pounding footsteps behind me, an unmistakable sprint, sent a lightning bolt of adrenaline through every inch of my body.

The other girl had found me.

Something moved over my shoulder, just out of sight, like wind fluttering the edges of a kite. I turned on my heel and felt my balance shift too far. I sucked in a harsh breath, in disbelief and denial, feeling myself pitch backward.

No, no, no, no.

Teetering at an angle impossible to hold for long, I pinwheeled my arms, frantic at what I knew was going to happen next, the thought emptying the air from my lungs and driving rational thought from my mind. As I hung there, time stretched out elastic, giving me plenty of opportunity to be afraid. I couldn't hold the balance; I couldn't stop it. My mind went blank and no sound came out of me. I kept my eyes on the blue of the sky as I finally tipped backward and down, dropping fast to the last place I ever wanted to be, falling. If there was anyone to witness, they would see me fall in silence, landing in the water but making no splash, what looked like water absorbing the impact, closing over me and instantly evening out as if it had never been disturbed at all.

SEVENTEEN

THOUGH THE WATER WAS STRANGELY VISCOUS, I fell fast and deep into a pond that had grown not only out but *down*. I thrashed against the pull, every muscle straining, trying to slow my descent, but it felt like trying to stop a train. With incredible effort, I managed to maintain my position but started getting lightheaded—if I didn't choose a direction right then, it wouldn't matter. The black water would hold me there forever; I could feel it closing in around me, rage and loneliness pressing against my skin, looking for a way in, to fill me up, own me, and sink me down to the bottom for good. Up, down, every direction felt the same and no light penetrated to give me a clue. Time was ticking by—it could have been seconds, or hours. The thought of spending eternity there in the cold, lightless depths broke me out of my torpor. I chose a direction and struggled with short, hard strokes, making very little headway, the black water unwilling to give up the shiny prize I was, tightening its grip with every inch of progress I made.

My stubbornness is what saved me. Disoriented and on the edge of consciousness, I broke the surface with a rasping gasp. Sucking in all the oxygen my lungs could hold, I looked around and for a moment saw only water in every direction, a vast gray ocean with no shore to swim to.

It's not true.

As soon as I thought it, the illusion failed, and the banks of the pond were there again. I struck out for the bank near the dock, panic making my strokes choppy and sloppy, every second expecting to feel something slither around my leg, tighten like a noose, and yank me under, this time forever. There was no thought in my mind, just an animal focused *gogogogogogogo* and tunnel vision for the bank.

The soft squish of mud between my fingers set off a wave of relief so intense it threatened to stall my progress. The whisper of strands of long grass caressing my ankle sent me scrambling onto the bank and out of reach of whatever was lurking in the water. I turned onto my back, with my pulse thundering in my ears, needing to make sure nothing had followed me—no Ragged Man, no faceless zombies—and saw only a pond, tiny waves lapping on the mud banks inches from my feet. No other me waiting to pounce—in fact, no one at all.

I stared down at the dark, fetid mud oozing between my fingers. Every time before I did it, burning the bones had put the black water to sleep. But now the black water was fully awake, just as malicious and grasping as ever. It had to be because of me. I'd tried, but somewhere along the line, I'd made a mistake, and it was right in front of me even if I couldn't see it. What was the only unexpected thing I'd done? I stared down and squeezed my hands into fists, hearing the wet suck of mud escaping through the tiny gaps between my fingers.

Key.

Maybe I'd been the black water's fool all along; maybe this was exactly what it wanted. I thought I'd broken the cycle.

Now I knew I hadn't.

I rose from the ground, dripping wet, a whole new level of fear unlocked. Something had climbed through the bathroom mirror. Something was wrong with Key, and whatever was still lurking in the pond now had a front-row seat in the fountain, easily coming into contact with the entire population of Crook's Falls and making FallsFest—the highlight of the summer—the most dangerous place to be.

Images flashed through my mind along with a rising sense of panic: Foster dipping his hands in and pressing the cold water to his neck. Stella plunging her arm in up to her shoulder. I squeezed my eyes shut against the violent shiver that shot up my spine.

I didn't turn my back on the pond until I was on the path to the parking lot, full of cars but passing no one who would look sideways at the dripping girl muttering to herself and tripping over her own feet. The sun was still high in the sky, but I didn't feel its heat and the breeze had disappeared, which meant my clothes wouldn't dry any time soon. All this was just background noise, thrumming against my one clear thought—*GET HELP*. I went down the sidewalk, sopping shoes squelching with every step, dark footprints following me like a ghost, when I stopped and looked back. There was no ghost; there was no one. The gatehouse was empty. There were no cars on the road.

I started walking again slowly, like there was a reason I should be cautious that had just slipped my mind. On Mercy Street, still several blocks from home, I stood and watched a sprinkler hissing, dragging an arc of water first one way, then the other over a pristine lawn. Back and forth. Back and forth, like it would go on forever, one side to the other, then starting all over again.

Tssssssssst. Tssssssssst.

I did a careful spin on the sidewalk, dread pooling in my stomach. There should be unseen children shrieking in a backyard. There should be birds chirping and flitting from tree to tree. There should be the rumble of a truck in the neighborhood and the distant sounds of FallsFest.

But there wasn't.

There was absolutely no life in the neighborhood, like everyone had been evacuated while I was thrashing in the pond. Based on my theory of what the black water was up to, evacuation was probably a good idea.

The familiar squirrelly spin of anxiety started slowly in my chest, but I forced myself to start walking again, the *squish, squish* of my wet shoes conspicuous in the unnatural silence. Had it been this quiet before? I'd been so freaked when I fled the house that I couldn't remember. Maybe everyone was at FallsFest. The thought soothed the agitation for a moment before I remembered what else was in the vicinity of FallsFest—the fountain.

Whatever else was going on, I needed to get home, rescue Buttons, and get help. I shook out my hands, trying to focus. Heading home as fast as my ruined shoes would allow, I slowed again at the end of a driveway where a maroon sedan sat idling, the low rumble made louder by the absence of any other sound. Finally. Sighing with relief, I stood waiting, because any second, someone would emerge from the house—maybe they had popped back inside to retrieve a forgotten phone. They would return and get in the car, and I would feel better. Maybe they couldn't help me, but they would at least be there. I wouldn't be alone. The veil of weirdness that fallen over everything would disappear.

Any second.

I bit my lip as I stared at the front door of the house, a painfully manicured yard that despite the perfectly symmetrical garden full of blooming flowers and bushes, felt dead rather than joyous. There was something fake about the house and yard, but some people overdid it—they made nature so sanitized and orderly that it wasn't nature anymore. The door didn't open; there was no sign of life inside at all, and the longer I waited, the more sinister the idling car became, the unbroken solitary noise sounding too much like a growl. Maybe it was the wrongness of it—the car needed a person to start the engine, but there was no person around.

Who had started the car?

I eyed the sedan warily, every inch of me vibrating with tension. The gleaming curved metal brought to mind the haunches of a tiger, and I started to get the creeping sense that if I moved, it would follow, driver or not. I would wait one more minute. I just needed to see someone, anyone, to shake this insane notion that something terrible had happened to the world while I was in the pond trying to figure out which way was up.

"Get it together," I muttered. A car wasn't alien, and despite the sound and the shape, the headlights resembling unblinking eyes, it wasn't a beast. Cars in driveways were normal. There was no reason it should unsettle me. But an endlessly idling car with no driver, one that seemed to be watching me back . . .

The minute passed and my desire to see someone wavered. Did I want to see whoever might emerge from the house in this dead neighborhood?

The longer I stood there, the more it sounded like the car was not just growling, but growling at *me*, a predator that had caught sight of something tasty, and was now waiting to spring into action. Light glinted off the silver grille, teeth bared in a snarl.

Maybe this was why the streets were empty.

I hadn't thought of that.

I took a few steps away from the car, unwilling to turn my back on it, waiting until I was almost at the corner to turn and run, soggy shoes or not, sprinting across the street without looking because now I didn't expect to see any cars. There were no vehicles to dodge, no cyclists, no strollers to leave the sidewalk for. It should have been a runner's dream.

But it wasn't.

One more block and I ran up my driveway only to slow, deciding to go around to the back door, which had a window that would allow me to scope out what I'd be walking into.

There was nothing suspicious in the backyard, just a lot of unmown grass slowly overtaking the tilted picnic table, like a jungle reclaiming a ghost town. I crept onto the back porch and peered through the back door window—the kitchen seemed clear, dishes in the sink and the yellow-checked dishcloth wadded up on the counter. Nothing looked disturbed and nothing was moving. Beyond that, the dining table was littered with junk mail, phone chargers, and reusable grocery bags. From the window, I could see a sliver of the living room, all the shapes familiar, no one in there unless they were crouched down.

Unless they were hiding.

I cracked the door open, wincing at the slight creak. One foot inside, then two. The house was still, holding its breath just like me. I eased the door shut carefully so that it closed with no more than a quiet *snick!* and stepped out of my shoes, creeping through my own house like a burglar. I stopped to scan the living room before continuing into the hall.

"Buttons," I whispered so softly I barely heard myself. "Buttons." I picked my way down the hall slowly, one hand trailing on the wall like I needed support.

The fact that the bathroom door was still closed was comforting, until I saw the sliver of light around the edges. It wasn't wide open, but it was no longer shut, either. I raised my right foot and gave the door a quick tap, ready to bolt at the slightest movement.

Nothing.

Another cautious nudge and the door swung open, revealing the floor covered with the shattered remains of the mirror. If I really wanted to be sure, I'd go in there.

If.

Instead, I backed away, until my hand touched the doorway to my bedroom. I looked back the toward the living room with my pulse booming in my ears. This was my house; everything was in place, and I didn't think the girl in the mirror was still here.

But something was off.

"Buttons." I poked my head in my bedroom and scanned for any signs of life. If the girl in the mirror had hurt my cat, I would freaking murder her. "Buttons!" My room looked the same as I'd left it, but was so messy it was hard to be sure. I dropped to my knees, flung up the edge of blanket, and peered under the bed. No one home but the dust bunnies.

"Buttons?" I knelt in front of the closet and then *in* the closet, digging through the pile of clothes on the floor. Still no cat. His two favorite hiding places and he wasn't here. The girl in the mirror had taken him, or he was in some hiding spot I didn't know about, too afraid to come out even at the sound of my voice. Either way, the girl was going to be sorry. I rose to my feet, fists clenched at my sides. I had never physically harmed anyone in my life, but messing with my cat was a whole other level of not-cool. Thoughts of Buttons, the idling car, and the girl in the mirror swirled through my head in a tangled mess as I paced the room, the mirror still half-covered with the T-shirt I'd thrown there. Mom had been oblivious to the thing by the TV last night. Only I had witnessed the girl in the bathroom. There may or may not be something going wrong in my brain, but I kept circling back to one inescapable fact.

The girl in the mirror had scared Buttons, too.

The thought made something in my absolute center go still. The spinning tornado of thoughts lost its form and dispersed. None of this was in my head. The girl had come through the mirror and chased me to the pond. There were now two of me running around—me and Other Avery. But what was she up to—what did she want? I flexed my fingers and took a deep breath in and let it out slow, the main weapon in Stella's Overwhelm Toolbox.

Okay. I lined up what I knew: My cat was missing. The house was empty. I sat down on the floor, considering what to do next. Who could help me? People.

I pulled my phone from my back pocket but got only a black screen.

"Okay." I rubbed my hands over my face. I needed to talk to

Frank and Foster. Something was really wrong, and they were the only ones who could help me make sense of it.

I shed my wet clothes, got changed, and left my useless phone on the desk. I sat on the bed to put on a pair of retired running shoes and stood.

Where to go?

The bookstore.

Who to see?

Frank. I'd get Frank's take on things. From there, we could go to Foster.

After locking the back door and making sure the front was securely shut in case Buttons was still in there, I headed downtown, nothing interfering with my course now. As I walked, I distracted myself by making a mental list of everything I would tell Frank. I'd tell him about the fountain and its source. I'd tell him about the girl in the mirror. And I'd tell him about Key; I just wasn't sure exactly what I'd say.

My walk downtown was just as eerily quiet as my trip home. Everything was normal except for the lack of people. Passing Mehmet's Kebabs, I stopped at the corner, the red "don't walk" hand flashing. But looking both ways, I couldn't see any cars. I couldn't *hear* any cars. The only sound was the *tick-tick* of the "don't walk" sign as it blinked.

"This is ridiculous," I muttered and stepped out into the street against the light.

The hum of generators was startlingly loud at the outer boundaries of FallsFest, but from what I could see, the area was absolutely devoid of people. There must be something I'd forgotten, an event that drew a crowd. That had to be it, but the tight knot of anxiety in the center of my chest wasn't a believer. I hadn't seen anything alive—no people, no birds, not even a mosquito.

In the vendors' area, the tables were laden with crafts but unstaffed, the tablecloths flapping like sails on a ghost ship. I walked through cautiously, frowning at the cashboxes out in the open and even the most expensive items alone and unprotected. It seemed a little too trusting even for our small town. Continuing on into the midway did nothing to lessen the dread that was starting to creep over me. The cotton candy machine was right where it should be, whirring and ready to spin clouds of sweet fluff onto paper cones, but there was no one staffing it and no customers waiting. I stopped at the fishy game and watched as the plastic fish circulated in the stream unimpeded, around and around. I reached out and plucked a blue fish from the water, waiting for someone to pop out and scold me, but no one did, and the rest of the fish continued on their loop.

Alone in the empty midway, I held up the fish in my hand. It was blue, but something wasn't quite right. I closed my fingers around the cold, hard plastic and took a good look at my surroundings. There was something wrong with all of this. Everything was where it should be; everything was running. Around the booths, multicolored lights twinkled and blinked just as they should—

Wait.

I opened my fingers and looked down at the fish, my stomach sinking and a flush of adrenaline shooting through my body. Suddenly I knew what was wrong with the gardens I'd seen, the blinking midway lights, with this blue fish. The fish wasn't blue. It was just the suggestion of blue—the approximation of color but not the real thing.

My breath was coming fast and shallow as I turned, taking in everything and finally seeing what I'd missed. The lights that should be bright were anemic and weak. The sun hadn't dried my wet clothes because it was just a muted disk in a gray sky. Everything here was colorless and without life.

I pocketed the fish and ran through a FallsFest that no longer smelled of sugar and sunscreen, where my footsteps were the only nonmechanical thing I could hear, each step ratcheting up the tension in every muscle. I darted across the street and came up to the front window of the bookstore, tears of relief filling my eyes.

"Frank!" He stood at the counter with his back to the window, writing out an order form like there was nothing at all wrong in the world. "Frank!" I banged on the window, trying to get his attention. Frank frowned over his shoulder but didn't turn, intent on the form. For an instant, he seemed to disappear. I blinked hard and he was back, but I had to really focus to see him, like my eyes were diverging. I banged both palms on the window again but got no reaction at all. He stayed with his head bent, following his finger and carefully copying a string of numbers onto the form. How could he not hear me?

I raised my hands to hit the window again and froze, the blood in my veins suddenly gone icy cold, my focus drawing in tighter and tighter, spiraling inward until the whole world constricted to a single tiny spot.

No.

I cupped my hands around my face and pressed them to the window, the skin over my entire body prickling.

I blinked and forgot how to breathe.

The store was empty.

Dead and quiet, just like the streets, just like FallsFest. The tall wooden shelves that stretched up to the ceiling, the display table of books I'd made by the front door—it was all there. But no Frank. I had seen Frank's reflection in the window, without the real Frank to cast it. Which was impossible. I backed away from the window, my skin tingling and everything inside me going quietly numb.

I understood now what was going on. I knew where I was. My breath left me and my legs went weak. I turned and slumped back, leaning against the cool brick, and stared blankly out into the street, letting my hands drop to my sides and feeling like my head was about to quietly detach and float free of my body.

I'd fallen in the pond and felt the presence of the black water. It hadn't wanted to let me go. I'd hovered disoriented in the cold depths and then struggled to get out. But I had. Like the girl in the mirror, I'd finally broken the surface of the Big Pond. I'd crawled out of the water.

On the wrong side.

EIGHTEEN

I STUMBLED ACROSS THE STREET ON LEGS GONE numb, not even bothering to look for traffic, and dropped down hard on the edge of the fountain where I'd been with Foster, trying and failing to quell the tsunami of panic rising inside me. Other Avery had broken through the mirror and climbed through.

I bent over and let my head hang, because the thought made my head go all swirly.

Would I be stuck here forever? With the other me around, would anyone even notice I was gone? I didn't know what to do and not only was there no one here to help me; there was no one here at all. Even as I sat, my heart beat faster and faster, pulse thumping in my throat and thoughts whirling around in my mind until they threatened to just become white noise.

Focus.

I straightened up and pushed back against the panic, pressing my fingers to the silver turtle around my neck and let a long, slow breath out through my lips. I had to get hold of myself and think.

If I was where I thought I was, why could I see Frank? I turned and looked into the water rippling in the base of the fountain. A red balloon, distorted by the moving water, floated into view. A hopeful glance over my shoulder showed nothing. There was no balloon.

Not on this side.

I leaned farther over the edge and gasped when a little face popped up, distorted by ripples but looking startled to see me. A little girl, the red balloon tied to her wrist, pointed at me with wide eyes.

She could see me.

If I could get Frank to turn around, would he see me too? Back on my feet, my thoughts came quickly, stumbling over one another. I could—I could write a note and hold it up to the window. I could tell him what happened. I could beg him to get me the hell out of here, back to where I belonged.

And warn him not to trust Other Avery.

I should go. I should do it and get out of here as soon as possible. I had to get back to the real world before Other Avery caused any damage. Who knew what her plans were?

A few steps toward the store, a sound stopped me in my tracks. From deep inside FallsFest, in the very center of the midway, a whining, grating sound rose, slowly at first, then settling into a rhythm. My stomach sank. The noise was vaguely familiar. And although I knew I should go back to the bookstore and find a way to make Frank notice me, I turned, the sick-sounding melody pulling me on like a siren, what I recognized now as a distorted version of the carousel music. Like the car, the carousel couldn't have started on its own. If there was someone else here, I needed to know.

I needed to see.

As I made my way slowly back through the midway with its games and rides, FallsFest looked different to me now. I hadn't noticed at first how open the game booths were, how much painted metal there was. Now that I knew reflective surfaces were my only way of seeing what was really going on back in the real world, I realized how very little glass or bare metal there was around me. I had to fix that.

As I entered the midway, my stomach rumbled, which was ridiculous. I was trapped in another dimension, a poorly constructed hellscape version of my world, and my body wanted to eat. I passed by a popcorn stand on my right, red and white stripes matching the bags of popcorn already filled and hanging, waiting for customers who would never come. I thought about it, rejected the idea, then doubled back to stand in front of the vat of popcorn that should be sending out a delicious salty, buttery aroma but here smelled like nothing at all.

I'd never stolen anything in my life, but I was hungry and there was literally no one here. Still, I glanced around self-consciously, thinking of Ru slamming down the five dollars in front of Frank. My stomach rumbled again, casting the final vote.

"Screw it." I reached around the kiosk and scooped a handful of popcorn from the vat and started walking fast before shoving it in my mouth, half-convinced that some nightmare version of the sloucher would pop around the corner hitching up his belt, shambling and dead-eyed, but somehow still on his feet.

That'sssss ssssstealing.

He'd clap cold metal cuffs on my wrists and drag me somewhere worse than I already was. The image was so clear, I stood stock-still for a moment, waiting. But nothing happened, and two chews later, I leaned over and spat the mouthful into a trash can anyway. The popcorn tasted just like it smelled, which was not at all, as tasty as chewing a mouthful of Styrofoam peanuts.

I leaned over and spat again, desperate to make sure my mouth was empty, my mind filled with fragments of a myth about a girl eating fruit and being eternally confined to hell. I frantically wiped at my lips with the hem of my shirt until they were raw. I straightened up, pressed my fingertips to my eyes, and exhaled slowly. I couldn't afford to spiral here. I needed to focus before I made a mistake that would make my situation even worse. One benefit of being an eternal pessimist—knowing that things can always get worse.

I wiped my hands on my shorts and continued following the stilted music, vaguely familiar but sending pings of unease through my body. I wound through the empty fest, signs flapping, lights blinking. I rounded a corner and found myself in the center of the midway, where the carousel, the crown jewel of FallsFest, resided. It seemed more than a little shifty to start up the carousel and hide, but I'd never felt so alone in my life. I was desperate to find someone here—anyone.

What I found before me was a still a proper, Victorian-style carousel with horses—different colors, in different poses—everything else painted in muted pink or dirty white and edged in dull gold. This carousel was drab and tired, and when I got closer, I saw that the horses looked tortured—wild-eyed, with heads rearing back in terror. Round and round it went, just a little too fast and wobbling slightly, the music shrill and off-key. The music got louder and the carousel spun faster, making me take a step back and clap my hands over my ears. The whole thing was turning so fast now that I could only glimpse the mirrored center, where flashes of faces smiled, then mouths stretched out in soundless screams like they were trapped in the little squares of glass. I spun around to check that those faces weren't behind me but there was only more of the empty midway. My hand drifted up, nervously rubbing at the silver turtle like a charm as I stood and watched the carousel warily, thinking of the idling car.

Faster and faster, the carousel spun, the limpid colors bleeding together. Watching it made me feel nauseous and unbalanced, like I was suddenly at sea. As much as I wanted to look away, I felt myself take a step closer, my body feeling faintly distant. Something was taking shape at the center of the carousel, dark and nebulous, rotating around the center pole. What was that? The darkness grew like a cloud forming in a time lapse video when suddenly a wisp shot off and up, away from the carousel and up into the sky. The violence of it startled me, but before I could recover, another piece of the cloud broke off and rocketed away like particularly nasty cotton candy slung at high speed. More wisps peeled off, rising into the sky over FallsFest like a swarm of something dark and biting.

The terrified horses kept rotating, eternally trying to flee and failing, the carousel now rotating too fast for me to see any faces in the mirrored center. But it gave me an idea. I turned away from the carousel now shooting dark wisps like sparks from a flame. The faces I'd seen had to be from the other side, from real people standing around the real carousel. I needed a bigger mirror, and where was the most reflective place in FallsFest? I'd already been there once and hadn't liked it, but it would suit my purpose now. Keeping a wary eye on the dark wispy things, I threaded my way past the little kid roller coaster.

The fun house.

It felt good to put the carousel at my back, go back past the popcorn stand and deeper into FallsFest. The thought of being able to see people urged me on, and I picked up speed, running past the test of strength Stella had conquered the other night, then faster past the water gun shooting gallery where I'd won Key a huge stuffed rabbit last year. I shoved that memory away and after that, tried not to look at what I was passing because each game, ride, and food stand held a memory and all of them involved Key. I rounded the corner and past the unwinnable ring toss game, skidding to a stop and gazing up at the giant clown lounging atop the fun house like it had been waiting for me all this time.

Welcome back.

Walking into the clown's mouth the first time had been unsettling enough, but as I stepped up to the double doors, I noticed that this version of the clown was grayed-out and hungry looking, with eyes that were mostly white and rows of teeth like a shark, tiny but sharp, lining its whole mouth, which was stretched in a manic grin that held no joy. I hesitated, turning back to look at the deserted midway, but if I wanted to see people—real people—this was my best chance. A creak from above made me go still. The clown remained sprawled above me, but was the mouth . . . wider? Dark red paint flaked at the corners of its lips, looking like the dry, crusted remains of a meal that hadn't satisfied. My hand hovered over the door, resolve faltering. But one look over my shoulder showed the dark wisps still shooting up and away from the carousel. The strained melody warbled through the air. With one last suspicious glance up at the clown's wild eyes and a full-body shudder, I pushed through the swinging doors and stepped inside.

Everything I'd seen so far on this side of the black water was a thin, watered-down version of my world. The fun house was the opposite, the extreme of its real-world counterpart. The corridors with unstable floors sent me lurching from one side to the other, slamming my shoulder into the wall. The optical illusion hallway left my chest feeling tight and panicky. It was actually a relief to pass through to the hall of mirrors—each pane of glass stretching up into the darkness that seemed to go on forever, the space now impossibly large, the ceiling unseen but feeling so far distant it may as well not exist at all. I'd hoped to see people reflected in the mirrors like the little girl in the water. It wasn't totally reasonable, but I just needed to make sure that there still *were* people out there. If Other Avery had watched me through a mirror and broken through to the real world, surely I could reverse it and get back to where I belonged. But there were no reflections in the mirrors here.

None.

I walked up to a mirror and stretched my arm out until it touched glass.

Nothing. No reflections. Not even mine.

In every direction I turned, the mirrors were empty.

For a moment, I stood uncomprehending, and discovering that standing in front of a mirror and seeing nothing is really disturbing. I stepped up close to the mirror. Touched it again with the tip of one finger to be sure. Leaned in close enough to see my breath fog the glass, frowning.

This made no sense. Maybe there were no other people in the fun house right then. But the mirror was here. I was here. So why didn't it show my reflection? The air here was still and dense, but a cold chill touched the back of my neck.

I gasped and fell back two steps, trembling like a leaf about to fall.

I *was* the reflection; I couldn't cast one, like I was on the wrong side of a two-way mirror.

I remembered the girl in the bathroom, the other me, breaking through the mirror *like it was a window*. It had granted her access to my world and I'd ended up here in hers. That's why I'd been herded to the pond. She'd never been a reflection; she was someone else entirely. What I'd mistaken for reflections was the black water's version of my world on the other side of the glass. I'd been staring at it the whole time.

And it had been staring back at me.

I wrapped my arms around myself and backed away until my shoulder bumped the mirror behind me and I jerked away, afraid to let anything touch me. The air here was still and damp; there was no sound but my own breathing, like the fun house existed in a void. All around me was . . . nothing. I was in the black water. Alone. My throat tightened but I pressed my lips together hard. I couldn't afford to start crying now. I needed to get out.

With no reflection to guide me, I stretched my arms out like a sleepwalker to touch the mirrors, trying to find the open way. Each time my fingers made the barest contact with glass, I tensed, afraid that the girl from the bathroom would appear and grab me, and my world would go from dim and gray to complete darkness.

One step forward—solid.

Quarter turn to the right—solid.

Another turn—solid.

Each breath was shakier than the last, my resolve to keep it together fading fast. I was biting down on my lip so hard I expected to taste blood any moment. This had to be the direction. This had to be the way because there was nowhere else to go. A sudden vision sprang into my mind of the fun house as a trap, of turning fruitlessly forever, boxed in by empty mirrors in an empty place, a fun house tomb in the belly of a clown. Holding my breath with my eyes closed, I stepped forward, then shuffled forward again, my fingertips meeting no resistance. Two more little shuffle steps and I dared to breathe again. I'd found the way. I wasn't trapped. I would get out of here and find some real people. I opened my eyes and stepped forward again.

And then I found one. A real person.

Slumped on the floor, head hanging in dejection. A real person who also had no reflection. Long, slender fingers curled palm-up on his knee, like something small that was ready to give up and die. A strangled sound came out of me, and the figure on the floor slowly raised his head, turned to me, and froze.

Key and I stared at each other, too shocked to speak.

NINETEEN

"AVE?" KEY BREATHED MY NAME, RISING TO HIS feet slowly, like I was a wild creature that might startle and disappear at any sudden movement.

But I'd been shocked into immobility, not flight. My mind was a blizzard, thoughts churning so fast and thick that all I could do was stand while they swirled around me like snowflakes, impossible to catch. My brain wanted to know how he was here; the rest of me just wanted to wrap my arms around him and not let go.

Be careful, the little voice in my head whispered. The black water had played tricks on me before. But I could never be truly cautious when it came to Key.

Key was wearing the same blue T-shirt and green cargo shorts he'd worn the night he went missing weeks ago, that night when he'd held my hand in both of his and things between us had changed for the first time. His face now was drawn, and there were dark circles under his eyes, but there was a spark in them that something in me answered, some part of me that hadn't spoken since he'd woken up in the hospital. I'd stubbornly refused to acknowledge it, but I knew now: not only had something been wrong with him from the very beginning, but it hadn't been him at all.

"Is it you?" He crept forward, inch by inch, equally unsure, the shock on his face turning to wonder. "How did you get here?" The dark that surrounded us greedily swallowed each word as soon as it was out of Key's mouth.

"I fell," I whispered, watching as his hand reached out, closing my eyes at the feel of his fingertips ghosting over my cheek. Was this really him?

"Ave."

The sadness in his voice was a password. A door inside me swung open and everything I'd repressed, all my doubts, flooded out and away. This was the real Key. *My* Key.

It was him. I knew the instant he touched me.

"Key!" I stepped forward and into his arms.

Key wrapped his arms around me, but unlike the other night, he held me to comfort, not contain. He was solid and real, the only real warmth I'd felt since I fell into the pond.

But if this was Key, who had I been hanging out with?

Who had I pulled out of the pond weeks ago?

I tipped my head back to look into his face. Part of me had been missing him without even knowing it. That was pretty much all I knew. The rest of what I was experiencing was a tangled mess.

"The reflections . . . I saw a girl who looks like me."

He nodded, looking more exhausted than I'd ever seen him. "And she saw you, too."

"But—"

"Not the Unfinished." Key read my mind and waved the idea away. "These are the Others."

"The Others."

He nodded grimly. "They look just like us."

"I'm so confused." I admitted. "We're in Crook's Falls, but... not?"

Key rubbed his mouth and slipped into his teaching persona, familiar from the hundred times he'd tried to educate me about his favorite things. "We're still in Crook's Falls." He leaned forward and held my gaze. "But like a parallel version. We're in the same physical space, but our world, where we came from, is on the other side of—"

"The mirror." I finished for him.

He nodded. "Every mirror, window, water—any reflective surface. It's the only place where the two versions of Crook's Falls meet. Both versions of Crook's Falls can see the other. And pass from one version into the other." He tilted his head, and I knew he was gauging how well I was taking this news, that we were living the plot of his favorite movies.

My head had started to ache with the impossibility of the situation, a vise tightening just behind my eyes. The girl in the mirror had never been my reflection; she was someone else altogether, from the start. And the mirror wasn't a mirror—it was a door.

"In front of the store." I'd dropped my coffee in shock when I'd seen him in the window.

"That was me." He smiled softly. "I wasn't sure if you saw or not. Windows are hard."

What was hard was realizing how badly the black water had played me.

"I'm so sorry." I leaned back to look into his eyes. It made sense in a ridiculous way—his weirdness since he'd gotten out of the hospital that everyone chalked up to fatigue, the things he should have known but didn't, just not being himself. It hadn't been him at all. I thought I'd saved him, but I hadn't. I'd pulled some other version of him out of the black water, an imposter like the girl in the mirror. And he'd been stuck in this empty parallel world. Alone.

"It's okay." Key shook his head, smoothing my hair over and over.

"It's not! I can't believe I thought he was you." I shook my head, because it was so obvious. Now that I was with the real Key, I could see what a pale imitation the other was.

"That guy," Key said, his face darkening.

"You've seen him?" I couldn't imagine it—to see yourself doing things you didn't like and not be able to do anything about it.

Key nodded. "Like I said, reflective surfaces are where the two Crook's Falls meet. If there's a surface, I can see the other side, the real side. But it's summer, and people are outside a lot, so . . ." He shrugged. "There's a lot I miss. But I saw him after Sian's the other night."

The flutter I'd seen in the car window.

"He's a dick," Key muttered, looking away.

He'd tried to fool me—Other Key. Sometimes he'd done a passable impression, but then he let his performance slip and I'd known something was off. He'd come close, though. If it weren't for the fountain running with water for the first time in my life and quickly freaking me out, in time I probably would have gotten used to the new Key and just accepted him. I shivered at the thought and docked my chin into the dip in Key's shoulder. In my defense, how could I have guessed that my real boyfriend was stuck in a parallel world? I realized with a sinking feeling that there must be a lot that Frank and Foster didn't know, although maybe Foster had tried to warn me.

You don't know what you're bringing through.

Whatever I'd brought through hadn't been the real Key, but I was with him now. I held him close again, and we stood in the lifeless silence that hung over the hall of mirrors, cocooned for a moment from the depthless emptiness that this place had to offer. I wasn't alone anymore; being with Key made everything seem more manageable, even something as horrifying as being stuck on the wrong side of the black water. We'd find a way out of here together. This time, I wouldn't let go of his hand. This time, I wasn't going anywhere without him.

"I'm so sorry." They seemed like the only words I had for him.

"It's not your fault." His voice was soft next to my ear. "I went into the forest that night, looking for the pond, thinking I could help, and then . . ." He sighed deeply. "Next thing I knew, I was on the street here. Alone. I guess the Ragged Man got me. And now you . . ."

"Fell into the pond," I said dully.

Pushed.

"So here we are, in this crappy fake world." He spread his arms, then closed his eyes and let his arms fall slack, getting hold of himself.

I'd never seen him like, this, looking like he was on the brink of unraveling. But he'd been stuck here in this dead imitation world for weeks.

"So this version of the town is . . . empty? You've been alone the whole time?" I asked softly, hating the idea, but the image of the girl in the mirror was itching in my mind. Had other imposters climbed through other mirrors?

I didn't even know what I wanted him to tell me, because if there were others trapped in the black water, was that better or worse? But he didn't answer my question at all.

After a moment, Key stepped back and framed my face with his hands, eyebrows drawn together in sadness. "You're not going to like this," he said softly. "But I have something to show you."

I opened my mouth to question him, to know what he had to show me and why he seemed to dread doing so when there was a sudden rustling behind us, farther back in the hall of mirrors. Key froze with his hands on my face. The rustling stopped, then came again, sounding like something big slithering along the floor, something ponderous and searching. Key's face went tight.

"What is it?" I whispered, seeing the clown's tiny shark teeth in my head, the hunger in its eyes.

Key gave a shake of his head and gripped my arms. "We should go," he said, voice low and quiet.

The rasping slithering came again, followed by a thud, still behind us but closer. Something was in here with us. I imagined the clown as a shadowy serpent, huge and bloated but squeezing through the maze just the same, shedding skin as it went, driven on by our scent and hungry enough to swallow us both whole. "Come on. This way." Key pointed to the left.

"Are you sure?" I had moved so slowly through the maze of mirrors. I took his hand and let him lead me, carefully but steadily threading our way through the mirrors.

"I memorized it," Key said grimly. "This place has been a good hiding spot." I squeezed his hand but he raised his finger to his lips, preventing me from asking the question already forming on my lips.

Hiding from what?

Key got us safely out of the fun house but didn't even slow down when we burst through the door. He kept a firm grip on my hand as we wound through FallsFest, ducking between rides and booths, taking a shortcut and coming out at the opposite end and onto the street. Suddenly, he stopped short, and I ran into him.

"You didn't eat anything, right?" He was staring at me so intently, it was unnerving.

He looked so concerned that my first instinct was to lie, just to soothe him. But if I'd learned anything—and at the moment that was questionable—it was that lying never got me where I wanted to go. "I—I tried." I knew immediately that was not what he wanted to hear. "Some popcorn."

"You actually ate it?" Panic bloomed on his face.

I shook my head. "It tasted like nothing, so I spit it out."

"All of it?" At my nod, Key's shoulders sagged. "Okay." He released a breath that puffed out his cheeks. "Just—don't. Nothing." With no further explanation, he took my hand again and crossed the street, walking down the sidewalk like we were late for something.

"Where are we going?"

Key nodded but didn't look at me. "It's hard to explain. It's not far." He squeezed my hand, but I wasn't comforted. Key was not an evasive person. I was the secret-keeper, the avoider, the procrastinator. A knot of tension started twisting in my chest.

We passed an empty golf cart where the sloucher should be lounging, judging people and exulting in his delusion of authority. Then on past the Pink Unicorn, the doors open, freezers full of ice cream humming and the bubblegum pink interior lit up, but no one behind the counter and every pink picnic table empty. The only movement came from the breeze lifting paper napkins one by one off the stack on the counter and sending them slowly rolling onto the ground and around the patio like a ballet of the inanimate.

The streets Key led me through were just as still and dead as the others, but at least there were no idling cars or creepy carousels. And I was with him, putting to rest the unnamable agitation I'd had ever since I pulled something that looked like him from the black water. I'd been missing him. Some wiser part of me had known that he wasn't with me; I hadn't saved him.

I was with him now. And this time I'd save him or die trying. I squeezed his hand and matched his speed, in a hurry to get wherever he was taking me.

TWENTY

WE HURRIED ALONG THE SIDEWALK THROUGH a residential area I knew but didn't frequent. Now aware that the black water had trapped us in a parallel world, I looked around more carefully. It was a pretty faithful replica of the town, just empty and silent. Everything was where it should be, but there was a thin quality to it. It reminded me of a movie set waiting for actors.

Were we the whole cast, or would there be more?

I snuck a look at Key's profile as we went—the same nose, the same strong chin with an almost-indetectable childhood scar. The same curl that always hung over his left eyebrow, forever rebelling against any and all products and his habitual attempts to brush it back. Despite where we were, being with him filled me with the same warm glow as always.

I thought I was being subtle, but he caught me looking and smiled. "I missed you, too," he murmured.

Key was walking fast, and I hoped it wasn't because of the things I caught moving, just in the corner of my eye—dark fluttery shapes like afterimages from looking at something too bright that vanished when I tried to look at them squarely.

"Stay ahead of them," Key said without turning.

I didn't ask what "they" were, just tightened my grip on his hand and kept pace with him.

When we turned left on Matilda Street, I knew where we were going.

"Frank's not here, is he?" A whole new level of fear sent my heart knocking in my chest. Had I been working with Other Frank all this time? Was no one around me real?

Key frowned. "Frank? No, he's not here. But we *are* going to his house."

I'd only been to Frank's house a few times and found it unsurprisingly Frank-like. Classic but modern; old-man appropriate but cool. His Craftsman bungalow was perfectly maintained but managed to retain its warmth. The border gardens in the front yard were bursting with white and soft pink hydrangea that drooped over the picket fence. The front porch was decked out with a sisal mat, two wicker chairs, and hurricane lanterns on either side of the door. A big front window displayed the living room and Frank's artfully curated furniture, but it wasn't the mid-century light fixture or harvest table that stopped me dead in the gate, grabbing onto Key's arm with my free hand for support and sucking in my breath in a sharp gasp.

Key turned to gauge my reaction, sympathetically rubbing the back of my hand with his thumb.

"No," I whispered, trying to be quiet and not scare away what I hoped with every shred of my soul was a ghost.

"Ave." Key reached out to hold my arms, but I brushed by him, unthinking and numb, through the gate and up the stone walkway that led to the painted porch.

"No." It came out a little louder as I walked, because in the history of things that were not fair, this was the most not-fair thing conceivable. I stepped off the walkway and onto the lawn, speechless. For a moment, we hung there, the slight figure in front of the window and I. Then the tension in her shoulders changed as she registered my presence and she turned slowly, like we both were hoping to be figments of imagination or wisps of half-forgotten dreams.

But she looked real enough to me.

Ihstá Lily stood in front of the big window, her mouth falling open in a delicate O of recognition, immediately followed by despair. "Oh! Oh no. No, no, no." She rushed forward, reached out to touch me, and stopped short, pressing both hands to her mouth and looking past me to Key. He nodded, his mouth downturned. All I felt at the moment was confusion laced with fear around the edges.

"Ihstá?" I said hesitantly, because she was Lily, but wasn't. How could this possibly be Lily? My ihstá lived in a retirement home. Her hair was white, she was unsteady on her feet, and her mind was unreliable. The woman in front of me stood straight and her eyes were clear. This was the Lily that I remembered from my childhood, but this—this couldn't . . .

Oh my God.

"Ihstá?" My voice cracked. How much farther down could I fall? How many people had the black water stolen from me?

Lily clasped her hands in front of her, at the waist of a pale blue dress I'd never seen, short-sleeved with a full skirt. Her hair was longer and pinned up in a twist, shot through with silver but darker than it had been in decades.

"Avery." Tears glistened in her eyes. Shaking her head in dismay, this younger version of my ihstá opened her arms and I fell into them without thinking, inhaling the same scent of lilac as always. It was her. Just like Key, she'd been taken by the black water. Just like him, she'd been trapped here and no one knew. But Lily had been on this side, in this empty place, for much, much longer, since before I was born. How could that be?

Lily craned her head up to search my face for clues. "How did you get here? Why didn't I see this coming?" she muttered to herself, the frown on her face getting deeper, her lips hardening into a line as she came to a conclusion. "I knew it."

I jerked back at the sudden brush of Lily's finger against the silver turtle around my neck.

"You wanted the earrings," she said, a dreamy smile on her face. "But I wanted to give you something that would last, something you'd have forever."

I remembered being at the powwow and looking at the vendor's table. I'd been interested in some beaded earrings, but Lily had picked out the necklace and laid it around my neck, and we'd looked together in the mirror the vendor held up. Lily's reflected face had been so soft and wistful.

"This was from me." Lily delicately tapped the turtle.

"That was you?"

"That was me."

I wrapped my fingers around her hand and felt it—I knew that somehow this *was* my ihstá. My throat went tight as Lily and I gazed at each other. By my shoulder, Key kept his eyes down and swept his right foot over the grass, just barely skimming the tips of the blades, over and over, giving me space to grieve a loss I hadn't been aware of.

"What were you looking at just now?" I needed something else to focus on. Learning that two of my favorite people had been suffering while I was going to parties and eating ice cream was . . . It was a lot to deal with. Turning to the front window gave me time to swipe at the tears threatening to spill.

"Oh," Lily waved toward the house and slipped her hand into mine, and we took the few steps to the window together. "Just this silly goose."

The living room was empty, but talking about things that no one else could see was not new territory for my ihstá.

"Look at the window, not the room," Lily instructed, leaning close to me. "You kind of have to let your eyes go."

"It's like those optical illusions." Key was suddenly at my other side. "Relax your eyes."

Like seeing Frank reflected in the store?

I closed my eyes and willed the muscles to relax. When I opened them again, he was there. Right in front of us. Frank's living room was empty, but in the reflection of the room, Foster stood at an ironing board, lips pursed in concentration, expertly pressing a shirt.

"He's there? At Frank's?" I whispered.

"Yes," Lily said, smiling. "On the other side. Why, I can't imagine."

I could. "Did you see his house?"

Lily shook her head. "I don't go out there—too much of a walk."

Key's eyes were burning a hole in my head. Judging by the fondness in Lily's eyes as she watched Foster, it occurred to me to just keep my mouth shut, but just for an instant. I'd learned my lesson about keeping secrets.

"All the glass was broken, at Foster's house." I watched Lily's face carefully for a reaction, but if what I'd said upset her, she didn't show it.

"He was right to do it," she murmured, never taking her eyes off him.

But that wasn't what I'd said. I turned to Key, who shrugged, apparently not knowing what to make of her nonresponse either.

"Can he see us?" I watched Foster pick up the shirt, shake it out, find something not to his liking and lay it back down on the board again, smoothing the fabric with his hand.

"If he were to look our way, he might." Lily had a faraway look on her face. "But he doesn't know to look *at* the glass, not *through*."

This was all confusing and didn't seem to make a lot of sense. "I saw Frank in the store window, but he had his back to me."

Lily nodded. "I've always thought it best that way."

"So he doesn't know?" I asked cautiously, not sure what she meant. "That you're here?" In all this time, couldn't Lily have tried to contact Frank or Foster?

"I've always thought it best that way," Lily said again, making it sound like the final word on the subject.

We stood in the middle of Frank's lawn, in front of what should be a beautiful house, in the middle of what should be a fragrant garden. But it wasn't. None of it. A cold sense of unreality seeped into my body, like standing in rising water. Of all the unbelievable things that had happened to me since I stumbled on the pond in the forest, this was somehow the worst. She'd been trapped here before I was born. She seemed strong enough to stand out there all day. Her mind and body were intact, able to enjoy life, but she was stuck here where there was none. I remembered Foster visiting and bringing flowers to whoever I'd grown up with. The thought produced a kind of claustrophobic panic, a swirling tightness that rose in my chest and threatened to cut off my air. Who was the woman I'd grown up with?

Key's hand slid into mine, holding firm, anchoring. I looked at him gratefully. He understood. He knew.

"I've seen everything," Lily said quietly, still watching Foster wrestle with the shirt. "I've seen you grow, and, Avery"—she turned to me with tears in her eyes—"I'm so proud."

"You've watched like this?" I pointed to the window, where Foster had moved on to another shirt. He lined up the seams, caught his finger on the edge of the iron and winced, shaking his hand.

"Oh, dear." Lily turned away.

Childhood memories of my great aunt—or her imposter—flooded my mind, flipping like pages in a book with one constant. "The mirrors," I said, wonder in my voice. Lily's apartment and her little house before had been full of mirrors, glass, and shiny surfaces. Even at restaurants, Lily had always insisted we sit next to a window. Mom and her family had always shrugged it off as a quirk and later as evidence of Lily's failing mind. But it was intentional, allowing my real ihstá to see us.

"So at restaurants . . . ," I said.

Lily nodded, smiling. "You all thought she was just batty, but she was making sure I could see. Although . . ." She tilted her head. "That's why she did go batty, the strain of keeping our connection."

"But how did you . . ."

"We talked about it, she and I," Lily said, like it was the most normal thing in the world to negotiate with the imposter taking your place. "We've had a long time to get to know each other."

"You can talk to your . . . Other Lily?" What did you even call something like that? Imposter? Changeling? I couldn't imagine rationally discussing anything with the girl in the mirror.

"It's not easy. It took time." Lily lifted a fluffy hydrangea bloom in her hand and then let it drop. "She was willing to keep that connection between us open. Others . . ." She nodded at Key, who shook his head and looked down, his lips twisted in disgust. "Others are not willing, and they snap that tether the first chance they get."

"So *she* set up all the mirrors in your apartment." This was blowing my mind, a reverse-engineered puzzle finally making sense. "For you." How often had I looked into a mirror not realizing I was looking into a different world completely?

Lily nodded. "Mirrors are much easier than windows. You can just look straight through. Easy peasy. She didn't have to do that. They're not all bad, the Others." She shrugged. "Not completely, anyway. We came to an agreement long ago, me and her."

Long ago.

"So, all my life . . ." I hated to ask but had to know.

Lily pursed her lips and gazed out at the street. Maybe even after all this time, she still expected to see life out there. "It's difficult to explain," Lily said, "but yes. It's been her with you. She and I had so long to negotiate that by the time you were born, she was willing to share a little, even though it was a strain for her. We knew each other so well by that point that no one noticed she wasn't me. No one noticed I was gone." She dropped her gaze and let out a deep sigh.

I took Lily's hand, and she raised her eyes to meet mine. "I knew it wasn't Key," I told her. "If I'd ever met the real you, I would have known. I would have noticed, Ihstá."

Lily smiled and pressed her palm to my cheek. "I think you would have, my beautiful niece. You see everything."

The three of us stood, hands linked in love in that horrible place.

"Now." Lily's face went serious as she folded her arms and turned her body to face me. "Why are you here?"

TWENTY-ONE

I NEEDED A MINUTE TO FIGURE OUT HOW TO explain something I didn't understand myself. "I fell into the pond. When I came back up, I didn't notice that things were wrong right away." It seemed incredible to me now—that I had ever mistaken this flimsy grayed-out version of my world for the real thing.

"You fell?" Lily's emphasis on that word—*fell*—sharpened my gaze. They were both looking at me so intently.

"I—" I'd felt someone else there. I'd seen something. I'd been pushed. But before I could answer, Lily cut me off.

"Why were you at the pond?" This rapid-fire, deadly serious version of Lily was as disorienting as anything else.

"I didn't go there on purpose." I tried to give her concise answers. "I knew there was something wrong with Key—" I shot him an apologetic smile. "Another me came through the mirror and chased me, and the fountain—"

"That blasted fountain," Lily muttered, shaking her head.

I'd just told her I'd been chased by another me, but the fountain was what she latched on to? None of what was going on made sense. The only thing I cared about was getting out, getting back to the real world, but there was one niggling question, one question I didn't want to ask.

Lily had been here for so long. If there was a way out, she would have found it. Which made me wonder if there was one.

The angle of the light hitting the window now made it hard to see Foster, and trying was making my headache worse. I looked up to find that the weak sun had moved in the sky.

"What time is it?" I frowned at my watch.

"Whatever time it wants to be," Lily said drily. "I've aged, but slowly. It's the one thing that really vexes her." She smiled wickedly. Her, the other Lily. I was still trying to wrap my head around that.

Key shrugged. "Time is weird here."

Lily patted my shoulder sympathetically. "We should get settled," she said, looking up. "It's not good to wander too much at night."

I was too numb to ask why.

Lily took my hand and started across Frank's lawn toward a gap in the hydrangeas. At the fence, she gathered up her dress in one hand, gripped one of the pickets, and hopped over, landing lightly on the other side, smoothing down her skirt and turning, waiting for us to follow.

My mouth hung open. The Lily I knew couldn't even get into a car by herself.

Key smiled at my amazement. "It does take some getting used to." He held out his hand in a "you first" flourish.

"There is a gate," I pointed out to both of them respectfully, but neither seemed to hear.

Hurdles were never my thing, so I didn't manage to clear the fence as gracefully as Lily had. Key cleared it with no problem, but I guess if he was hanging with this spry version of Lily, he'd gotten some practice in. The thought made my heart clench—at least the two of them had each other.

Lily led us down a laneway, a holdover from the days of horses and the need for carriage houses. "He's done a good job, with the house," Lily said over her shoulder. "Louisa always kept the yard neat as a pin."

"You knew Louisa?" Frank's wife had passed before he bought the store, so I only knew of her through Frank.

"Oh, yes. We were all friends back in the day." Lily's tone had a hint of sharpness, a glint of steel peeking out around the edges of happy words.

I looked at Key, who caught my eyes and gave a micro-shake of his head.

Don't talk about them.

Got it.

We strolled down the leafy tunnel, with Lily calling out milestones. "That was your kindergarten teacher's house." She pointed at a large house with a wraparound veranda in dire need of paint. "They've really let it go to hell."

"See that big old oak tree?" She waved at a massive tree towering at the edge of one of the yards. "You and I both climbed that as children. I didn't see you do it, of course. I only heard about it from her secondhand. Better than nothing, though. Right?" She sounded like a Crook's Falls tour guide, but her tone was increasingly bitter, calling up an answering darkness in me that promised to take me down the same resentful road.

I tightened my grip on Key's hand, listening to Lily get caught in a current of negativity, a whirlpool of bad thoughts that would suck her down and under. I tried to stop it by blurting out the first thing that came into my head.

"When Ru was thirteen, she stole two chocolate bars from the general store."

Lily stopped in her tracks and turned to stare at me like I'd sprouted another head, then burst out laughing. "Did she tell you that?"

"She did. She tried to pay back Frank the other day."

Lily shook her head and continued walking. "That girl," she said over her shoulder with one finger raised, "has always been a lovable menace. Do you know her mother—"

Lily stopped walking, and Key and I came up beside her.

"Listen," Lily whispered, raising her finger.

I strained my ears but heard the same nothingness that had been there since I'd climbed out of the pond.

Then a distant rumble.

"Thunder?"

Neither Lily nor Key answered, both of them looking ahead with a haunted focus.

The rumble came again, but this time it was something I felt as much as heard. Lily and Key spun, searching the horizon all around, but the rumble seemed to come from everywhere and nowhere at once.

"Shit," Key whispered.

Was a storm that big of a deal?

The next rolling rumble made the trees shiver.

Maybe not a storm.

"What is it?" I whispered, but Key touched my mouth, his eyes hard.

Lily started to back up, pointing to the east. I turned to look and suddenly, I was back at the black water, in the rain, the Ragged Man dragging me away from Key. I'd seen the leafy treetops shiver and shake, something huge and lumbering making its way through the forest.

Thud!

Close enough and strong enough to set off a car alarm. Whatever it was, it was coming this way.

"Come!" Lily was already moving back the way we'd come, waving her hands for us to hurry. She grabbed my free hand in an iron grip and we ran.

Beside my kindergarten teacher's old house, in the weed-studded driveway, a peeling wooden shed sat tilting against the house, creating a gap. Lily shoved me into the cramped, musty darkness, then Key after me and finally herself to block the small opening.

The steps were thunderous, like Godzilla had come to Crook's Falls. I covered my ears.

Over Key's shoulder, Lily pressed one finger to her lips like a threat, her eyes wide like the carousel horses'. I curled up small against the wall, squeezing my eyes shut and feeling the ground tremble under the progress of something enormous. Foster had said the Ragged Man wasn't the worst thing in the black water. I hadn't believed him at the time.

The ground shook, the shed groaned, and everything seemed to fall into shadow, something massive eclipsing the sun.

Key's arms were wrapped tight around me; his head tucked against my back. I could feel him holding his breath and understood that he was terrified, which bled straight into me. Key had always been fearless about all the things that scared me. If he was cowering, there was good reason to make myself small and hope whatever was thundering by wouldn't notice us. I reached up to squeeze his hand gripping my arm, and he squeezed back.

Huddled together in the nook between the leaning shed and the house, the smell of damp earth made me think of a graveyard.

A rush of air, laden with stink and rot, swirled around us in the tiny space, forcing me to cover my nose with one hand. The next step was thundering. The little shed shook, raining dust and old leaves down on us. The rumble that had been distant was now practically on top of us, not one sound but a cacophony of voices, many shrieks woven into a single agonized roar. The sound pierced my head, reaching into me and teasing out something deep inside, something long-hidden that, if I let it, would rise to the surface and attract the monster's eye. It would find us. It would snatch us up and consume us, adding our voices to the tortured choir. Panic coiled in my chest, on the verge of breaking out, when another hand gripped my wrist, smaller than Key's but just as strong—Lily's. Though there was no way to hear over the roaring like the crashing surf of the ocean, I felt her message—*hold on*. I took my hand from my face and wrapped my fingers around the turtle pendant. It glowed warm in my hand and I focused my mind there.

The vibration from the next step wasn't as strong. The shrieking clamor was now a rolling roar. The foul smell dissipated. Whatever the beast was, it was moving away. We listened, still tense and huddled, as the sounds faded into the west. I twisted around as Key lifted his face, where instead of relief, I saw sadness.

Lily's shoes scraped on the ground as she turned in place, peering out and around the edges of the shed. "Hold on," she whispered and then darted out.

Key and I turned toward the opening. I rested both hands on his back, his shirt now plastered with sweat. His heart beat through my palms and I focused on that, finding my heart slipped into rhythm with his easily. We kept our eyes on the opening, waiting for Lily.

The moment stretched into a minute and the minute felt like a year. Then Lily was back, smoothing down her dress and hair, a shaky smile on her face.

"Come." She motioned us out.

I crawled out after Key, who stood but then bent over, hands resting on his knees and breathing deep. The neighborhood looked the same except for some branches lying in the street, but the air smelled burned, an acrid tang that clung to the back of my throat.

"What was that?" I still crouched on the ground. My joints were stiff and leaden.

"That, my dear, was the black water." Lily spoke around the pin she'd taken from her hair. She redid the twist, reinserted the pin, and offered me her hand.

What?

"It's everywhere; it takes different forms—some slivers, some larger chunks," she said, pulling me to my feet. "That was a very big chunk. But it's all one."

"What was it looking for?"

"Well, it's looking for us." Lily said like it was the most obvious thing in the world.

And I had felt that; I'd felt some part of it reaching out, questing, and part of me had threatened to answer.

"That's the point of all of this, don't you see?" Lily peered into my face. "To consume us, to gobble us up one by one until there's nothing left, until we're part of it, indistinguishable."

"That's what the Others are for?"

Lily nodded, still watching me like she was waiting to see if I could reach the right conclusion.

"But why now?" The black water had been waking and sleeping for decades at least with no sign of the Others. "Why are the Others invading now?"

Lily patted her hair, pursed her lips, and looked away.

Apparently, I'd failed. This was not good. I went to Key, who was still bent over, staring at the ground vacantly. I put a hand on his back and he straightened up slowly. Between the two of them, his reaction seemed more reasonable, but maybe this "being stalked by a monster" thing was old hat to Lily.

"Well." Lily sighed and looked around, getting her bearings again. "Shall we continue?" She brushed off her dress and headed back down the drive to the sidewalk, like we hadn't just narrowly escaped something big enough to shake the earth under us.

"Key," I whispered, taking his arm.

He shushed me with a slight gesture of his hand. "She knows what she's doing," he said quietly, meaning to reassure me but answering none of my questions about this Lily at all.

TWENTY-TWO

I WAS USED TO SIDEWALKS AND ROADS, SO THE meandering route that Lily took, traipsing through backyards and alleyways, disoriented me. We popped out of a hedge and into a backyard that looked like it was owned by people aspiring to life off the grid. Three clotheslines stretched from the back porch to the fence and all were covered in bedding—sheets and pillowcases, mostly white but a few sets of pale green and purple. Everything in the yard was in subtle but constant motion, stirred enough by the weak breeze to undulate gently. The fabric rippling around me was thin enough to make shadows, moving patches of darkness that were there one moment and gone the next. I started at the brush of a sheet against my skin, pulling my arm in tight to my body.

"Do you know where we are?" I asked Key, keeping my voice low.

"Kind of," he whispered.

He didn't seem as bothered as I was, as wary of the swooping, darting shapes that surrounded us. I hurried to stay close to him.

Without missing a beat, Lily snatched a comforter off one of the lines, making it twang and sending a vibration all the way down the line, like a fly tripping a spider's web. She continued striding along, unconcerned. I shot Key a look, but his eyes were on Lily's back, like he didn't want to lose sight of her in this labyrinth of linen as she wound around, under, and through.

Key and I followed slightly behind her, leaving me with no idea where we were going until we stepped out of the backyard and into the parking lot of the conservation area.

The last time I'd come here because of the black water, the sky had been purple-black and pouring rain. I'd been with Stella, frantic to burn the Ragged Man's bones, thinking it would end the madness bleeding into my world. Tonight, the darkness would be total; when I looked up, the sky was empty—no clouds, no moon, no stars. Nothing. With the new path, I knew from here we were only a ten-minute walk from the pond, the source of all our problems. I didn't find that comforting.

"Should we be this close to it?"

Lily chuckled but there was no humor there. "The black water? It's already gotten us. What does it matter now?" Lily's mood had gone south, reminding me of dinner at the Willows, which reminded me that the Lily I'd grown up with wasn't really Lily. Without a word, she walked off toward the pavilion in the center of the field. Unsure if we should follow, I looked to Key.

"Fire supplies," Key explained.

Right. Of course, my ihstá would be retrieving fire supplies in the middle of the park, in the growing dark, in the black water's imitation world. I bit my lip gently and willed my mind to not fly apart.

Key retrieved some blankets folded neatly under a picnic table and spread them on the ground. "I liberated them yesterday." Key shrugged and sat, took my hand, and gently pulled me down beside him.

"Liberated?" We were going to sleep outside on stolen blankets? I looked down at our hands clasped on the blanket and it struck me that for him, this was still new. For him, our relationship had changed that night in the bookstore, and then—

I took his hand in both of mine. "After you were gone, I said something to you," I began slowly, the horror of seeing him in the cellar returning. "You weren't really there, but—"

"I heard." So softly, the words were barely audible, but he looked into my eyes.

"I meant it." The words that had taken what was in my heart and made it real.

"I know," he said, then a mischievous smile spread over his face. "Back at you."

I had to laugh. "Back at you? This is your response to my profession of love?" If nothing else convinced me that this was my Key, here it was.

He shrugged. "Concise. Effective. And it made you smile." He gazed at me like I was the only thing in the world. "It's the sole quality I have in common with that guy."

That guy. Other Key.

"Hmm." On to the next uncomfortable topic. "So . . ."

"So I know you kissed a me who wasn't me," he filled in, always making things easy for me.

"In my defense"—I let go of his hand and raised mine—"evil twins had never occurred to me."

He grabbed back both my hands and held them to his chest. "Forgiven. Totally."

Which was such a Key response, and yet there was definitely

a different edge to him, a hardness that hadn't been there before. I was probably different, too. When we got out of here and back to the real world, it might take some getting used to—this new us, the real us. But I wanted to. I wanted it all, greedy in a way I'd never been before.

I looked around, feeling exposed in the middle of the field. Lily was making her way back carrying two plastic bags. "There's no hiding here," I observed.

"It's better to be somewhere like this, where you're not expecting to see people. Mentally, I mean." Key tapped his temple. "Staying in my house or hanging out in the middle of town and being the only one there is depressing. Waiting to be found by people who don't know you're gone . . ." His voice trailed off.

Like me. Key had watched me going about my life like everything was normal. He'd watched the other guy take his place, and even his parents hadn't noticed. I squeezed his hand but didn't know what to say.

"It does things to your mind," Key said softly.

I bet.

Rather than deal with that thought, I got to my feet ready to take the bags from Lily, but she walked right by me like I wasn't there.

Lily dropped the bags, settled herself on a blanket with a sigh, toed off her shoes, and leaned back on her elbows like she was at the beach. Key arranged some kindling in the firepit in front of us and lit it, leaning over to gently blow and help the flames catch. All his zombie apocalypse skills were really paying off here.

"It's just nice to have a fire," Key explained, slipping the matches into his pocket. "Makes it festive. Less depressing."

Depressing was realizing that he'd been here long enough to develop a routine.

"You stash all this here?" I asked.

"It's one of our favorite places." Key gestured around us. "Open. Quiet. Kind of a stark beauty vibe." He smiled, but it only made me feel worse for him. The idea of any beauty existing here seemed odd, but maybe the absence made any little bit even more valuable.

"Come and sit, dear." Lily patted the ground beside her.

I stretched out beside this slightly unnerving version of my ihstá. She'd been so blasé about the lumbering thing that had forced us to hide. She was stern and serious in a way the Lily I knew was not. But like Key had said, being here as long as she'd been—it must have done things to her, changed her in ways I couldn't yet name. I just hoped she wasn't *too* different, that the core of who she'd been had managed to survive.

My eyes kept drifting up, expecting to see twinkling points of light in the sky, only to find a blank void, which was unnerving. In the companionable silence, I worked up the courage to ask the question I'd been shoving away for days.

"Why is it doing this? Sending the Others?" I was a little afraid to ask but had to know.

Key picked at the blanket and Lily was silent for so long, I thought she wasn't going to speak.

"If I'd been paying closer attention"—she sighed—"maybe I could have done something. Probably that's why she kept me distracted."

"She?"

Lily turned to me, her lips a tight line and slightly downturned in disappointment.

Right. Other Lily.

"I didn't see the Ragged Man until it was too late," she continued, looking into the flames that were crackling quietly. "After all these years, I thought I could trust her."

"But we got rid of him. And yet . . ." Here we were, victims of the Others. I'd done everything I'd been told to put the black water back to sleep. It clearly hadn't worked, and I thought I knew why, but what about now?

"The black water has a lot of tricks, dear. Don't feel bad." Lily's face softened and suddenly I wasn't afraid of her anymore. However different she was, this was my ihstá, who loved me.

"It's smart. It hides and when it's discovered; it makes people's memories fuzzy. But I've come to believe it's also no better or worse than people are. Look at what people do to each other every day." Lily spread her hands like the world was before us. "Not everything is ever good. Not everything is ever bad. Everything works together in balance."

"Like day and night. Like Maple Sapling and Flint." The black water seemed pretty thoroughly bad to me, but I got what she was saying. Foster had told me the story of the twin brothers—one a creator, the other constantly trying to destroy.

Lily's face lit up. "Yes!" She patted my hand and left hers covering mine. "Each of them needs the other to define him. The black water seeks that through us. Through being us. It has more than enough darkness but no light. It sees our joy and wants to take that; it uses the Others to make us a part of itself, to become whole. But taking someone by force is not going to end in joy." Lily stared out into the darkness that had stolen over the field. "It's so lonely, Avery. So empty."

I searched her face because right then, she sounded sorry for the black water, like she pitied it. There definitely wasn't any pity in my heart for the monster who'd swallowed us whole, but Lily had been trapped here for decades. If it were me, I'd have become the most bitter, resentful, and unstable person ever after just a few weeks. But Lily was . . . Lily. A more somber version, yes. But also stronger in every way.

"Anyway." Lily smiled at me. "That connection, it's also why we have been the ones to deal with the black water for so long—the strength of the community has allowed that. Even though we don't always win, we don't lose, either."

She was right, I knew that. That strength had allowed the community to survive against almost impossible odds. And I had been trying to weave myself into the community.

Until the black water had snatched me.

Was that *why* it had brought me here?

"I've been trying," I told Lily. "Learning from Foster and trying to speak the language more."

"I know; I've seen." She nodded. "You can keep working on that when you get back."

"When *we* get back," I corrected her, but Lily said nothing, just smiled vaguely down at her hands.

It seemed there was no more to say. We all lay back, the false forest surrounding us like a moat. I hadn't thought there was even a chance of me sleeping, but as I wedged myself securely between

Key and Lily, my eyes started to get heavy and my body relaxed. But my brain couldn't let go completely. I fell asleep thinking not about Lily or Key, but about Mom and Dad, Foster, Frank, and Stella. I drifted off, but with no sense of peace, only worry about Other Avery and what she might do to the people I loved.

TWENTY-THREE

I WOKE TO MY SHOULDER BEING GENTLY ROCKED back and forth, tiny movements, just enough to bring my consciousness back to a very intriguing sight.

I opened my eyes to find Key's inches away, which was not how I usually woke up, my sluggish brain confirmed. "Oh. Hi."

But I wasn't complaining. In fact, waking up next to him was a scenario I'd played over a million times in my head, and even though it was happening on the wrong side of the black water, it was still good.

Key's hair was wild, sleep crusted in the corner of one eye, but he was beautiful as always. He smiled like he was trying to hold something in, and I knew he was thinking the same thing about me. The knowledge spread warmth through my chest.

"Ahem." Lily cleared her throat loudly, already up and on her feet, folding her blanket neatly and giving us the same stern look I'd seen on my mom's face my whole life.

"Sorry." I scrambled to my feet, getting momentarily stuck in the blanket, not knowing what I was apologizing for. "Help me," I muttered to Key, trying to kick free.

"Stop kicking and I will," he muttered back, tugging at it until it fell away from my legs.

Our blissful moment was officially over.

"Are you quite finished?" Lily phrased it as a question, but I knew it meant we'd better be.

Key and I nodded in tandem. I quickly smoothed my hair back, trying to make myself presentable. I'd been awake for thirty seconds and I was already in trouble.

The sun was back, but it was hazy and dull; morning here had no brightness, no birdsong, no life. Back in the real world, Mom would be getting up to go to work like it was just another day.

"My mom's going to lose it when she sees I'm not there." Especially after what had happened with Key going missing and almost drowning, my mom's determined version of events.

Key looked away, scratching at the back of his neck. Lily was watching me, her head tilted and a pitying look in her eyes.

"She won't notice, dear."

Right. Other Avery.

I felt the knowledge hit me with a jolt. The girl in the mirror was there in the real world to take my place, just like Other Lily and Other Key. One by one, the black water would absorb us all. And those left behind would be none the wiser.

"But..." It hurt me to think that Mom wouldn't notice. "I mean, she's my mom." Would the woman who made me really not notice I was suddenly someone else, a slightly altered, off-brand version of her daughter?

"You'd be surprised," Lily said softly. "People see what they want to see."

Lily was living proof of that fact, but there was a small part of me that straight up didn't believe it. Deep down, I'd known something was wrong with Key, and I refused to believe that my family would just accept an imitation of me. Key must have witnessed his parents welcoming that imposter into their home. Anger and hurt burned in my chest but I steeled myself. If I was going to stop the black water from assimilating me, I would have to stop thinking about what may be happening in the real world and focus on getting there.

And ending Other Avery in the most satisfying way possible.

I clenched my fists at my sides. "What's the plan, Ihstá?" Because this Lily? I knew she had one.

"We're going to find some help," Lily said and started walking briskly toward the parking lot. "It'll be easier for you to get back if there's someone waiting."

I had no idea what that meant, so I turned to Key.

"We're going to try to contact the other side. Oooooh!" he said, doing the spooky hands.

That didn't make things any clearer, but I followed Lily off the field and onto the gravel parking lot. It wasn't even where we were going or what we were going to do when we got there that was setting off a twinge of unease in my stomach. When Lily said *you*, she meant *us*. We were all going back.

Right?

"Ihstá—" I trotted up beside her. Damn, this Lily was fast.

She stopped short and spun to face me, a steely look in her eye and her jaw set.

"You're going to have to trust me, dear. I know what our options are, but you need to do exactly as I say." I nodded, struck silent. Lily turned and continued walking, her skirt swishing around her legs, at odds with her determined march. "I'm not having you rot in here," she muttered, but I didn't think she was talking to me anymore.

Key caught up and slipped his hand into mine. I automatically fell into step but kept my eyes on Lily striding ahead of us, single-minded and serious. I leaned in toward Key.

"Is she . . . okay?" I whispered. That was as close as I could get to voicing the doubts creeping around the edges of my mind.

"She'd been alone until I got here," Key said, keeping his eyes on Lily's back. "I didn't figure out what had happened to me for—well, it took me longer than it should have."

"What do you mean?"

Key adjusted his grip on my hand, like he was afraid to let go. "That night, when it happened, I thought if I could go find the pond and get a few pictures, get you to see it from a different perspective, it would help. But . . ." He took a long breath, and I realized it was hard for him to tell me this, to go back there in his head. "Next thing I knew, I was alone, in the forest—"

"Like that time—"

That got a little laugh out of him. "Yeah. I pulled an Avery."

My turn to laugh, a little relieved that he'd gotten the joke.

"But my camera was gone." He sighed. "I got home and there was no one. Anywhere."

Been there. I squeezed his hand in sympathy.

"I lost it," Key confessed, shrugging. "I thought maybe I was in a coma, some kind of fever dream, then considered the existence of actual hell. Weird that after all the movies I've watched, the idea of a parallel dimension didn't really occur to me. Then those things found me, and I ran—literally—into Lily."

Just hearing him recount the story made me hold my breath.

"She was surprised and . . . really upset," he said, keeping his eyes down. "I think the black water kept her . . . distracted somehow. She felt like it was her fault, that she hadn't seen what it was doing."

I knew all about guilt. I'd been on the other side blaming myself for setting the whole cycle in motion and Lily had been here, doing the same thing. "She left me for a while," Key continued. "I think she went to talk to Other Lily. When she came back, she was . . . not better, exactly, but calmer."

This calm Lily was disturbing enough.

"Hey." Key touched my arm. "This sounds stupid, but . . . is my camera okay?"

If there was any shred of doubt left in my mind about who he was, it vanished. Sucked into an alternate reality and trapped, he was worried about his precious camera—peak Key. I took his hand.

"He isn't even using it," I assured him. "Such a tip-off." That I was pathetically slow to notice.

"Good." Key looked satisfied. "I don't want that jerk touching my stuff."

"So you just—what have you been doing?" I hated to ask, to make him relive all of it, but I needed to know; I wanted to share as much as I could.

"We walk a lot," Key said slowly, like he was censoring what to tell me. "We watch when we can. Sometimes it's not too bad, but most of the time, it really sucks. That's when I go and sit in the fun house, just to be in the dark and see nothing around me. It's the closest I can get to disappearing."

What could I possibly say to that? We walked on in silence.

"But now you're here," Key said with a sigh. "I don't know how well she's actually handling that."

Lily had apparently thought she had an agreement with Other Lily, but it seemed like the black water wasn't great at fulfilling bargains. The grimness in Lily may be from being trapped in the black water for so long—if that wasn't a good excuse, I didn't know what was—but she must also feel betrayed. She thought she'd had a handle on things and then I got myself stuck here and proved her wrong.

We stepped out of the trees and came to a stop on the sidewalk, Lily standing still and appearing to calculate our next move, the weak breeze stirring strands of salt and pepper hair around her face. I felt like so far, I'd been deadweight, the slowest member of the team. They both knew far more than I did about this place, but surely I could contribute to getting us out.

"What about a note?" I said, remembering my original idea. "I could hold it up to the bookstore window. Would that work?"

If it would, wouldn't she have tried it?

"I'd rather not involve Frank." Lily sighed. "He seems so tired lately." She looked at me for confirmation of her interpretation, and I realized how hard it must be, to get glimpses of the other side but not be able to know for sure that what you thought was going on was what was actually going on. It would be like watching a movie with no sound and sketchy Wi-Fi.

I nodded. "It's been . . . a lot for him."

Lily gazed at me shrewdly, as if I had more to say and just didn't know it.

"Do we know for sure what time it is there?" I asked.

"Not really." Key shook his head. "It's approximate."

"If he's already at the bookstore, it's probably not going to work anyway," I conceded. The bookstore was the least reflective place I could think of, full of paper and wood. The only possibility there was the huge front window, but Frank sat with his back to it all day. "I already tried."

"Your mother won't be able to see. She won't be looking," Lily thought out loud. "It has to be someone who knows."

Someone who knows.

Ru had given me the impression that she knew or believed more than my mom.

You can talk to me anytime.

"Ihstá?"

Lily and Key turned to look at me.

"I have an idea. Follow me."

TWENTY-FOUR

MY RIGHT FOOT WAS ALREADY STEPPING OFF the curb when a firm hand on my wrist pulled me back.

"We need to stay off the streets," Lily said quietly, in the voice my mom had used after a fight we'd decided we were going to just ignore.

"What does it matter?" I asked, bitterness creeping into my voice. "Nobody can see us."

"The people on the other side may not, but things here will."

"More things here? That's just great." I gently pulled my hand away.

"Avery." Lily frowned at me. Behind her, Key twisted his hands together, looking uncomfortable.

I took the longest, steadiest breath I could and gripped the turtle pendant in my hand. "I'm sorry, Ihstá. It's just—"

"It's a lot, I know." Taking my hand again, Lily said patiently, "I'm getting you out of here, Avery." She looked me in the eyes. "I have no doubt about that, and neither should you."

She was being a little scary again, but I actually felt better. "But, Ihstá, if you know how to get back, why are you still here?"

"Now, listen." Lily turned to us, taking one of my hands and one of Key's. "Your handsome boyfriend and I are here because the black water took us." She nodded at him. "We remained here, replaced by the Others, keeping the door open, giving it the strength to flood rather than close, even after the Ragged Man dissolved into nothing." She wrinkled her nose at the mention. "We were taken here. We need someone to take us back." She reached up to brush my hair from my face. "But you, my dear, you weren't taken by the Ragged Man. You came on your own somehow. You can get back the same way you got in."

"All this time, you couldn't get anyone's attention in the real world?"

"I never tried," Lily said softly. "Once I was on this side, I felt it, how lonely the black water was, and I knew that it would never stop. When I saw how well Other Lily was accepted, that everyone on the other side was okay, I thought I could keep everyone safe from here. I thought that my presence, my company, would be enough for the black water." She sighed and let go of our hands. "I was, of course, spectacularly wrong," Lily said bitterly. I couldn't imagine what it had been like for her, alone all those years with all that bottled up inside.

"I thought Other Lily and I needed each other." She shrugged. "She was willing to share, to help me see you all and I was willing to stay here. I thought we had a deal."

"Well, she screwed you over bigtime, Ihstá." I patted her shoulder.

Lily let her hand rest over mine. "She did. You can never know another person, not really. You see what they allow you to know and nothing more."

Very true. Other Key had managed to fool me for a while for this very reason. I thought I knew who he was, and as long as he kept up the charade, I didn't know any different. He'd been a good actor, but not a perfect one. Every mask had to slip sooner or later.

"So you had this agreement, you'd stay here, she'd stay there, and the black water would leave everyone else alone." I hated to press, but it was so hard to wrap my head around Lily being friendly with her Other.

Lily nodded. "She was amenable, even though it was difficult for her to sustain our connection."

"And Other Key?" I said cautiously. Key snorted and turned away, folding his arms across his chest.

Lily shrugged. "They're all part of the black water, but they're not all the same. He hasn't been in the real world very long. It's still shiny and new to him." She and Key exchanged a look. "Also, he seems to be something of a jackass."

Fact.

"Maybe he'd mature." She drew the possibility in the air with a careless wave of her hand. "In time."

"But we're not going to give him that chance," I said firmly, wanting to make sure we were all on the same page. A few leaves stirred limply on the little tree growing in a tiny patch of dirt cut out of the sidewalk, but other than us, there were no sounds or signs of life.

Lily looked me in the eye for a moment, her expression unreadable, before a gentle smile broke over her face. "No, we're not," she said quietly, then turned away and started walking.

"I think I have an idea—"

"Avery." Lily closed her eyes and raised her hand like I was tiring her out. "Getting you out is my responsibility. Trust me."

"But—"

"Avery." Lily fixed me with a steely gaze that permitted no further argument. "Let's go."

Key was already following behind her like a duckling. No one wanted to listen to me and I wasn't certain enough of my idea to make them.

"Okay," I whispered to myself and fell in line. I'd see what my ihstá had planned, but Other Lily still loomed large in my mind, maybe a key Lily didn't know I'd brought with me.

It was weird and disorienting to move like this. I was passing through neighborhoods I knew well, but I was used to the front gardens, the street-facing sides of the houses. Now, moving through only backyards and laneways, it was like the town was in disguise. Creeping through the back of a big corner lot, the quiet gurgle of a pool filter and the whisperings of tiger grass in the garden gave me a hint to where we were. The tiger grass lined the front yard, too. The house belonged to a snooty couple who'd given my dad's car a disdainful sniff when he'd picked me up from school. But that wasn't what interested me now.

I crept up beside the house and peered over the wooden gate.

Yes! I knew it. I gripped Key's arm in excitement.

Directly across the street, my little gray house sat just as I'd left it, except for one thing. Ru's convertible was parked in the driveway.

"Wait, wait, wait!" I whispered. "Look!"

"We have to go." Lily's voice was low and firm.

Why would Ru be at my house in the middle of the day, when both Mom and I were at work?

"It'll take two minutes." A tiny seed of hope dared to sprout. If I was right, it could change everything. I unhooked the latch on the gate and gently pushed it open, but thanks to obsessive home maintenance, it swung open soundlessly.

"Avery—" Whatever Lily had been about to say died when she saw Ru's car.

This could not be a coincidence.

"You think?" Key bit his lip, a new habit he'd picked up here.

"Two minutes," Lily said.

Through the gate, I checked both ways and saw nothing moving but the leaves in the breeze. Even if I did see something, this was too important. I sprinted across the street with Key and Lily close behind me, up the driveway, and onto the porch, where my nerve almost gave out.

The last time I'd been here, Other Avery had chased me, herding me to the black water like livestock destined for the butcher's case. But Other Avery was in the real world now, and I was here, so . . . Thinking about the logistics made my head hurt. I turned the knob and stepped in more cautiously than I'd ever entered my own house. Just in case.

"This is a long shot," Key said, like he was trying to prepare me for disappointment again.

Maybe. Maybe Ru was just dropping off food she'd made. She did that often enough now, cooking being one of her love languages. But.

Maybe she went to the bookstore and noticed that I was not . . . myself. Maybe she remembered telling me about Bee.

The three of us stood crowded together in the hall, listening.

Shut the door. I motioned to Lily, because Buttons could still be here. The black water had taken a lot from me; I'd be damned if it would take my cat, too. Lily eased the door shut with a quiet click that sounded loud in the stillness.

I looked around, seeing the house with new eyes. The living room—not much shiny in there. The kitchen was better.

But there was only one place I really expected to find what I was looking for.

"Ave?" Key followed me down the hall. The bathroom door was still slightly ajar. "Why the bathroom?"

I always left Bee a secret message on the bathroom mirror.

I was hoping Ru had left another.

I carefully pushed the door open, because everything on this side of the black water seemed quiet and sneaky, but the bathroom was empty.

"What happened?" Key asked, stepping in behind me, eyes widening at the glass everywhere. "Is this where . . . ?"

The mirror over the sink was gone, just like in Foster's house. But here, someone had swept the shards into a neat pile against the wall, someone caring, who didn't want anyone to get hurt. Ru had been here, if she wasn't here still, and after seeing all the glass, she must have known *something* was wrong.

"Get the shower." I said over my shoulder and turned the hot water on in the sink as far as it would go. The center of the mirror was gone, but the outer edges still clung to the wall. I'd stood and looked into it so many times, mistaking the girl in the glass for me, when she'd been on the other side watching me like I was an animal at the zoo. I leaned over the counter and started breathing close to the glass, trying to hurry the process along, desperate to prove my theory right.

"I get it." Key turned the shower on as hot as it would go, closed the glass door, and stood back, staring at it.

I glanced over to see Lily standing guard at the door, leaving it open only a sliver and wringing her hands, looking anxious for the first time. Maybe she'd never been this close before to making anyone see. But Ru would. I knew it. I could get us out. I could save my ihstá. I could save us all.

Steam began to billow over the top of the shower door, and the mirror remnants slowly fogged over.

Lily gasped and pressed her fingers to her mouth.

On every bit of mirror left, on every inch of the shower door, smiley faces emerged.

A full body shiver started on my scalp and raced to my toes.

I picked up the hand mirror on the counter and saw a big smiley in the dead center. I smiled back, choking back tears. A message. Someone knew I was here. We were going to get out.

"Ave." Key wrapped his arms around me from behind, squeezing like he could hold together every part of me that was threatening to spin away.

"We're getting out of here." I sniffled. Lily stood in the corner, taking in the messages that for her, were coming from an impossibly distant place and time. "We're getting out of here," I said, looking her in the eyes. Back to the version of Crook's Falls I belonged in; that was *mine*. She gave me a shaky smile.

"Okay." I swiped my hand through the smiley face on the mirror, ready to replace it with my reply. Ru's car was outside. For all we knew, she could still be in the house with us.

Help! Pond!

Pretty concise. I propped it up against the wall behind the sink, easy to see for anyone who knew what to look for.

Picking up the towel from the floor—like my mother always dreamed of—I carefully wiped away the smiley faces on the mirror remnants, then turned to find Key and Lily watching me.

"Let's get to work!" When had I ever bossed my ihstá around? Never, that's when. But this was a weird situation and as soon as I spoke, she and Key started wiping at the shower door and repeating my message in letters big and small. Everywhere.

When every inch was filled, we shut the water off and surveyed our work.

"We've been here too long," Lily said quietly. She seemed like she couldn't wait to leave.

Outside, the driveway was empty but it didn't matter. Ru had seen the shattered mirror, and she was a busybody at the best of times. She'd know something was wrong and she wouldn't let it go. She'd left the messages, which meant she at least suspected something. I nodded to myself. This was going to work. I took Key's hand, stepped off the porch, and nodded to Lily. We headed down the street and around the corner together. I was ready to go home.

TWENTY-FIVE

A DISTANT SCREECH FROM SOMETHING OUT-raged, like metal on metal, snapped Lily and Key to attention. "Now, remember," Lily whispered, her eyes still scanning the neighborhood like a hunter. "Quietly and away from anything shiny. We don't need any interference."

Interference from what? I trotted up a driveway and into a backyard after my suddenly spry great-aunt. If I challenged Lily to a race, I would still win, but probably not by much.

"Well, the black water, of course." Lily raised her eyebrows at me, reading my mind. "You have to go back through the door. It would be easier with someone on the other side, but we've waited long enough."

A wave of nausea rose up at the thought. This is what I had been dreading. It made sense, to go back the way I came, but the thought of willingly going into the water again made me shiver. "Isn't there any other way? What if I go into the pond just to pop up here again? Up is not up and it's so cold and dark. It's very confusing in there, you know."

Both of them stopped and stared at me, and the realization of what I'd said made me bite my lip in shame. They both knew exactly how confusing it was.

"You got out once, Avery. You're the only one. You can do it again."

As soon as she said the words, I remembered. I remembered everything. Running through the rain as the Ragged Man dissolved, diving into the black water and being lifted back up. The knowledge of how I'd done it, that I hadn't been alone and I wouldn't be now, coursed through my body and gave me new strength. I set my jaw and made a vow to myself. Other Key wasn't going to have time to settle in, and Other Avery was going to get the shock of her life.

Lily and Key were still watching me. I nodded and Lily nodded back, satisfied. We understood each other. The black water may have been a match for my ihstá or me separately, but together, I had no doubt about which side was going to win.

"Let's do it."

Lily turned on her heel and I followed.

She led us on a circuitous route for the Big Pond, scurrying through backyards and side streets, staying away from the houses with gleaming patio doors and windows, and all the cars. I had never seen Lily like this, steely-eyed and focused, sure in her directions for shortcuts and setting a pace that Key and I had to work to keep up with. This was who she was. The real Lily wasn't a doddering, delicate old lady. The real Lily was a badass warrior and her blood was in my veins. The fact gave me hope.

Stumbling through someone's vegetable garden, I turned to Key as he came up beside me. "Why do we need to stay away from—"

"It can see us. Track us. Like when Frodo put on the ring," he muttered, keeping his eyes on Lily's back as she shimmied through a gap in the hedge into the next yard.

"Frodo?" I wrinkled my nose. I knew the name but couldn't place it.

Key stopped for an instant, wrinkling his nose back at me. "Have I taught you nothing?"

It felt like a fist squeezing my heart. The two of us curled up in the dark, watching one hero or another save the world in flickering blue light—it felt like another lifetime.

Frodo. I flipped through my mental file of Stuff Important to Key. "Precious?" I think I had it.

"That's my girl." Key patted my cheek.

"So the black water can see us in the glass," I clarified. "But you were in the fun house. Lily was watching Foster by the window. You two weren't afraid of being seen then."

"It's you." Key pressed his hand against my back, urging me on. "We don't want it to see where you're going now. Like she said, we're here because we were taken. You weren't. You're special. You're Frodo," he whispered.

The explanation helped, but it didn't comfort because I couldn't remember what had happened to Frodo at the end of the story and was afraid to ask. I tried to focus on following Lily, but was distracted by a little tickle of anxiety. It had already sucked me in—what more could the black water do to me?

When we crept through the bottom of Sian's yard like thieves, I cast a glance up toward her house, remembering when everything had changed, when my dreams of a perfect summer had crumbled.

"Keep going, Ave." Key tapped my shoulder. I hadn't realized I'd stopped, remembering the night. Had Key seen himself at Sian's, all of us reflected in the patio doors? Had he watched Other Key enjoying the party while he was stuck in this wasteland? I pushed those thoughts away and kept going, over the fence I'd almost crashed into during my ill-fated slide, down an overgrown patch of brush, and popping out into a laneway, standing behind the back fences of some of the nicest houses in Crook's Falls.

I tapped Key's shoulder. "This is Stella's street." Which meant we were almost there. I'd gone down this street on my way home. A curl of dread unfurled in my stomach. Lily motioned us down, and we moved low along the fence.

"Wait!" I grabbed the edge of Key's shirt and tugged. "Ihstá!" I hissed.

Lily turned back and frowned, but she stopped, dropping into a crouch. "Avery—"

Key and I dropped down too. "I came down this street," I whispered.

"We have to keep moving," she chided.

"Yeah, but—"

"Ave, trust me. We need to go." Key gave me a little push, but I held my ground.

"There was a car." They weren't listening to me.

"There are lots of cars," Lily said quietly, turning away to evaluate our options once we reached the end of the fence.

"This one was different." It was crouched and waiting, a tiger flicking its tail in anticipation of a meal.

"You have to trust us, Ave."

I did, but what if they didn't know what I was talking about? What if the car was something new, something they hadn't encountered before? If I was so special, shouldn't they listen to me?

"Wait!" The panic in my voice finally got their attention.

Lily cocked her head. We all went silent. And even though I didn't want to hear anything, even though I was finally more than okay with a totally quiet, dead neighborhood where nothing stirred, I wasn't surprised when I heard the low, droning rumble.

RrrrrrRrrrrrRrrrrrRrrrrr

Lily frowned.

"Shit," Key spat.

"What is it? Who started the engine?" It was suddenly very important to me that some*one* had started it rather than some*thing*. Like maybe the car was yet another little part of the black water, a little "bet you didn't see that coming!" twist in an otherwise faithful replica.

Lily shuffled close to me—the Lily I knew, her knees would never allow this kind of maneuvering—and spoke in a low, urgent voice. "I don't know quite what that is, but we have to go this way. It's the most direct route and we can't afford to get cut off."

"Cut off by who?"

"By *what*," Lily said flatly. "There are things here, like splinters of the black water, smaller versions of the big one we hid from."

A chill danced down my spine. What else could the black water have waiting for us? Sentient cars? Slithering giant clowns?

Lily caught and held my gaze. "We have to make sure they don't see you. We may run into them, but if we do, Avery, don't look. They have a way of latching on to you and digging in, festering in your mind like an infection." Lily shot a look over my shoulder to Key, who nodded solemnly in agreement, and I suddenly understood that what they'd told me of their experiences here was only the beginning of a much longer story.

Lily peeked around the end of the fence, extending one protective hand behind her to make sure Key and I stayed back. Now that I'd pointed out the idling car to Lily and Key, the sound dominated the silence lying over the neighborhood like a heavy blanket.

RrrrrrRrrrrRrrrrRrrrr

Rising and falling but steady, as if to let us know that it wasn't going anywhere, that whenever we chose to stand up and come out from hiding, it would be waiting.

Somewhere behind, a long rising whistle pierced the air, containing a note of triumph that I didn't like. "We have to go." Key crowded up behind me.

Lily nodded tightly, pointing down the street to a silver van parked at the curb, our next destination. "Stay lower than the windows," she reminded me, then sprinted away.

I slid into place next to Lily, Key's hand gently on top of my head to make sure it stayed below the windows. We froze at another whistling shriek, no longer behind us but running parallel.

Something dark and shifting, an elongated stretch of shadow, darted through the lilac hedge across the street. I caught a glimpse of it, then wasn't sure I'd seen anything at all, as if my mind was disregarding the information sent by my eyes, denying it.

"They're trying to cut us off," Lily whispered.

There was a grinding wail on our side of the street, and now I saw it—a fleeting, flitting wisp of darkness, a thin flickering—not a person, but people. One face after another, none staying long enough for my mind to grasp hold of; it swept past us and was gone with a shrill call.

My skin went cold, and for a moment, my breath caught in my

throat. "What was that?" The thought of that thing getting hold of me made me want to curl up and hide. One touch and I knew something inside me, something important, would freeze solid, never to thaw. It was a mobile shard of a void, a portal to an even greater nothingness than this, space-cold and silent. Something that would bleed me dry for a very long time.

I was jerked out of the vision by Lily's hand griping my wrist and pulling me down the block and into the middle of a garden of sickly pale sunflowers in a front yard.

"Those things are after us? They're people?" I huddled between Lily and Key among the stalks, but no longer felt safe.

"They're not people." Lily patted my shoulder like it was a consolation. The sunflowers towered around us, swaying in unison from our entry. These anemic versions, sunflowers but not, disturbed me, so I kept my eyes down, away from them. "Those things, the other Key and me, they're all just facets of the black water. Splinters of it."

"And they want me." Just to be sure I understood.

Lily shot Key a glance, which I didn't like at all.

"If they latch on to you, it would make getting you back to the other side significantly more complicated." After a moment's deliberation, Lily continued. "And Key can't just go back through the water. He has to be brought through, the same way that he was taken. He can't go on his own like you. So you have to get out first, dear." Lily's fingertips brushed the turtle pendant around my neck. "For him to have a chance. But *she'll* be there."

"'She,' meaning . . ."

"You," Key said softly.

"Me." Trying desperately to understand. "Other Avery."

"Now, listen, dear," Lily said quietly. "The Others are different parts of the black water—some nice, some not. The other me, for example, was reasonable. But the fountain offers freedom to so many. Now that they're so close to being able to cross over, some of the Others you encounter will be vicious."

"Other Avery." She was going to be waiting for me.

Lily nodded. "She's unlikely to be cooperative."

"Yeah." I nodded. Understatement. "Okay, but meeting yourself—" I turned to Key "Won't that . . . disturb the . . . the . . ."

"Space-time continuum?" He smiled. "Like she said. It's not you, Ave. It's the black water. It just looks like you."

"And you?" I asked him. Getting me out of here was one thing, but not the most important thing.

"I'll follow you." Key pressed his hands into my shoulders and looked me in the eye. "As soon as Lily says. I'll meet you at the pond."

"At the pond on the other side. But what do I do?" I sputtered. "How do I bring you?"

Key shook his head. "You just go. Your passage will clear the way and I can get through right after you."

This didn't make any sense. I went numb as a thought hit me— was Key lying? I was doing this for him, to make sure he could get out of this hellish place.

But what if he was doing the same thing for me?

"One in, one out," Lily said clearly, like she wanted me to memorize the words.

One in, one out. The one thing I'd done differently from every other time the black water woke. And the one thing I could do to put things right.

"Key." I held on to him, but he seemed to know what I was going to say.

"Ave, I promise. I'll be right behind you. Trust me."

This wasn't going the way I'd planned—all three of us were supposed to leave together, but using Key was pretty good motivation. I'd run enough races to know that running for yourself isn't always enough to get you through a tough course. Competing for a team, though—that was a sure-fire way to get the absolute best effort. My ihstá knew what she was doing.

"Even when I'm back, the fountain will still be there," I pointed out. "The water in it is coming straight from the pond!"

"You let me handle that," Lily said. "But when you get back, tell Ru the water's not safe. That'll speed things along."

"Okay, but after that," I took Lily's arm. "What about you? How do I get you back?"

Lily patted my hand, already peering through the sunflower stalks, charting a new course, dismissing my concern. "Don't worry, dear. We're almost there."

Which wasn't an answer. Not at all.

TWENTY-SIX

"OKAY." LILY TURNED BACK TO US, AND WE huddled like a team in the last quarter, or homestretch or whatever. I was so nervous now that I couldn't even keep my sports analogies straight. "Fast as you can, down Maitland and past the gatehouse."

What? After prowling through the neighborhood like crafty raccoons, Lily's plan was to just go out in plain view, right through the proverbial front door?

"Umm . . ." I chewed my bottom lip.

Lily seemed to read my mind. "The faster we get this done, the better. And you, my dear, are very fast." Lily's eyes twinkled with mischief, like she was playing a game with the black water that would end with everyone having a laugh, not an eternal time-out for one side or the other. My heart swelled at the conspiratorial wink she gave me, but doubt lingered. Lily had been here with only the black water for company, for a long time. She was definitely sharper than the Lily I knew, but did that mean there was nothing wrong with her mind? Did she really know what she was doing?

Key took my hand in his and looked into my eyes. "Trust us, Ave."

Lily took my other hand with a gentle smile.

Trust. That's what it all came down to. Either I did or I didn't. I did.

"Okay."

Key moved aside to let Lily give me a hug. She still hadn't answered my question.

One in, one out.

But there were three of us.

"I have to stay," Lily said softly, reading my thoughts and telling me what, deep down, I already knew. "I can make a difference here, be an anchor on this side. I'll be more vigilant from now on. I'm going to have a word with her," she promised darkly.

The top of Lily's head came only to my chin. She was slight, like Other Lily, but solid. I understood now that Other Lily's paperiness, the thin, insubstantial quality of her, came not from age but from the fact that she belonged here, in this place, not in my world.

"It's going to be weird, to know she's not you," I whispered into Lily's hair, my voice cracking.

"Don't think that way." Lily shook her head. "She's not me, but she does love you. And wherever she is"—Lily leaned in and looked up into my eyes—"I'm there, too."

She held my gaze for a moment, and then Lily collected herself and spoke quickly, aware that she was running out of time. "Now. Make an effort with your father. If you don't try, you'll regret it later. Don't blame your mother for the way she is—she grew up very differently than you did." Lily pulled me in close again and held me tight, one hug that would have to last us a very long time. "And remember to talk to Ru."

"Isn't there anything I can do to help you?" I turned to look at her through my tears. Just leaving her here wasn't something I could wrap my head around.

THE OTHERS

Lily drew back and looked into my eyes like I was the only thing in the world. "Live your life," she said firmly. "Live your life as the Creator intended, my wonderful girl."

She carefully centered the turtle on my chest and tapped it gently. I nodded, my throat too tight for words. I would. I'd live an amazing life, I decided then. I'd be generous and brave. I'd live the life Lily couldn't. I'd give her joy by being happy.

Urged on by two people I loved most in the world, my reluctance didn't stand much of a chance. If Lily was wrong, the three of us were going to be together in this place for a really long time, but I had no better ideas, and I trusted my ihstá with my life. I gave the only answer possible. "Okay." I nodded and squeezed their hands. "Let's go."

Lily cautiously parted the sunflower stems and peeked out. "Don't wait for us." She said over her shoulder. "Look straight ahead and don't stop for anything, no matter what you see or hear."

My heart was a thudding background to her voice. My focus narrowed and sharpened, as it did before a race. This was the most important run of my life so far, because if I didn't beat those splinter-wraith things, Key would never leave this place. Coming in second meant coming in last.

"Go!"

We burst out of the garden, Key immediately falling behind but Lily close at my heels. Speed must run in the family.

Down the sidewalk, past the empty gatehouse, and onto the short gravel path. At this speed, the fresh layer of thick gravel was the worst footing imaginable, no better than a sheet of ice. Behind me I heard the long scrape of Key skidding as he rounded the corner.

Down the path, thick green bushes rose shoulder-high on either side of me like a corridor, providing either the perfect cover or the ideal ambush. The only sounds I heard were my feet crunching on gravel and the air rushing by my ears. My eyes were locked on the end of the path; I saw, heard, and thought of nothing else. I was firmly in race mode, focused on one thing—getting to the finish line first and claiming the biggest prize of my life.

Right on cue, the gravel path ended abruptly and opened up onto the Big Pond; like everything else on this side, it was similar to the real thing but not the same. When I'd crawled out after fleeing from Other Avery, I must have been so panicked that I didn't notice that this water was definitely not clear. The surface of this pond was still and black, looking more like an oil spill than water. The edges of the pond were ringed with the very tips of the long grasses floating on the surface, trapped in a greenish scum like things drowned. The scent of something unseen and rotting hung in the air. This version of the pond was stagnant and still. No sunlight glinting on the water, no fresh breeze rippled the surface.

The path and dock stood empty. Nothing challenged me; nothing blocked my way. I slowed, stopped, and looked around anxiously, my skin crawling.

This was too easy.

"Go!" Lily appeared at the end of the path, her skirt billowing around her, her eyes steely.

But I was fixated on the tree line trembling; something in the forest, something big, was lurching ponderously toward us, setting even the biggest trees swaying. Like a ripple in water, the swaying in the trees advanced, the ripple of green getting closer to us.

"Avery! Go!" The panic in Key's voice snapped me out of it.

I spun on my heel, dug in, and took off, spraying gravel as I went, my eyes focused on just one thing: the pond that had haunted me for too long. I flew over the steps and up onto the dock, the sound of cracking, splintering wood close behind me, but I didn't stop to look. The black water had distracted me long enough; it was time to see things clearly and finish this.

Two steps brought me to the end of the dock, the dark, stagnant water waiting below. Every fiber in my body screamed at me not to jump, but if it was Key's only way out, I had no choice. Besides, somewhere on the other side of this pond, Stella, Frank, Foster, Ru, and my parents were all clueless and vulnerable. I clenched my jaw.

And Other Avery—that bitch had my cat.

I ignored my clammy skin and my racing heart. The black water was lonely? Too bad. Sharing a life was one thing; stealing was another. A tremor sent a jolt through the dock; the footsteps of something huge and lumbering exiting the forest. I heard Key's voice raised in panic but didn't register the words. The water in front of me reflected nothing of the gray sky above. Lily would be the last person trapped in the black water's mirror world; I would make sure of it. One drawn-out, thundering roar, and fetid air rushed over me from behind. I pressed my hand to the turtle over my heart, filled my lungs, and jumped.

TWENTY-SEVEN

THIS TIME I DIDN'T THINK; I JUST SWAM, EYES closed and legs kicking hard, trusting that I would come out on the right side. I surfaced with a gasp and struck out for the shore, noting that the water was clear and fresh. So far, so good. When my feet touched bottom, I stood and sloshed through the shallows to the bank, drawing the plastic fish from my pocket. It was robin's-egg blue, and the silly plastic smile on its face made me smile back in relief. I was back on my side of the black water, the real side. I was here, where I belonged. Tears of relief rose, but I pressed both hands over my eyes. Other Avery was here, too.

Relief could wait. I had asses to kick.

I shot down the gravel path and past the gatehouse. This time, my strides were measured and firm with no hint of panic; my legs felt strong enough to run forever. The summer guy did a double take as I passed.

"Hey, there's no swimming," he called out mildly, but I ignored him and slowed down only enough to allow my soaking shoes to navigate the turn onto the sidewalk without wiping out.

I didn't care who saw me or what they thought. The distance I had to run to get home went by in a flash, but I still had time to think about what I was going to do when I got there: rescue Buttons and deal with Other Avery.

One in, one out.

The only thing that slowed me was the maroon sedan, still in its driveway but silent and still. I gave it a wide berth, but also a firm finger as I passed. The version on this side wasn't going to hurt me, and even if it wanted to try, I felt like I was fired up enough to take it.

Yeah, I felt like I could beat up a car.

A screech of tires to my left startled me out of that mental brawl. "Avery!"

I'd know that bellow anywhere. A silver convertible screeched to a stop beside me in the middle of the road.

"I was on my way to the pond." Ru leaned her whole upper body out the window, her voice a notch higher than I was used to hearing it. "What is going on?"

"You got my message." I knew it.

Ru's jaw dropped. "It's real," she whispered.

I stepped off the curb and up to her car. "Can you do me a favor?"

Ru looked up at me, dripping and deadly serious, and blinked.

"Can you go to the bookstore, make sure Frank and Foster are okay?"

"Avery." I'd never heard Ru's voice so quiet and unsure, but today was a different kind of day. "What is going on?" she asked again.

Even the little I knew would take hours to explain. I leaned on her car and she drew away from me, just a bit.

"You know how you said you'd never experienced anything weird yourself?"

"Yeah," Ru said cautiously, still looking at me like I'd appeared from another dimension. Which—fair.

"Well, congratulations."

"Oh my God!" Back in full form, Ru slammed both hands on

the steering wheel in triumph, shaking her head and sending long dark hair flying. "I can't believe it. I knew it—"

"Please hurry, Ihstá." Other Avery had access to an oblivious Frank and Foster. I didn't know what she'd do if she sensed that things were not going her way.

"Get in!" Ru jerked her thumb at the passenger seat. It was tempting. I wanted to see Frank and Foster safe for myself, but that had to wait.

"I can't." I stepped back onto the sidewalk. "There's something at the house I need to get."

"Will you be okay?" Ru asked, in protective-auntie mode once again.

Excellent question. I shooed her away and she pulled a U-turn, then peeled away with an arm raised out the window. At least I knew she was taking it seriously. She'd keep Frank and Foster safe while I did what I had to do. I trotted down the sidewalk, every ounce of focus riveted on my house.

Lily had said she and Other Lily kept their connection open to keep tabs on each other, but when I thought of Other Avery, I felt nothing but loathing. Our connection had definitely been severed, which meant although we were now both on this side of the black water, I didn't know for sure where she was.

But that also meant she had no clue where I was, either. I cut across the neighbor's lawn, slowed to a cautious creep, and made my way to the front door, staying low and away from the windows.

The driveway was empty, as it should be with Mom at work. I snuck up the front steps, pressed my ear to the door, and heard my own voice, unintelligible but unmistakable. She was in my house.

I eased the door open and stealthily stepped inside, crouched low in the foyer.

"Okay," Other Avery said in the living room.

It made me sick to hear her, to think about this imposter who thought she could just take over my life and leave me with nothing. My fingers tingled with adrenaline. There was no one to stop this but me. Key and Lily were depending on *me*. I slowly straightened up and stood, stepped out into the hall, and glared at the black water's imitation of me, lounging on the sofa wearing my best running shorts and a purple T-shirt from the only fun run I'd done with my mom. Around her neck gleamed something silver—who knew where she'd gotten it, who she'd stolen it from. It was a silver pendant of the right size and approximate shape, but it wasn't a turtle. It wasn't the real thing.

Neither was she.

"Yeah." She locked eyes with me across the room and slowly rose from the sofa, still holding the phone to her ear. Her face seemed to shimmer, to shift out of focus slightly before settling. Neither of us moved. "Yeah, of course I'll pay for it. I just wasn't paying attention and threw the shampoo bottle. I'm sorry." She was talking to Mom. My mom. My skin went hot all over, and I clenched my fists so hard my nails bit into my skin. Other Avery's voice was light and unbothered, but her eyes were flat and dead, her face a mask of hate. If I'd doubted it before, I was certain now: Other Avery wasn't going to be like Other Lily. Other Avery wasn't going to want to share.

"See you later," she singsonged and put the phone—a new phone, most likely bought with *my* money—down on the table. Although she kept her face blank, I could tell that Other Avery was shocked to see me but still defiant, unwilling to give up her new life as a daughter.

"You don't belong here." My voice was quiet but shook with anger. I took one deliberate step into the living room. Even if she were amenable like Other Lily, that agreement had taken decades to forge, and in the end, Other Lily had broken it.

"They don't know that." Other Avery sneered, and her voice didn't sound like mine anymore—it was tinny and tight, like it was traveling a long distance on a bad network. "I'll be a better daughter than you ever were. You should have been nicer to your dad." She pointed an accusing finger. "Me." Pointing to herself. "He's going to love me."

"You're delusional." My face screwed up in disgust. My dad had almost broken through the black water's spell and remembered Jackie. He wouldn't fall for this fake. Sooner or later, he'd know something was wrong. Ru already knew. And Frank? Foster?

"Frank and Foster, we know them." Other Avery smiled slyly, reading my mind. Maybe our tether wasn't as severed as I'd thought. "We've known them for so long. But they'll never see us coming. Not this time. The last thing they'll see? Will be your face."

A chill ran up my back because she was right. Frank and Foster didn't know about the Others, and who would they look to for an explanation? Me. The black water would be able to get rid of anyone too strong, anyone who even thought of fighting back. It would dump them in the pond or suck them through a mirror. There would be nothing to stand in its way of taking over completely, replacing all of us and swallowing this town whole. The black water would get its wish and become us.

"Ru, Pearl, Mom." Other Avery stepped around the end of the sofa by the wall in slow motion and I mirrored her, putting her the sofa between us. "All potential trouble. But not for long." Her lips curled in contempt.

Like in the fun house, I stared at her but couldn't hold her eyes. Then I realized why. She wasn't looking at me. She was looking covetously at the turtle hanging from my neck, the only missing piece in her Avery costume, the one part of me I swore she'd never get.

Buttons slunk out of Mom's room and into the hallway. He stopped and stared, raised his hackles and hissed, then scooted over to me, winding around my ankles before hissing at Other Avery from behind my legs.

"See?" I shrugged. "You're not me."

"People aren't as perceptive," Other Avery snapped. "I promise you, they'll never know."

But was there a glimmer of doubt in her eyes now?

I shifted my weight imperceptibly toward my back foot.

"You think I'm going to make a deal with you?" Other Avery scoffed. She obviously knew about the Lilies and their arrangement.

"Nope." I looked back at her steadily. Her eyes darted to the left and I knew. However much she looked like me, however strong her desire to take my place, Other Avery was a coward. When it came down to it, I was willing to stand and fight for what I believed in. Other Avery was fighting just for herself, while I had the weight of everyone I loved and generations at my back. The knowledge made me calm. My heartrate settled and a sense of peace flowed through my body. Other Avery saw this and knew. She saw it and flinched.

And then she bolted.

"I knew it!" I lost a second trying not to trip over Buttons before I burst through the back door after the pathetic coward wearing my face. I got onto the porch just in time to see her squeeze through the gap in the fence into the neighbors' yard.

Other Avery obviously hadn't been training. I was faster, but she was reckless. She darted out into traffic, zigzagging across one street after another, tearing through yards and weaving through parking lots.

Close to downtown, I pursued her past a car parked haphazardly at the curb, the right front tire on the sidewalk and the driver's side door hanging open. But what I noticed the most was that all the windows were shattered. The sight triggered a faint note of alarm, but I couldn't think about it just now.

Ahead, Other Avery ducked underneath a tarp serving as a wall at the back end of FallsFest, shimmying between two trailers and a bank of diesel generators chugging. Through the midway, under the Ferris wheel, people spun in shock to watch us fly by until we reached the fun house, where I stopped in my tracks. The dark gray double doors that formed the clown's mouth were pulsing, pushing out and falling back like the clown was breathing. I squinted, unsure of what I was seeing, vaguely aware that whatever it was, it wasn't good. The doors bulged to the breaking point and I took an involuntary step back, just before Sian and a few others rushed screaming from the entrance, forcing the doors the wrong way and snapping one off the top hinges in their desperation to get out. They scattered, jumping off the plywood ramp and racing off in all directions.

Other Avery shoved her way through a family of four holding

hands, and I took off after her. Across the street, I could see the metal gate over Mehmet's grill drawn and locked when the place should be jumping. What the hell was going on? I was close enough to reach out and graze the back of her—my—T-shirt when Other Avery reached the crowded vendors' area by the fountain and got into the crowd and away from me.

There seemed to be a commotion around the fountain, with the sloucher presiding. A crowd had gathered around a muscular Asian man who had one foot braced on the ledge and a white woman with a bad sunburn pulling with both hands around his waist as they struggled to haul something out of the fountain's basin.

"It's not real!" the man cried, his voice cracking with panic.

Some of the crowd must have come from the Pink Unicorn, because it was like a ghost town, paper napkins drifting off tables and onto the ground in an eerie echo of what I'd seen on the other side.

"Stand back, folks," the sloucher drawled, stepping closer and parting people to get a better look, most likely expecting to find a dog or toddler reluctant to get out of the water. He pulled his notebook from his shirt pocket as he went, clearly relishing the ticket he was about to write. "Holy crap!" He jumped back, dropping the notebook. His hand went to his hip.

I caught a flash of purple zipping across the street and I followed, leaving the panicked shouts and voices murmuring like a hive of bees behind me. Other Avery seemed to have gotten her second wind. She ducked down the walkway that intersected the alley behind the bookstore.

Frank.

I had to catch her, had to stop her before she got to him.

From the fountain came more shouts and what sounded like the footsteps of a startled herd. I hoped Frank had stayed in the store and not joined the crowd. The plastic fish in my pocket had confirmed that this was my side, my world, but from what I'd seen so far, it might not be that way for long. I didn't know what was going on but had the feeling the black water wasn't just going to give up. I had to get Key back here before it arrived in full force.

I leaned into the turn to gather speed and broke into the alley just in time to skid to a halt right behind Other Avery, who was face to face with Stella. She stood in front of Ru, Frank, and Foster, feet planted and gripping the golf club in her hands like a baseball bat. Four jaws dropped in unison.

"Holy. Shit." Ru clapped both hands to the side of her head like she was going to remove it.

I took a step away from Other Avery and slowly raised my hands. I was pretty sure I'd watched this scene in more than a few of Key's superhero movies.

"Stella," I said cautiously. "It's me. She's not me."

"No, Stella!" Other Avery raised her hands in supplication. "It's me! Help!"

Stella's eyes darted between us.

"Stella." Other Avery took a step forward, and Stella and her little group took a step back. "I trust you. You know it's me."

The five iron dipped, Stella's confidence wavering.

"Help me get rid of her, and we can end all of this," Other Avery said. She sounded like me. Her voice was gentle and calm.

Frank and Foster huddled together. A full head shorter than both of them, Ru stepped protectively in front. Stella bit her lip and flexed her fingers on the comfort grip of the club. "Stella. Stell," Other Avery said soothingly.

It dawned on me that none of them was sure which one of us was the real me, and I felt more insulted than I might have imagined. But even *I* hadn't been sure at first, so I'd help them out.

I stepped up beside Other Avery and caught Stella's eye. I didn't have time to mess around. "What happened when I got lost?"

Other Avery turned to me, mouth downturned like she smelled something bad. "What?"

"When I got lost," I said, enunciating every word but locking eyes with Stella. "What happened?"

Other Avery turned away, with just enough time to open her mouth and take a breath.

Stella swung like she was on the green, and Other Avery hit the ground like a bag of rocks. Frank hissed and Foster covered his eyes with both hands.

"Shit!" Stella staggered back. "Did I kill her?"

"Stell!" I rushed forward and grabbed her arms, peering into her face.

Stella was shaking her head slowly, staring down at Other Avery, who lay still, facedown in the dirt of the alley. "Flashlights," Stella muttered.

"Stella."

"Yeah." Stella's eyes looked a little glassy, but taking down your best friend's evil twin must suck.

"Are you okay?"

"Sure." She bobbed her head.

"But you weren't more—uh, surprised? To see two of me?"

Stella paused and then shrugged.

"Stella. Have you seen . . . things?"

"Seen?" Stella straightened up and seemed to regain her focus. "Like Window Stella? Yeah. That's why I'm here."

"Window Stella." This was news to me.

"Yeah." Stella nodded, swallowing hard. "She told me to forget about you and Key, to just let you go, and that it was for the best. But I said I couldn't do that because you're my best friends." The words tumbled out in a rush. She swiped the back of her hand across her mouth. "She said in that case, I should get going because shit's going down. So here I am."

Huh. Lily had said the Others wouldn't all be the same. Leave it to Stella to have an evil twin who was helpful.

"You saw a window Stella and didn't say anything."

Stella flapped her arms, sending the golf club swinging dangerously wide, making Ru, Foster, and Frank shrink back. "At first, I thought it was just my imagination. And . . . I didn't want to worry you."

"At first?"

"Well, yeah. When she started talking, that's just not normal. But—" She shrugged. "This is Crook's Falls, so."

I pulled Stella in for the biggest, tightest hug I could give without crushing her. "Love you, Stell."

"Yeah, yeah." Stella blew her hair out of her face. "So what do we do with her?" She pointed at Other Avery with the club.

"Is everyone else okay?" I could see that they weren't hurt, but Foster, Frank, and my auntie had been standing speechless and were still staring down at Other Avery. "Guys?"

"Holy. Shit!" Ru broke the silence. "She's, uh, okay?"

I shrugged. Other Avery's health and welfare were not a super-high priority for me.

"She's . . . not you," Ru clarified.

I shook my head. "Nope."

"Your mother called earlier." Frank's eyes scanned my face like he still wasn't sure. "She and your aunt here were worried. They think you're not yourself."

"Ha!" Stella barked a laugh, leaning over, hands planted on her thighs like she was out of breath.

"Well, I guess they're not wrong." Foster clucked his tongue.

Ru bent over to get a better look at Other Avery. "I knew it!" she crowed, pointing triumphantly. "The necklace! I knew something was wrong, and then I saw Bee and went to your place and there was glass everywhere—"

"Bee?"

"Yeah." Ru's eyes were huge. "Like Window Stella. I saw Bee!"

Why were all the Others so helpful and mine was evil? Did that say something about me?

"Avery what is going on?" Frank asked, wide-eyed.

"I was going to ask you the same thing," I said with a sigh. If I'd hoped that Frank and Foster would have answers, that clearly wasn't going to be the case. Based on the commotion I'd seen on the run in, and the fact that they'd all been out here with Stella armed, of all people, whatever was happening was getting worse. "All I know is Key is not Key. That is not me, and the black water is definitely not asleep."

Now was not the time to talk about Lily.

The sound of glass shattering—a lot of it—came from the street.

"What do we need to do?" Frank spread his hands open, turning from me to Foster, who gave a massive shrug.

"This has never happened," Foster said to himself, shaking his head.

"The real Key is going to follow me through the pond, which means this"—I kicked Other Avery's leg—"needs to go back through."

"He's stuck in there?" Foster's eyes went wide. "All this time?"

"We're going to dump her in the pond?" Stella shifted her grip on the club nervously.

Everyone seemed to be latching on to a different aspect of this, which was supremely unhelpful. I needed to get everyone on track, because I needed their help.

"She's not me!" I couldn't see what the problem was, and Other Avery belonged on the other side, not here.

"But she's somebody," Frank said gently, "and she's alive."

I spun on him and Frank took a step back, almost like he was afraid of me. Actually, as I looked around, they were all watching me with the same caution. I took a deep breath and tried to explain the impossible as reasonably as I could.

"One: She's not actually alive. She's a piece of the black water."

Foster gasped and stepped away from Other Avery.

"Two: Whatever she is, she doesn't belong here. We're just sending her home before more can join her here."

"How do you know all this?" Frank pressed. "Who told you?"

I took another long breath to give me the time to say what I'd been dreading. "Lily."

Whatever they thought I meant, they both went quiet, recalculating.

A siren pierced the air.

"That's not good," Foster muttered. Right then, it was the only thing we all knew for sure.

"We don't have a lot of time." I tried to stay calm. They didn't know what was happening on the other side.

"So what now?" Ever-practical, Ru stood beside Frank with her hands on her hips, looking at each of us in turn. I wished I'd had Ru with me from the beginning.

"We have to get her out of here." I pointed at Other Avery.

"We can take my car!" Ru raised her hand, inappropriately enthusiastic.

"Frank's is right here," Foster pointed out. "It sounds like mayhem out there." He pointed with his chin toward the main street.

"Well . . ." Frank wrung his hands and grimaced. "Let's load her up then. Where are we headed?"

I grabbed Other Avery's limp wrists and nodded to Stella to get her feet.

One in, one out.

"Take a wild guess," I said darkly.

TWENTY-EIGHT

GETTING A BODY INTO A CAR IS ACTUALLY NOT that easy.

Thanks to the black water, this was something I now knew.

With both back doors of Frank's car open, Stella and I pushed and pulled until we managed the feat. Ru hovered nearby holding the five iron, while Foster monitored the increasing sounds of mayhem in the street from the safety of the front passenger seat.

"Should we tie her up?" Stella mused, looking down at Other Avery.

"I am not comfortable with that," Frank said loudly from the driver's seat.

"She's not going anywhere, Stell." I assured her. Other Avery looked like a life-size me doll, still and quiet, and I felt not a bit bad for her. "Get in."

"Auntie?" I gestured at the car. It was going to be snug in there.

Ru waved me off, already backing away. "I'll meet you there," she said.

"Please just get in!" I didn't have time for this.

"I'll meet you there," Ru repeated, a strange smile on her lips. "I've got a stop to make." She turned and trotted toward her car at the other end of the alley.

THE OTHERS

I hoped my auntie would be okay with the chaos we could hear downtown, but she was probably worried about Pearl. Everyone has their own choices to make.

"Ave?" Stella called. "Ready?"

I watched as Ru gave a beep and burned rubber out of the alley. If anything happened to her, I didn't know what I'd do.

With Other Avery propped up in the back seat between Stella and me, Frank backed out of his space and started a responsible three-point turn in the alley. About to shift into drive, he stopped, hand on the gearshift.

I leaned forward to look through the windshield. At the end of the alley, where it opened onto Pine Street, a white man in flipflops and neon green board shorts stood motionless, staring at us with absolutely no expression.

"Well." Once again, it seemed the black water knew exactly where I was and what I was doing. But how? It certainly wasn't getting any information from the unconscious me with her head lolling back.

Come.

"Did you hear that?" Stella scrunched her nose. "Did you hear that or is there a voice in my head?"

"Oh, boy," Foster whispered to himself and rolled up his window. "Turn the radio on. Loud. Don't listen."

Good advice. I knew what happened when you listened to the voice in your head in this town.

"Frank."

Frank sat, one hand on the gearshift, the other resting on the wheel, transfixed by the man standing there.

"Frank!" I shouted and was satisfied to see him jump a little. "Radio!"

"Right, right." Frank tapped the console and the car was flooded with the aria from *Madama Butterfly* at an extremely high volume.

Stella clapped her hands over her ears. "Something else and lower!"

"Foster, change it!" I was too far away. How Frank drove at this volume was unthinkable. The windows were vibrating.

"I don't know how!" Foster jabbed at the console.

"It's a playlist!" Frank yelled. "Just let me—let me do it!" He slapped Foster's hands away, not noticing that the man in the flip-flops was stomping toward us, looking increasingly angry with every step.

"Frank." I tapped him on the shoulder as he fiddled with the console. What harm could a man in flip flops do?

I didn't want to find out.

"Well, now we're in the default playlist," Frank said with disgust before looking up. "Oh!" He finally registered the man, who unfortunately was no longer our only problem.

The dented metal door of the florist banged open and the walking definition of *grandma* stepped out like a sumo wrestler entering the ring. A white lady with white hair set in careful curls, white slacks, and a flowy top, clutching a large silver purse in her hand, sighted Frank's car and glowered at us, her lip raising in a coral lipstick snarl.

"Doris?" Stella twisted around. "She's from my aquarobics class!"

"Frank, just go!" I pleaded.

"Doris is really strong," Stella warned, gripping the back of Frank's seat.

"What do you want me to do—run them over? I can't!" Frank's voice cracked.

Doris dropped her purse and charged the car like a bull. Frank threw the car into reverse and jammed his foot to the floor.

"Hold on," he said tersely, throwing one arm over Foster's seat rest to navigate through the rear window. Outraged Doris and the furious flip-flop man gave chase.

We flew backward through the alley until we shot out onto Pine Street and screeched to a halt, the front of a bus inches away from my window. Other Avery's arms flew up and hit me in the face.

"Holy shit," Foster breathed, both hands still braced against the dashboard.

With the flip-flop man and Doris closing in, Frank pulled onto Pine Street and headed toward the park.

"There." He nodded to himself. "Driving forward is much better."

But as we pulled away, I turned to watch our pursuers, wondering how many other people had come into contact with the water while I'd been gone and if they were all going to turn.

We traveled in silence for a few moments until Foster twisted around.

"Okay back there?"

Stella and I nodded, but it seemed like a lie to say the word *yes*.

"Is she okay?" Frank asked. "Stella, make sure she's breathing."

"She's fine," I muttered.

As Frank turned into the park driveway, I looked out the window and sighed. This forest, the trails, had always been my happy place, but it felt more like a battleground now. The lot was predictably packed on such a nice day, so Frank prowled the rows, looking for a spot as close to the pond path as possible. I hoped the people here were people and not Others, but it still wouldn't be good to have too many witnesses to Stella and me toting a body.

"Right there!" Foster pointed up ahead.

"I see it," Frank groused and eased the car into the second to last spot in the row.

Once the car was off, we sat in silence. I was going through the plan in my mind—send Other Avery back and help Key through—but I knew the rest of them were wavering. I could feel it.

"I mean..." Frank turned around in his seat. "She's not conscious. She'll drown."

I'd known this was coming but felt my blood pressure rising just the same.

"She's. Not. Real."

"Avery," Frank chided.

"Stella was the one who hit her with the golf club!"

"That was a reflex!" Stella protested. "She was threatening you. But now she's . . ." She gestured at the limp form between us.

"We're just sending her home," I insisted but got no reply. "What about Jackie? And Cara Messer? When we burned the bones, they went right along with them," I pointed out.

"But they were already gone," Stella shot back. "And we didn't even know that was going to happen to them. We know what's going to happen to her."

Why could they not understand? I had to get control of myself because there was no way I could do what I had to without help.

"She tried to take my place here and send me there. There's a Key somewhere that did the same thing. And a Lily." I didn't want to say it, after she'd let them live in ignorance all those years, but it was the only way to make them understand.

"What do you mean? *A Lily?*" Frank frowned, but Foster paled.

"We made a mistake," Foster whispered, his eyes vacant.

"What mistake?" Frank demanded.

"You know."

They stared at each other for a moment, then Frank looked away, shaking his head. "Well, that's not possible. We were very careful," he tried to convince himself. "That just can't be true."

"And if it is?" Foster countered. "If it's been true all this time, all these years?"

Frank's face crumpled, and he put his head in his hands.

Now I understood why Lily had let them think what they wanted. Tears welled up in Foster's eyes, and I felt like absolute garbage. Lower than the useless lump beside me. Whatever mistakes they thought they'd made, I'd just told them the truth was even worse.

A deep, dense silence enveloped the car and I didn't know how to navigate us through.

"Then, I guess," Frank said suddenly, swiping at his eyes and rallying, "I guess we have no choice."

"Frank—" I said softly.

"No." He blinked quickly and waved away whatever I'd been about to say. "Let's just finish this. The rest can wait."

Getting Other Avery out of the car was significantly easier than getting her in, mainly because I wasn't too concerned about what happened to this other me—this lying, devious husk who'd tried to claim my life. If we bumped her a bit, I wasn't going to shed any tears.

"I'll pull, you push," Stella directed, getting out of the car on her side.

I waited in my seat while she got hold of Other Avery's ankles.

Of all the things I'd planned to do this summer, getting a body out of Frank's car was not one of them, and one look at Frank's face as he stood by, arms folded firmly across his chest, told me that he was thinking something similar.

"Ready?"

"Yup." Was I ever. It felt like I'd wasted far too much time already while Key was still trapped, hopefully still waiting on the other side of the pond.

Now it wasn't that hard to maneuver Other Avery, so she was sitting, feet on the ground and head lolling against Stella's shoulder.

"Well." Stella patted Other Avery's head apologetically where a thin trail of blood ran onto her forehead. "At least with the head wound we won't have trouble telling you apart anymore."

Seeing an unconscious, bloody me slumped against Stella was more than a little creepy. For a moment, my vision doubled and tilted uncomfortably, but I blinked it away. Other Avery looked like me and was wearing my clothes, but she was not me.

"She's not me," I said firmly, not realizing how random that sounded until I saw them all staring at me.

"She's not." Foster patted my shoulder.

"We'd better go." I grabbed Other Avery's right wrist and hauled her halfway up onto her feet.

"Just give me a sec." Stella rubbed at her shoulder.

"Stell—"

"Relax. That guy was in flip-flops, and Doris has bad knees," Stella said, grabbing Other Avery's left wrist. "We've got time."

"But Key is waiting. And there will be others," I said, uneasy. Other Stella might be okay, but how many people in town had

scooped up just a handful of that water in the fountain to cool off?
"Ready? On 'three.'"

Stella didn't reply, and I felt irritation prickle. I didn't know how long I had to get Key, and things were getting worse here. We had a body to move before trouble found us.

"Stell." I turned to find her staring wide-eyed at the car next to us, where an older white man with thick black glasses snarled from the passenger seat window.

"What?" Frank glanced down at the window and then saw it. "Oh!" He quickly edged to the back of his car.

Trouble was here.

The four of us huddled together at the back of Frank's car, slowly turning and finally seeing the trap we'd walked into. The whole time we'd been standing around, going back and forth about what to do, we'd been surrounded by the mirrors and glass in a lot full of cars. The Others were already here. They were everywhere. The windows might have been empty when we pulled in, but they were rapidly being filled with glowering faces and hands pressing, banging against the glass, ready to break through the way Other Avery had in the bathroom.

"There's no one in the car, just in the window. So they can't get out, right?" Stella peeked out from behind me, her nervous fingers plucking at the back of my T-shirt. I tapped Other Avery's legs, still dangling outside the car. "She did." I wasn't happy to see Others so close, but it did provide my reluctant little team motivation to move.

"Get going," Foster said, nodding at me.

"But what about—"

"We'll take care of this." He flipped his cane to hold it like a bat, looked at Frank, and suddenly what had happened to all the glass in his house and why he'd fled to Frank's was a mystery no longer.

"Bring them back, Avery." Frank stood beside Foster. I knew he meant Key and Lily, but I didn't have the heart to tell him—one in, one out. I'd gone in; Key would come out. There was no *them*. I tried to focus on what I had to do.

"Ready, Stell?" We got Other Avery vertical, an arm draped around each of our shoulders, her head drooping down to her chest.

Stella nodded, silent and serious. One more second to adjust my grip on Other Avery's wrist, and we were off, half carrying, half dragging the first of two imposters I had to deal with. Despite what I'd said to the others, I didn't know exactly how I'd feel when it came time to actually put Other Avery in the water. I didn't believe she'd drown; I didn't think I was killing her. But even though I hated her and wanted her gone, it was hard for me to put something that even looked human in danger; it made me feel a little sick inside. But I also didn't see any way around it.

"Over there!" Frank shouted in the parking lot, but whatever they were dealing with, I couldn't stop now.

I glanced back once, to see Foster raising his cane and Frank brandishing the golf club, each of them striding purposefully toward a car. Stella and I hurried down the gravel path, the sound of shattering glass behind us. I didn't look back again.

TWENTY-NINE

THE GRAVEL PATH HAD TAKEN ME LESS THAN seven minutes the last time, but the last time I hadn't been toting a body and listening to Stella groan.

"We're almost there." The corridor of bushes lining the path still made me uncomfortable, but at least they weren't reflective.

"Okay," Stella panted. "I can do it."

We had to. It wouldn't stop the black water from fulfilling its grand fountain-expansion plan, but leaving Key there was a deal-breaker. Besides, Key was smart and he'd learned a lot on the other side. Together, we'd figure out a plan to stop the black water, get rid of the Others, and help Real Lily.

Once I found Key.

Which turned out to be sooner than I expected.

At the end of the gravel path, the bushes thinned out. The knowledge that we were almost there—so close—made me jog faster.

Then I saw the dock, and the figure waiting on it.

Key. But not mine.

I stumbled over Other Avery's feet, almost taking all three of us down.

"Oh!" Stella recovered and saw Key. "Is that . . . ?"

We slowed to a walk, skirting the edge of the pond, giving me one precious minute to think, because this wasn't a scenario I'd planned for. Other Key was so obviously Other; he even stood differently than the original, a hint of arrogance in his posture. Now that I'd met Other Avery, the imposters were so easy to sniff out. Their only strength had been that we weren't expecting them. Now that I was, I could see that they were obviously wrong, twisted versions of the original.

They had to go.

"Ave!" Other Key smiled and waved his arms, but he stayed on the dock. You'd think that seeing his girlfriend carrying an unconscious copy of herself would warrant a few questions.

I glanced over my shoulder as we neared the steps. The forest was quiet, a breeze I couldn't feel moving through the leaves creating a rolling *shuuushhh*. There was nothing behind us on the path.

"What's going on?" Other Key frowned, but the concern was too late, too delayed. As always, this Key was a step behind.

"Stay here," I instructed Stella and took Other Avery's full weight as I carefully climbed the steps.

At the end of the dock, Other Key smiled and exhaled in a show of relief.

"Ave." He pressed a hand to his heart. "I've been looking all over for you! Are you okay?"

I kept my eyes on him but said nothing, awkwardly climbing the metal steps with Other Avery hanging off me like an unwanted growth.

"There's something weird going on," Other Key said, wide-eyed. "I needed to find you."

"So you came here," I said dully. "To the pond." How stupid did Other Key think I was?

"I've looked everywhere!" He raised his hands and let them fall to his sides. "We need to get inside somewhere safe—people are going crazy out there."

I nodded, staring at him. People were.

"Let's go home—you, me, and Stell. We'll figure out what to do."

He was smooth-talking, sounding a lot less like Key now and more like an evil used-car salesman, telling you things you know aren't true but desperately want to believe.

"What about her?" I nudged Other Avery.

Other Key shook his head helplessly, then shrugged. "We can take her with us."

"Don't listen to him, Avery." Stella stood at the steps, blocking the way back.

"Look, I'll help you." Other Key took a step toward me, reaching out and offering to share my burden.

"You'll help me?" The black water had a very twisted sense of humor. "Then jump."

There was a beat of silence as we stared at each other.

"Are you kidding? Ave, we have to get out of here." He took another step closer.

"Jump." He was not Key. I was talking to the black water, and the knowledge made my voice cold.

"What?"

"Jump into the water."

"Look. Dump her in." Other Key's eyes went hard; he was apparently changing tack.

My pulse pounded in my throat. Behind me, I heard Stella gasp.

"As soon as she goes under, she'll get sucked back to the other side." He gestured to Other Avery dangling off my shoulder and took a slow step closer, trying to crowd me. His smile made my skin crawl. "That's fine. I like *you* better."

There it was. Admission of who he really was, of what was really going on. He was done playing, but so was I.

"I am sending her through. But you're going, too." I tightened my grip on Other Avery's wrist and held my ground. One in, one out. But what if I sent two?

"Don't," Other Key said in a voice I'd never heard before—flat and threatening, at odds with the words he spoke. "Avery, we can be happy." He took a step toward us, hands open and wide in front of him. "I'll be just like him."

"His family—"

"Will never know, either," Other Key said firmly. "We can replace people and no one notices. No one will go looking."

He meant it to be soothing, but the idea enraged me, and my Key would have known that. The idea that the black water could steal the essence of a person, the best parts of them, and leave behind what remained, made my face burn. The black water had taken Lily and left me with a shell of who she'd been, a poor bargain no matter how much the replacement loved me. That would never be a deal I'd accept if I could stop it, not for anyone.

"Come on," Other Key cooed. "Drop her in and we'll just pretend this never happened, any of it. I'll be just like him."

"But I'll know you're not. I'll know it's an act." Despite my resolve, a wisp of panic started swirling in my chest.

"How can you ever know it's not anyway?" Other Key chided. "You think he never lies to you?"

I blinked.

I adjusted my grip on Other Avery. "He might. He might lie to me sometimes." And he did; I knew it was true. Sometimes I drove him nuts with my weirdness and he pretended it didn't bother him. "But I'll take 'might sometimes' over 'always definitely' any day. I want my Key." I took two steps forward, and something in my face made Other Key finally take one back. "You're not him," I said firmly, two more steps, building speed, momentum, and commitment to my new plan. "And she's not me. And neither of you belong here."

Other Key's eyes went wide. He twisted to get out of the way, but my Key had never been an athlete, and apparently this version wasn't, either. He was too slow and outweighed. Other Avery and I hit him like a truck, taking the three of us off the end of the pier, falling together for an impossibly long time before the surface of the water broke, closed over us and the black water swallowed me down once again.

Down.

Down.

I kicked as hard as I could, wanting to make sure that the other two went in the right direction. I dove so deep my ears popped. Other Avery was still and limp, her arms drifting up over her head and tangling with her hair, sinking fast. Other Key seemed to be getting sucked down much faster than me but reached up and tried to grab my ankle until I kicked free of him, some current I couldn't feel dragging him down. Maybe those two really were being transported back to where they belonged. The truth was, I didn't want to end Other Avery. I just didn't have that in me. But knowing that she would wake up on the dim, lifeless side felt right. She belonged there.

I gave one hard kick back the way I'd come but I was deep already;

it was a long way up and the water had become thick and resistant. It didn't want to let me go, but the black water had forgotten how stubborn I was. I'd come out on the right side or not at all. Ignoring the panic and the burning in my lungs, I stopped struggling and treaded water for a moment, trying to calm myself. In my head, I recited the words I'd heard Foster and others speak, making the words my own.

I'm thankful for Mother Earth.

I'm thankful for the waters.

Suddenly, as if answering to its name, the density of the water changed. I followed the fresher, lighter current with long, strong strokes.

I'm thankful for the plants and animals.

I saw sunlight above and kicked with every bit of strength I had left.

I'm thankful for the sun, moon, and stars.

I broke the surface, gasping for air.

Now our minds are one.

I was alone in the water and the sky was clear and blue.

"Ave!" Stella knelt on the end of the dock, reaching out and waving me over.

I did it. I'd made it back.

I swam for the dock, because that's where my Key had said he'd meet me.

I gripped Stella's hand and climbed onto the dock, flopping on my back for a moment to catch my breath. What should I do now? Where was Key?

"Avery!"

My head instinctively snapped up and I turned on my side, because—no way.

But yes. My mom was leaving the gravel path and rushing toward the pond. For an instant, I thought she'd take the shortcut and just walk straight into the water, but Ru put a hand on her arm, slowing her and making soothing sounds. Mom looked at Ru and back to me, wide-eyed and confused but *seeing* for the first time.

"Mom!" My heart swelled. Whatever happened next, my mom was safe and she was here.

"Is it her?" Frank called from where he had taken Mom's other arm, patting her shoulder on one side. Foster was beside him. Ru still held Mom's right arm with one hand and a tire iron dangled from her left. Clearly, none of them was letting my mom go until they were sure that I was me.

Stella squinted down at me. "She doesn't have a lump on her head, so I think we're good!" She turned to give Frank a thumbs-up.

Key.

I turned on my knees, staring intently at the pond.

Tiny waves danced in the breeze.

Had I failed?

I suddenly felt cold and small, like I was shrinking in on myself. That's what I'd be without him—less. I kept my eyes on the center of the pond, watching and waiting for a bubble, a ripple—anything. Other Key had gone back where he belonged, but my heart clenched at the thought that I may have engineered a universe with no Key at all.

Then one bubble floated up and delicately popped on the surface. I held my breath. Another bubble, then three more.

"Is it him?" Stella whispered.

Something was coming, the only question was: Who would it be?

More bubbles rose to the surface, grew and languidly popped.

I remembered the lumbering thing we'd hidden from and rose to a crouch, just in case. Although if that's what was coming through, we were all pretty screwed.

The center of the pond boiled with bubbles and Key broke the surface with a burst of spray. He treaded water for a moment, turned, saw me, and dog-paddled to the dock. Behind me, Stella's hurried footsteps clattered as she darted off the dock and then returned with Frank's golf club, backed up by Ru with her tire iron and my mom, who I now noticed was toting a baseball bat. A prudent move, but I thought it was going to be okay. It had to be. I didn't know what I'd do if it wasn't.

"It's okay, Stell," I called over my shoulder, though it may have been desperation talking.

Key started swimming like a drowning man, his eyes locked on mine as he thrashed toward the dock. I knew the panic he was feeling, the animal desire to get out of the pond. I wasn't completely sure it was him, but I now knew that playing it safe wasn't always the best course of action. Other Key had never looked at me like this, like I was an island in the middle of the ocean, like I was safety. I knelt down on the end of the dock, and as he neared, I swallowed any lingering doubt and extended my hand to him.

Key grabbed onto my hand with such force he almost pulled me in with him.

"Ave!" Stella squeaked behind me and grabbed a fistful of my T-shirt. Ru grabbed Stella's arm, and Mom looped her arm around her sister's waist.

I leaned back and set one foot into the dock, everyone behind allowing me to hold steady as an anchor while Key hauled himself up and flopped onto the dock like a landed fish, panting.

Stella stepped up beside me, brandishing the club.

"Stell." I waved her off. It didn't matter who this was at my feet. I would take care of him, one way or the other.

"Ave," Key croaked, getting to his knees.

I couldn't stop myself. I took his hands to help him rise and he stepped in close, wrapping his arms around me.

"Key." I couldn't explain how I knew. It was him. I held him close, and something inside me settled down, content.

Key dropped his head on my shoulder and cried, deep, rasping sobs like an exhausted child, gasping for breath with his whole body.

I rubbed soothing circles onto his back but kept my eyes on the water over his shoulder. There were no more bubbles. The water was rippling freely, stirred only by the breeze now. Deep down, I'd been hoping that Lily would emerge, but the longer I watched, the more I understood that wasn't going to happen. Two in, one out. And one staying behind, by her choice. I held Key close and felt his breathing even out. It was too much to expect a fairy-tale ending, I knew that.

But it would have been nice.

Key hung on to me, and I finally looked away from the pond. Frank and Foster stood by the end of the dock, each with a hand on the other's shoulder, looking both relieved and somber. Ru rubbed Mom's arm like the big sister she was. Stella stood close to the steps, her face as open as always, but still holding the club in her hands.

"Is it him?" She waggled the club.

"Oh my God, Stell." Key lurched from me to Stella and hugged her hard, like he hadn't seen her in years, which might have been exactly how he felt.

I picked at my T-shirt, holding it away from my skin. My clothes were clammy and cold. Would I ever not be dripping and drenched?

Key left a teary Stella to go on shaky legs to shore, where he was embraced by Foster and Frank, my mom and Ru, all at once, a little knot of love with Key at its center, as he should be.

"There, there." Frank placed a kiss on Key's forehead and petted his hair, his other hand patting Foster's shoulder. They were holding Key like he was precious, but I knew who they were thinking of just then.

"I have no idea what is going on," Mom said to no one in particular. She sat down heavily, brain overloaded.

Stella patted her shoulder sympathetically. "It's a lot."

There was so much to explain to my mother, and for once, I was happy to do it. I was thrilled she'd be able to listen.

Alone on the dock, my shoulders sagged. Tension left me and exhaustion flooded in.

"I need to call Pearl!" Ru flapped her hands and pulled out her phone.

I'd gotten Key back—for real this time. Everyone here was fine. I'd done as my ihstá had told me.

One more thing.

I lay down on my belly, peering over the end of the dock and under, where a nest of pipes and meter brooded. And one valve.

"Lefty loosey, righty tighty." It wasn't rocket science.

I reached under the dock with both arms and turned, tighter and tighter, squeezing the life out of the black water.

"Ave?" Stella and her mass of curls dropped down next to me. "Oh!"

The valve was as closed as it was going to get. Now to make sure it stayed that way.

"Stell. Club." I held out my right hand like a surgeon.

"Not sure what you're doing, but I know sabotage when I see it. This is better." Ru appeared at my shoulder and offered the tire iron, phone still to her ear.

"Nice." I shoved the end through the valve for leverage, pushed forward with my left hand, and pulled back with my right. As I strained, I looked down into the water. If there was anyone watching from the other side, I wanted them to see. I wanted the black water to know it was me thwarting it yet again. It would always be me.

Just when I thought I might not be strong enough—*pop!*—the valve flew off, landing in the center of the pond with a *plop* and disappearing from sight. It wasn't a permanent fix, but it should stop the fountain for now. I sat up, flexing my burning fingers. Mom still sat on the shore, staring at the water where Key had come up, her mouth slightly open and her face blank with shock.

"I just..." She shook her head. I felt for her. It was a lot to take in, but I had received so much knowledge in so many stories—maybe now I had some of my own to share.

I knew the black water wasn't finished with us, but as Lily had said—we may not always win, but we don't lose, either. Even if this was just a lull in the action, I'd take it. I had what mattered most to me.

"Pearl is safe!" Ru cried, pocketing her phone and hauling my mom to her feet with a broad smile. "It's all good!"

It wasn't.

I stepped off the dock and slipped my hand into Key's. There were still Others out there, and I didn't know how to get rid of them. But maybe not everything was my personal problem. Maybe I didn't have to carry the weight of the world. Maybe for now, this one win was enough.

"We should celebrate with ice cream." Stella wrapped her arm around my waist.

Even the biggest badasses needed a rest now and then.

THIRTY

THE FALLSFEST RIOT, AS IT BECAME KNOWN, was the talk of the town for some time. But for a town whose last major excitement had been when a snowplow got stuck blocking both lanes of RR 5, the chatter died down a little too quickly. Property damage and mass hallucinations, you'd think that would stick in the memory; that meetings would be held, news articles would be written. But this was Crook's Falls—weird wasn't weird for very long. That didn't surprise me; it just meant that the black water was down but not out.

There were signs of hope, though. Not everyone forgot.

They were few, but I noticed them, trying to bring it up in overheard conversations at the Pink Unicorn or walking down the sidewalk. The listener's face would go blank and the person who remembered would frown and change the subject, feeling silly and second-guessing themselves. Had those things really happened: the broken store windows, people seeing doubles of themselves?

Every time I left the house—a feat accomplished only by accepting Mom's condition of practical surgical attachment to my phone—I scanned the faces of everyone I passed. They seemed real enough to me, but it had taken me too long to twig Other Key. For all I knew, there were still Others among us.

I didn't know what to do about that.

Three days after I'd pulled him from the pond—again—Key and I stood hand in hand in the elevator at the Willows, both of us avoiding the mirrored interior by studiously looking at the floor.

"Nice tile," Key said.

"Very even grout lines." I'd become a connoisseur of floors.

The second the doors started to open, we squeezed through, glad to be back in the land of wainscoting, wallpaper, and carpet. Neither of us had seen anything alarming recently, but we weren't complacent. It felt like the black water was regrouping, not defeated. Key squeezed my hand as we walked down the hall to Lily's apartment.

Key was Key. There was no doubt in my mind about that now. His parents were relieved that he was "feeling better," and he had jumped back into his life with a new appreciation. As far as they were aware, he'd just needed to recover and rest. If they only knew.

He still struggled sometimes, needed time to come to grips with what had happened to him, and I was going to give him all my support. There was still a lot he hadn't told me about his time on the other side and maybe he never would. But he had me, Foster, Frank, and Stella to talk to if he wished. We could all understand to some extent what he'd been through. Besides, Key was his own person; I wasn't entitled to any more than he wanted to give me. I just had to keep reminding myself of that fact.

But for all the things I had embraced, there was one I'd put off as long as I could. I was anxious about seeing Lily, who I couldn't stop thinking of as Other Lily, the one secret I still kept from Mom and Ru. I was afraid that when I saw Lily, I wouldn't be able to separate my feelings for her from my feelings about the black water because that's essentially what she was, a splinter that had worked its way into this world and into my life, embedded like a piece of wood in flesh. Now that I was aware of that, how would things be between us?

"Are you . . . ?" Key mimed knocking, and I realized that we'd been standing at her door for a few seconds too long. We both had moments like that now, and we were learning how to navigate them.

"I've got it." I did my special knock and steeled myself to come face-to-face with the part of the black water that looked like my ihstá.

But it was my other ihstá who opened the door.

"Avery!" Ru stepped aside, opening the door wide. "Look, Ihstá! Avery and Key are here."

Lily sat contentedly by the window, a cup of tea already steaming in front of her and the beginnings of a pale pink blanket on needles in her hands. After spending time with the real Lily, it was strange to see her so still and curled in on herself, so frail.

"Hi, Ihstá." I expected it to get weird, but as soon as I hugged her, I felt the tension in my shoulders leave me. Nothing had changed. This Lily loved me just like the original; I could feel that. I'd loved her before; I would again. I had two Lilies now.

"Oh, Avery." Lily held my hand and peered up at my face, and I thought I saw something in her eyes, searching. Did she know? I let my face relax and smiled, making sure that whatever she was looking for in my response, she found it. "Aren't the willows lovely today? Come and see!" She waved Key over and pulled us to stand next to her, facing the window and the massive trees outside that gave the place its name. "You'd think that trees look the same every day," she said dreamily. "But they don't. They change, just like us."

This Lily had a more complicated past than I'd known; she had hidden facets to her that were kind of dark and a little scary, but didn't we all? I had to remember: She loved me, and she'd done the best she could. It wasn't her fault that she was a husk of the original. She could have cut her tether to the real Lily and entirely taken over. But she'd kept the connection between them, stayed in Crook's Falls, and been my ihstá, even though the strain of doing so was fraying her mind. Whatever this part of the black water had become under Lily's influence, she'd made sacrifices, too, just like the rest of us. Maybe she recognized that doing so is part of our experience, part of being human. One in, one out; day and night; gain and loss. Right then, I felt like I finally understood the precarious but generous partnership the Lilies had formed.

Standing there, I couldn't help but think that she'd herded Key and me to the window in case someone else was looking. Maybe someone else in the apartment who could only see our reflections. My chest tightened and my throat threatened to close up. Key took my hand. We both looked into the window and smiled.

"Tea." Ru approached the table like a tightrope walker, eyes intent on the two cups of tea she balanced, the tip of her tongue out in concentration. She set them down with a sigh of relief, stressed at transporting Lily's beloved china cups across the room. I noticed mine already had milk and sugar in it, which made my chin go all wobbly. These people *knew* me. And after everything I'd been through, all the time I'd spent hiding, I discovered it was actually nice to be known.

"So what's up? Working?" Ru unwrapped a stick of gum and folded it into her mouth. After offering the pack around, she slipped it in the back pocket of her jeans and adjusted her cropped *All Children Matter* T-shirt.

"Oh, at the bookstore," Lily confirmed, sipping her tea.

"Yes, Ihstá. At the bookstore."

Ru caught my eye, impressed. Lily seemed especially with it today, and if Ru didn't know why, I had an idea.

"I'm working full-time, actually." Out of the corner of my eye, I saw Key had turned with his tea and was looking at himself in a mirror framed with carved ivy leaves on the wall. The sight made my stomach clench, but I tried to ignore it.

"I suppose FallsFest is in full swing?" Lily looked up with a smile and even I was caught short.

Key, Ru, and I exchanged an awkward glance.

"Um, yeah." I nodded. FallsFest had made a quick recovery from the "riot," everything repaired and cleaned up and glossed over at record speed, only possible in Crook's Falls. "I've been setting up tables every day, for the sidewalk sale. People really like them. I've sold a lot." Bragging, maybe. But it was true. In spite of everything, Frank's Books was killing it this summer, and I was more than a little proud of that.

Lily picked up her needles and I felt Key rejoin me.

"That's wonderful, dear." Lily started a new row. "Frank and that store." She clucked her tongue, chuckling to herself.

I knew I should just be happy with what was in front of me. I knew I should just leave things alone.

But I'm me. I always have to go a step further. I always have to know.

"The fountain in the square, it's gone dry again," I said as casually as I could.

Lily's needles faltered for a fraction of a second; only someone watching for it would have noticed. "Oh?" She cleared her throat, intent on her stitches.

And there it was. In that one syllable I knew that although I did love this Lily, and she was the only Lily I'd really ever known, I'd never be able to forget that this was not the original. There would always be something missing.

"We should get going." Ru grabbed her bag from the sofa. "Ihstá and I are going to play bingo in the games room. You want in? Starts in ten minutes."

I laughed as I rose to my feet. "No thanks." I bent to hug Lily. "See you later." I kissed her papery-soft cheek.

"Goodbye, dear." She was still focused on her blanket, so I got an air-kiss in return.

Crossing the living room, I glanced back. Lily was turned in her chair, looking out the window, one finger tapping her teacup gently. My gaze slid to the window where her reflection made eye contact and smiled. Which Ihstá was I seeing—the original, or what the black water had left behind?

Maybe Real Lily was right and the black water wasn't bad, exactly. Maybe it had a right to exist just like everything else. But it wasn't benign. It did need to be contained and watched. I thought of the twin brothers, Maple Sapling and Flint. Despite his connection to his brother, Flint had his nature. He may not have been evil, but he'd always be a destroyer.

So would the black water.

I turned to leave.

"Seriously?" Key followed behind me to the door. "No bingo?"

"Yeah, seriously?" Ru had followed as well.

I slipped on my shoes and poked Key in the chest. "Do you want to go up against a woman who owns her own dabber?"

Ru smiled wickedly and patted her bag. "I'm going to school these people."

Waiting for Key to tie his shoes, as he had never adopted my tie-once system, I remembered I had one last task.

"Ihstá." I pulled Ru closer to the door. "I wanted to talk to you."

A frown immediately crossed Ru's face. She'd been a little on edge ever since her introduction to the real Crook's Falls. "What is it?"

I glanced at Key, and he nodded. "The water in the fountain," I said. "It's not safe."

"What do you mean? Not safe how?" Ru's voice was low and soft for once, like she knew this wasn't something for Lily to hear.

"It comes from the Big Pond."

I couldn't explain everything. I hadn't told Ru the truth about Lily—I just didn't see the point. Not all secrets were bad. But the fountain had to be stopped for longer than my guerilla tire-iron assault could guarantee, and Lily had instructed me to go talk to Ru.

"But it's off now," she said. "You—" She mimed twisting the valve.

"They'll fix it. It will come back," I said slowly, willing her to understand what "it" was.

Ru's eyes held mine, and then she nodded, pursing her lips. "Got it," she whispered. "You leave it to me, niece." She pressed both hands into my shoulders and said, at her normal volume, "I'll deal with it."

I hoped she would.

Back in the elevator, Key and I obeyed the universal law of elevator etiquette and stood in silence. I was relieved to have visited Lily and found that it was okay, but I was tired of looking at the floor. I couldn't live the rest of my life afraid of what I might see in a mirror or window. Really, it was more dangerous *not* to look. If there was something lurking, the sooner I knew about it, the better. If the black water did plan on making a comeback, I could do something to stop it.

And I would. I always would.

So I rolled my shoulders back and raised my eyes to look in the mirrored door.

I saw me, real me—same hazel eyes, same long dark hair, same glint of silver dangling in the center of my chest. I raised my eyebrows, and my reflection did the same. Checked out. And Key was standing beside me, his shoulder touching mine. His hair was short now—he'd cut it the night he got home for real. I hadn't asked too much about that decision. If he wanted to share, he would. His glorious curls would grow long and wild again, but it wouldn't be exactly the same. Neither of us would.

But different didn't have to be bad. Different was just . . . different.

I slipped my hand into his, and he drew his eyes up. We saw nothing there but ourselves—Avery and Key—looking into each other's eyes. A smile bloomed across my face and clear across my heart.

THIRTY-ONE

BEFORE WORK THAT MORNING, I'D GONE FOR a quick run along the shady main loop, still quiet first thing in the morning. Parts of the parking lot were still cordoned off as crews cleaned up the vandalism spree that had damaged many cars on Sunday.

I still loved it—running like flying through the dappled green world of the forest, the air here smelling fresher and lighter than anywhere else. When I was done, I'd felt cleaned out inside, a pleasant kind of tired I could get only by running. Maybe this was my superpower. One of them.

After my cool-down, I'd stopped to check my watch, and out of the corner of my eye, the thing I was avoiding looking at wouldn't let me go.

The brush where the new pond path had been laid was starting to recover, the broken edges of branches now leafy and full again. It didn't look like it had always been there, but it didn't look brand new anymore, either.

One more glance at my watch and some mental math—jog home, shower, walk downtown—and I realized I could make it. I didn't particularly want to, but it now felt like my duty, like I was more of a protector of the town than the uniformed sloucher and his crew. I wiped my face with the hem of my T-shirt and walked the gravel path right to the end.

It was still there, water sparkling in the sunlight. I didn't go any farther than the end of the path, having decided that paths end for a reason. I stood for a moment, staring out at the pond. It was still here, but so was I. If it was still awake, if it was aware, I wanted it to feel my presence. I wanted it to know I was watching. We stared each other down for a moment, and then I turned and left it, alone once more, as it always would be, if I had any say.

The week had been a blur of busyness, the normal, boring *go-go-go*, punctuated by the occasional easy run, which was exactly what I needed. By Friday afternoon, what I needed was Friday night.

"Trying to move the clock hands with your mind?" I said to Frank, who'd been looking up at the big clock on the wall with increasing desperation for the last hour that afternoon as it inched toward five.

"You know what time it is," he muttered back as the next customer in a seemingly endless stream stepped up. I did know. We'd gotten past the midway point of FallsFest, which was when Grumpy Frank appeared, wishing for all the excitement to be over so life in his quiet little store could go back to normal. This year, the excitement had been considerably greater, so he was peak Grumpy Frank. And I couldn't blame him.

"You're leaving me?" Frank's eyes went wide with panic as I squeezed behind him and around the end of the counter.

"Just checking the tables outside." I waved.

"Don't be long!" The bell as I went out the door cut off the note of panic in his voice.

Honestly, the table was fine. I'd just wanted some fresh air. I tidied it anyway, in case Frank was watching, noting the graphic novels needed to be restocked.

This afternoon was beautiful, perfect summer weather—hot but not sweltering, sunny but not scorching. There was chatter and laughter drifting up and down the street, a nice change from panicked shouts and breaking glass. It was almost unbelievable that everyone was already forgetting. Almost. I filled my lungs and emptied them slowly. Somebody needed to keep an eye on these people.

A book about local birds toppled over and off the table. When I bent to retrieve it, I spied a quarter gleaming on the sidewalk. Found money was good luck, right? I understood now that luck didn't play as much of a role in my life as I'd once thought, but I'd also learned to get help wherever I could find it. I picked up the book and the coin and put one on the table and the other in my pocket.

Rapraprap!

The sound of Frank rapping his knuckles on the window startled me so hard I jumped. From inside, he raised his eyebrows at me meaningfully. He loved his store, but not when so many other people were in it.

I waved to let him know I was coming to his rescue, but took one more deep breath. The perfect summer seemed within reach again, and although I'd redefined *perfect*, I was going to try to make it happen.

Inside, Frank was flustered, trying to ring up a line of customers stretching down the fiction aisle, so I resumed my place beside him, the two of us ringing up and bagging behind the tall wooden counter like it was the last line of defense.

"Please form a single line!" he called out brightly. "I need a doppio," he added under his breath.

"Hey!" Key planted both elbows on the far end of the counter.

"The line starts back there," the second-in-line customer snapped, a middle-aged white woman from out of town with a hairstyle that boded trouble.

"He works here," Frank soothed her with a smile that went nowhere near his eyes. "Listen." He bent over, nose-to-nose with Key. "I will pay you anything you want—"

"Hey!" I objected. I was happy to see Key, as always, but *anything?*

"Shush." Frank gave me a delicate elbow and turned right back to Key. "Anything you want, to stamp a few stacks of bags."

"Anything?" Key stroked an imaginary beard.

"Within reason." Frank pointed a warning finger.

"Sure." Key relented as he was always going to. "As long as I'm not horning in on Ave's territory."

Frank shook his head and waved the next customer forward. "She's management. Above such menial tasks."

Key and I gave each other the "ooh!" face over Frank's shoulder.

"In your office?" Key knew the store almost as well as Frank and I and was already headed to the back.

The impatient woman wanted separate receipts for each of the three books she was buying because of course she did. Once she was safely out the door, I cast an accusing eye at Frank.

"You'll pay him anything?"

Frank shrugged and handed the next purchases for me to scan. "These are desperate times. This is why you should take some business courses."

Huh.

"I can't do this forever, you know." Frank handed over the books in one of our dwindling supply of stamped paper bags. "Thank you so much. Come again!" He must have said that a hundred times today, but he meant it almost every time. He really did love this store.

Come to think of it, so did I.

Business courses . . . I mentally stroked my own imaginary beard.

Once the line was gone, the FallsFest evening shift started to take over, which consisted more of people interested in rides and food than shopping. With just a few browsers strolling around the store, Frank looked up, and the clock finally showed him what he wanted to see.

"You're sure you're okay to lock up?" Frank grabbed his cardigan from under the counter, obviously counting on an affirmative answer.

"Yup." I sipped from my glass water bottle.

"This is it." Key dropped a stack of one hundred paper bags stamped with *Frank's Books* onto the counter and massaged his wrist. "You need to reorder."

"Already done." Frank waved that away and patted his pockets down for his keys. "They're supposed to arrive on Monday."

He was so on top of things in the store. The longer I worked there, the more I learned what was involved. Could I really do that someday?

When his cardigan pocket yielded the key fob, Frank made his way out from behind the counter. "Are you staying?" He pointed at Key.

"I am." Key smiled at me.

"Okay. I'm off, then." Frank looked around distractedly. "There's a lot to do still." He headed toward the back door, muttering to himself and listing things on his fingers.

"Pretty frazzled." Key slid behind the counter and sat next to me on Frank's stool. He leaned in with an innocent smile.

"I'm not sure occasional employees have the right to the boss's stool," I said primly.

Key slowly twined his fingers with mine under the counter.

"We'll take these." Two men with salt-and-pepper hair placed a few wedding magazines on the counter.

I completed the transaction, all four of us smiling for our own reasons.

At the stroke of seven, I locked the back door, and then we left through the front.

"Hold on." I ran around to check that the back door was truly locked, then returned to Key leaning against the wall beside the window.

"Ready?" He stood.

"Just one more." I ignored the eyeroll as I checked the front door. He didn't understand—locking up a store that I may perhaps possibly someday partially own was a big responsibility. "Okay."

"Are you sure?" He held my eyes and smiled. "Are you sure the handle didn't seem a little loose?" He jiggled an imaginary door handle. "Maybe not completely closed?"

I tried to stare him down, but he had me and he knew it. Finally, I cracked. "You're the worst," I said before scurrying back to the door to check it one more time while Key chuckled at my expense.

"You're so adorably predictable." He wrapped both arms around my shoulders as we stepped into the street. "Your loyalty as an employee is very admirable." He said it seriously, but I could hear the laughter in his voice.

I shook my head and booped the tiny scar on his chin fondly. "The worst."

We strolled hand in hand through FallsFest, a deliberate choice. We wanted to reclaim a place we'd loved, to cleanse it of bad memories and fear. We'd already hit up the food trucks for snacks, so we stood and watched the carousel before making our way to the fountain. Brave as we were trying to be, there was no way we were going anywhere near the fun house.

Key's camera was back around his neck where it belonged. He raised it, framing a shot of the Ferris wheel rising up over the town, the colored lights just visible against the darkening sky.

"Amazing light," Key murmured.

It made me feel calm and warm inside to see him taking photos again; somehow, to me, it meant that things with him were finally all right. I waited patiently while he took one shot and then another, finessing the angle, content to watch him do what made him happy.

I reached into my pocket for the coin I had found, looked at Key's profile sharp against the sky, and strolled over to the fountain. I made a wish—a big one—and tossed the coin toward the fountain, where it bounced on the edge, spun, and dropped with a clink onto the concrete bottom. I closed my eyes and smiled at the sound. The fountain was just seating again, a place for leaves to collect in the fall. Maybe not forever, but as long as I was around.

"Okay?" Key carefully replaced the lens cap and reached for my hand. "We don't want to be late."

"We definitely do not." But in truth, I was in no rush. I drew in a deep breath and found tension nowhere in my body. No dark thoughts lurked in my head. I laced my fingers with Key's and felt the warmth of his palm against mine. "Let's go."

THIRTY-TWO

WE WERE ON OUR WAY TO THE BARBECUE THAT Frank insisted on referring to as a "soirée." He'd organized it ostensibly for FallsFest, but for those who knew, there was a lot more than that to celebrate.

At the front gate of the little house on Matilda Street, we paused, remembering the last time we'd stood there. Although the party was around back, we walked up to the big front window, looked into the glass, and smiled. You never knew who might be watching.

On the other side was Frank's same furniture, but instead of Foster at an ironing board, I spotted a big sleek TV on the far wall, one of Foster's prize possessions.

"He's really made himself at home." Key followed my eyes and chuckled. "Frank must be grinding his teeth every time he sees it."

I nodded. "It's not vintage, that's for sure." Key was right. Frank had tried to talk Foster out of it, but I suspected that whatever pain the garish TV caused Frank was more than an even trade for company in the house. When the store was closed and I had gone home, Frank had never enjoyed living alone. The black water had solved that problem for him.

"There they are!" Key's mom and dad came up the walk behind us, carrying foil-covered casseroles. His mom looked cool and elegant as always, wearing a stylishly short pale green dress, her short hair showing off the perfect curve of her head. His dad walked half a step behind her, decked out in soft blue shorts and a coral short-sleeved shirt. When he came through the gate, I saw that they were trailed by Stella, wearing a lemon-yellow slip dress and white sneakers, who'd also been roped into casserole-carrying duty.

"Hey, Stell."

"This smells so good." Stella bit her lip and peeked under the foil as she passed us. "Would it be rude to just grab a fork and go to town?"

"Do we just walk in the yard unannounced?" Key's dad asked, shifting his dish from one palm to the other when it became too hot. Key's mom nudged him with her elbow. She was almost as tall as her husband, but her hands were too small to do the same skin-saving juggling. "You're not a king. You don't need to be announced. Now, this is hot. Let's go!"

We led them around the side to the backyard.

"I'll just take care of them." Key rolled his eyes toward his parents and took them to the deck, where they could relieve themselves of their steaming hot burdens. He hooked one arm through Stella's to force her to do the same and relinquish her dish.

"Just a taste!" she pleaded as he steered her away. "I'll split it with you!"

Frank's small backyard had been transformed. On the grass, a dozen small tables were scattered, each with a tea light and vase of hydrangea from the gardens. Folding chairs lined the perimeter. Twinkling fairy lights crisscrossed overhead, courtesy of Stella and me risking our lives on a ladder yesterday afternoon. Up close to the back deck were coolers of all sizes and folding tables groaning under foil-covered dishes and bowls, but the real action was next to it—the grill.

I headed straight over to see if I could help, given Frank and Foster's checkered past with grilling.

"How's it going?" I peered down on the array of grillables Frank was constantly shifting.

"We should have had Mehmet cater," Frank groused, too focused to look up.

"You're so cranky today," Foster observed from his folding chair, sipping a blue raspberry cooler. "You should start taking a nap in the afternoon. It's refreshing."

Frank poked at the coals and tilted his head, considering this. "Maybe after FallsFest. I could reduce my hours." He caught me listening. "Just a bit." He raised a clarifying finger. "I'm not ready for you to take over yet."

The second time he'd mentioned this today. Interesting.

I turned to survey the yard, catching sight of Key with his camera, weaving through the guests, surreptitiously framing, snapping, and moving on, like an explorer in a new world, totally in his element.

Some guests milling around I didn't know, but there were a lot of regular customers and neighbors. In a corner, the members of the Crooked Book Club were clustered around a lumbering white man, oohing and aahing over his little white dog on a leash.

I waved to Pearl, at the center of a group of girls by the fence. Pearl returned my wave, her eyes wide and awed. Ru had clearly told her everything she'd seen, but more importantly, Pearl seemed to believe and remember. Maybe stubbornness and speed weren't the only things that ran in my family.

Not far from the grill, Mayor Lewis stood at a table chatting with a red-haired man and a Black woman with chin-length twists holding their baby. "Thank God we caught it before it did any harm, thanks to Ruby," the mayor was saying, not a hair out of place and not a wrinkle in his khakis. "Well"—he raised his glass—"it's pretty, anyway. We're considering filling it with soil and making some sort of community garden."

The fountain. My auntie Ru had been busy. She'd gone in to work and started questioning the initial analysis of the water in the fountain, demanding additional testing, which had revealed that the water was highly contaminated with all sorts of bacteria. Apparently, the only way for the water to be safe enough to even wash your hands in would be to boil it, and what kind of modern society does that?

"I saw the notice posted at the library." The woman nodded, jiggling the baby in her arms. "People were upset at first."

"But there was obviously a reason it was dry for so many years," her partner added, offering the baby a stuffed giraffe. "We're actually lucky the valve broke."

"Yeah." The mayor drained his glass. "We could get into the whole water treatment thing, but it's too expensive for a little town like us, for something purely decorative. We can put that money to better use somewhere else. As soon as FallsFest wraps up and we can spare the staff"—he snapped his fingers—"we'll seal the valve and shut it down for good."

The little voice in my head sighed in relief. The town could do as much analysis as it wanted, but they could never treat the real problem with the water. I didn't know how she'd done it, but I knew why the water had gone bad. Somehow, on the other side, my ihstá Lily was making good trouble.

On this side, Other Lily and Ru sat together at the back of the yard, slightly apart from the action. Ru saw me and waved; she nudged Lily, who also spotted me. Her face brightened and she also waved, then leaned over to say something that made Ru laugh. I thought of her as just Lily now, but still called her ihstá out loud. Maybe in the future that would change, but right now it was the best I could do.

My real ihstá was not here, but not far away, either.

"Gentlemen, I'll leave you to it." I patted both Frank and Foster on the back.

"Yes, get yourself a drink, Avery." Frank waved distractedly, focused on flipping a burger.

"You're the one who needs a drink," Foster said, chuckling.

I went up onto the deck and popped inside, quickly closing the blinds on the patio door before slipping out again. If Real Lily was in the yard on the other side, the window would serve as a mirror, giving her a better view. She wouldn't have to strain to see us at all. She would almost feel like she was there, too. Almost.

Back outside, I turned to the patio doors, pressed my fingers to the turtle Lily had picked out for me, and smiled. Over my reflection's shoulder, I saw something that made my jaw drop.

My dad was standing awkwardly, a little apart from everyone else, but he was there.

"Dad!" Honestly, I hadn't known if he would come. I'd extended the invitation as casually as I could, trying to make him feel like I really did want him there but not pressuring him to show up. Not an easy balancing act.

When he spotted me, he smiled, and for a moment, I saw my dad the way he'd been, the way I remembered him from my childhood—happy. I had the power to do that. Time travel: add that to my list of superpowers.

As I walked over, Dad raised his arms slightly, a hug if I wanted but not too much commitment if I didn't.

I did.

I leaned in, resting my head against his shoulder like I had when I was a little kid. I was taller and he was leaner, but it was close enough. It was good.

"Thanks for coming." Like I was the host, like I'd already taken ownership of more than the store.

"Oh." He tugged nervously at the hem of his shirt. "I've never been back here. Frank's got a nice place."

"Frank and Foster now." I nodded toward the grill.

"Ah, the famous Foster." Dad rose up on his toes to look.

"Hi, Seth." My mom walked up casually, greeting him like she would anyone else, and my heart swelled. They were both trying so hard.

"Hi, Vi." They stood awkwardly for a moment. Dad smoothed the front of his shirt. I knew they were only doing it for me, but they were doing it and I loved them for it.

"Do you want a drink?" Mom asked for lack of anything else to say.

"Sure." Dad nodded, hands visibly clenched in his pockets.

"We've got a few coolers going. I'll show you what's what." Mom and Dad walked off side by side. He said something to her, and she laughed and nodded. I took a picture in my mind.

I turned to find a real camera lens pointed directly at me and for once, I didn't instinctively throw my hands up to shield my face. It was just Key behind the camera. There was nothing to protect myself from. I smiled softly.

A quiet click and Key checked and nodded, satisfied.

"You want to see?" He turned the camera toward me, but I shook my head. He would see the shot through his eyes, and I'd see it through mine. I couldn't see what he saw even if I tried. So I didn't. I didn't need to see.

"You know," Key said as we made our way to investigate the table of food, "I've been thinking. I've always planned to go far and wide, snapping exotic sights." He sketched it all in the air for me with a sweep of his hands. "But there's so much material right here in Crook's Falls. Oh my God." He broke off, squeezing my hand in excitement. "Someone brought mini cheesecakes!"

How had I ever thought he was anything other than exquisitely adorable? I smiled and waited for him to get back to his original and very intriguing thought. "As you were saying . . ."

"As I was saying, people think small towns are simple, shallow." He turned to me. "But they're not."

Not this town, anyway.

Small things are not always simple. Knowing how you feel about someone doesn't make navigating a relationship any easier.

I'd been thinking along the same lines as Key lately, even before Frank made his suggestion to take business courses. Like Key, I'd always assumed the future was to be found somewhere far away, something I had to leave Crook's Falls to discover. But maybe I already had a job, a purpose. The black water was never going to go away, and I was never going to forgive it for what it had done, the people it had taken. But maybe we could come to some kind of balance with it, if we were watchful. Real Lily on one side, me and Ru on the other. Maybe what I'd been looking for was here.

It was the perfect time of day, that summer evening freshness coming on, the scent of charcoal smoke in the air. I looked around and found nothing in my life to get away from, no need to run, only things to be thankful for. My dad was standing with Key's at the grill, helping Frank plate food while Foster supervised from a camp chair, arms folded over his belly and a contented smile on his face.

Stella was the star as always, the Crooked Book Club members rapt as she used pieces of cheese to teach the little white dog to shake a paw. When he finally got it, everyone broke out in a cheer, patting the beaming owner on the back in congratulations like it was his achievement.

Ru stood, the focus of a cluster of people, including Key's mom and the mayor. My auntie was sketching out something big with her hands, winning people over to whatever grand plan she was talking about. Lily sat in a chair, holding a beer on her lap and looking up, the fairy lights reflected in her eyes.

Everyone here had sacrificed. The two Lilies in my life had given up so much; so had Frank and Foster. It was unfair to leave the burden on them forever.

It was my turn. After everything I'd been through, everything I'd done to set things right in this town, I was willing to protect it.

I would stay and keep an eye on the black water. The next time it woke, it would find me here to greet it.

I followed Lily's gaze up to the sky, breathing out my thanks for everything I'd learned, everything I'd lost as well as what I'd gained.

I give thanks to the earth, to the water and animals.

The breeze caressed my cheek. I closed my eyes.

I give thanks to the sun, moon, and stars.

I opened my eyes to find Key standing next to me, licking cheesecake-sticky fingers.

"What?" He laughed.

I shook my head. Adorable.

I give thanks to the Creator, to family and community.

So much was different in such a short time. The me so focused on training, on achieving, the girl who was so afraid of the future she couldn't bear to think about it—she seemed long ago and far away. I now knew what was important and what was not. I was stronger now, surer; with Key and my family around me, I could look to the future with a welcoming smile. I would do as my ihstá had asked—live my life as the Creator intended, free of fear and full of joy.

Key pulled me close, his arm a comfortable weight across my shoulders, and joined me, looking up as the first stars in the sky glimmered brightly.

"This is good," he whispered.

I slipped my arm around his waist. My perfect summer had arrived.

Now our minds are one.

A NOTE FROM THE AUTHOR

Do you know who you are?

This is the first of two questions Avery has to answer in her experience with the black water, the question she deals with in *The Unfinished*.

It would be great if we knew everything about ourselves from childhood. Learning who you are is a process of exploring exactly what you believe, what you want, and how you envision your future life. Doing this isn't easy or necessarily pleasant but it's possible, with time and effort. This is the work Avery had to do in *The Unfinished*, and by the end of that book, she's figured out a lot of things. But not everything.

Do you know who others are?

This second question is what Avery is confronted with in *The Others*.

For example, I can sit you down and tell you all about myself—for hours—but by the time I finally stop talking, what have you really learned about me? How can you be sure that what I've told you is true? You can't. You see who I want you to see. Truly knowing someone else is almost impossible.

Avery discovers this when Key is not quite right, when she wonders what is going on in his head and has to admit she can't know for sure. This is how Other Key manages to fool her for so long. Similarly, she holds a grudge against her dad, thinking she knows how he feels, only to find that she's spectacularly wrong. What is real, and what she sees or hears, are not always the same thing.

Even the people we love keep secrets or parts of themselves hidden, either because they don't know themselves or they fear being hurt. Like the faces Avery sees reflected in windows, we can never be sure if what we're seeing is the original or a performance. At some point, we have to trust that what people are showing us is who they really are. If we believe that person to be worth the investment, we take that risk.

By the end of *The Others*, Avery decides that taking that gamble on the people in her life is something she's willing to do, and she's thankful for the chance, regardless of the outcome. Aware that she hasn't been easy to know in the past, she vows to live the life Lily would be proud of, to trust in others and to be trustworthy. Easier said than done, but very gratifying.

Be someone worth taking a chance on.

KANYEN'KÉHA GLOSSARY

ihstá (eeh-sta): auntie

Kanyen'kéha (gan-yen-gay-ha): Mohawk language

nyá:wen (nya-wa): thank you

oié:ri (o-yay-ri): ten

shé:kon (say-goo): hello/hi

tewáhsen (dey-wah-soo): twenty

wísk (wisk): five

To learn more about the language or to take an online course, visit onkwawenna.info.

A NOTE FROM CYNTHIA LEITICH SMITH, AUTHOR-CURATOR OF HEARTDRUM

Dear Reader,

Are you still reeling from all the revelations in this story? I am.

Amid this murky mystery, Avery gains a better understanding of who she is and of her purpose. She comes to fully, deeply recognize the truth of herself and of her loved ones. She more fully commits to the bookstore, and she resolves to watch over the black water.

Avery is young to have such a profound sense of who she is and of her place in the world. When I was her age, I was someone who embraced stories to help me think through life's big questions. I dedicated myself to those dear to me and to the places I thought of as home. Like Avery, I was someone my Elders could count on.

Maybe you share those qualities. Maybe not. Who you become is up to you.

The Others is published by Heartdrum, a Native-focused imprint of HarperCollins, which offers books about young Native heroes by Indigenous authors and illustrators. Have you read many books by and about Mohawk characters or other Native people? This book is a follow-up to Cheryl Isaacs' debut novel,

The Unfinished. If you haven't done so already, be sure to read that story next. It works just as well as a prequel or sequel.

In the meantime, maybe you'll catch a glimpse of Other You in the mirror.

Mvto,
Cynthia Leitich Smith

Cheryl Isaacs is a Mohawk/white writer from southern Ontario, Canada. She loves everything furry, anything that occurs outdoors, and running the local trails, where she's never encountered anything eerie. Not once.

Cynthia Leitich Smith is the bestselling, acclaimed author of books for all ages, including *Rain Is Not My Indian Name*, *Indian Shoes*, *Jingle Dancer*, *On a Wing and a Tear*, *Sisters of the Neversea*, *Firefly Season*, and *Hearts Unbroken*, which won the American Indian Youth Literature Award; she is also the anthologist of *Ancestor Approved: Intertribal Stories for Kids* and *Legendary Frybread Drive-In: Intertribal Stories*. She has been an NSK Neustadt Laureate. Cynthia is the author-curator of Heartdrum, a Native-focused imprint at HarperCollins Children's Books, and served as the Katherine Paterson Endowed Chair on the faculty of the MFA program in Writing for Children and Young Adults at Vermont College of Fine Arts. She is a citizen of the Muscogee Nation and lives in Austin and Denton, Texas. You can visit Cynthia online at cynthialeitichsmith.com.

In 2014, We Need Diverse Books (WNDB) began as a simple hashtag on Twitter. The social media campaign soon grew into a 501(c)(3) nonprofit with a team that spans the globe. WNDB is supported by a network of writers, illustrators, agents, editors, teachers, librarians, and book lovers, all united under the same goal—to create a world where every child can see themselves in the pages of a book. You can learn more about WNDB programs at www.diversebooks.org.